Mikelooney.com

Copyright © 2021 by Mike Looney

Front Cover illustration by National award-winning illustrator Bill Deore

All rights reserved.

Except as permitted under the U.S. Copyright Act of 1976, no part of this publication may be reproduced, distributed, or transmitted in any form or by any means, or stored in a database or retrieval system, without the prior written permission of the publisher.

Library of Congress Control Number: 2017963939

ISBN:	978-0-9774891-1-4	*paperback*
	978-0-9774891-4-5	*ebook*

Division of Human Improvement Specialists, llc.

www.hispubg.com | info@hispubg.com

PRINTED IN CANADA

TICKLE THE LIGHT

A NOVEL BY MIKE LOONEY

ABOUT THE AUTHOR

MIKE LOONEY is the author of the critically acclaimed book *The Big Shootout: The Untold Story of the Game of the Century*. "Untold Story" is a fascinating compilation of previously untold stories by the cast members of Mike's award-winning documentary *The Big Shootout: The Life and Times of 1969* which centers around the famous 1969 football "Game of The Century" between Texas and Arkansas that included President Nixon and what seemed like the entire federal government sitting in the stands.

Mike's non-fiction book, *The Battle of the Bulge: The Untold Story of Höfen* is a timeless story involving a false report filed during the Battle of the Bulge. The book received critical praise from the media, and political dignitaries alike. Follow Mike's journey as he discovers long buried secrets from World War II, revealed not only by his father's private notes after his passing—but also from Mike's interviews with his father's fellow soldiers. *The Untold Story of Höfen* reminds us that history often rewrites itself until we find the truth.

Mike Looney's first novel *Heroes Are Hard to Find* was also widely acclaimed by the media and public alike. Heroes delves into the theme of good over evil and exploits the pitfalls of taking the short cut in life and sports. In conjuncture with Heroes, Mike appeared on over fifty radio stations nationwide discussing the impact on society of cheating in sports.

Mike was born in Monticello, Arkansas but his parents relocated to Dallas in 1963 and he graduated from Woodrow Wilson High School in 1967. Mike graduated from Texas Tech in 1971 where he was a member of Sigma Alpha Epsilon Fraternity and earned a degree in marketing. Mike has enjoyed a successful business career as an insurance broker for over forty-five years, specializing in employee benefit plans and executive compensation. He still lives in East Dallas with his wife of thirty-nine years, Sandra, a former model and current local actress. The Looney's have three daughters and six grandchildren.

Over the years, Mike has spoken to countless civic organizations, schools, libraries, business, youth groups, churches, and prisons. Visit Mike's websites: *www.mikelooney.com* and *www.bigshootout.com* for further details on his award-winning film and books. Please contact Adrienne Perutelli at (214) 826-4949 to schedule Mike for your event.

CONTENTS

About the Author		v
Acknowledgement		1
Foreword		3
1.	The Duel	5
2.	The Duke	9
3.	It Was Twenty Years Ago Today or You Say It's Your Birthday	21
4.	My Dad Was a Coach	27
5.	This Is the Big Time	31
6.	A Will and a Prayer	41
7.	I've Been Away Too Long	49
8.	A Day in the Life	53
9.	King David	59
10.	Fantasy Camp	63
11.	Joe and Rocket Meet Again	69
12.	M. V. P.	73
13.	Life at Home	77
14.	Dad Comes Home	83
15.	An Unexpected Visitor	89
16.	Rocket Pays a Visit	93
17.	Frothin Green	99
18.	Back at the Office	103
19.	Spring Training	107
20.	Meanwhile	113
21.	Feeling Important	119
22.	Away from Home	123
23.	Point of No Return	129
24.	Candice Leaves Something Behind	133
25.	It's Deceptive	137

26.	The Holy Ghost	141
27.	Whack It or Whank It?	145
28.	Patrick Returns	153
29.	Liz Takes a Ride	157
30.	The Third Dimension	161
31.	Burdened with Concern	167
32.	They Turn on You in a Hurry	171
33.	Concentrate on What You've Got Left	175
34.	Cats Are Chasin' Dogs	179
35.	*Illegitimi non carborundum*	185
36.	Did Somebody Sneeze?	191
37.	The Bet	197
38.	A Plan	201
39.	The Exorcist	205
40.	Duke Pays a Visit	211
41.	Toothpick Johnson	217
42.	Like Another Joe	221
43.	Don't Make It Fair	227
44.	Falling Off a Turnip Truck	231
45.	Can Daddy Come Home?	235
46.	Joe and Joan Take a Ride	239
47.	Frothin Returns	245
48.	The Second Shot Was for You	249
49.	A Chapter from Liz's Diary Recorded a Few Days Later	255
50.	Safe at Home	259

DEVOTIONS

To the memory of my parents, George and Mary Washington Looney, parents devoted to that great endangered species—The American Family.

ACKNOWLEDGEMENT

A special thanks to my friend, the very real Dr. Duke Samson, former Head of Neurosurgery at The University of Texas Health Science Center, for his input concerning the medical fiction in *Tickle the Light*. Or is it fiction?

"If I live long enough, I'll perform that surgery," Duke told me, referring to the procedure used in *Tickle's* second chapter. Good news, no doubt, for those in quest of the ever-elusive fountain of youth.

In a prime example of fact trailing fiction like a shadow, on October 12, 2005, Dr. Samson and his staff performed successful lifesaving brain surgery on my mother a former school teacher and mother of three boys, Mrs. Mary Looney.

"The most interesting neurosurgeon in the world."
—Micheal J. Mooney, *D Magazine* October 2012

FOREWORD

"**P**LAYING baseball isn't real life. It's a fantasy world... it's a dream come true. "

Dale Murphy, the great Atlanta Braves outfielder, has unknowingly provided the best possible introduction to Mike Looney's hilarious fantasy tale about baseball and those of us who are "still crazy after all these years." If you ever imagined having Kershaw's heat, Koufax's hook, the sweet swing of Ted Williams, or Mickey Mantle's night life, this book is right in your wheelhouse. Regardless of why you didn't make it personally to The Show-couldn't hit the curveball, couldn't throw from the hole, couldn't run fast enough to get out of the rain- Mike offers you a free pass to the unexpected life and loves of a forty-year old rookie sensation who, thanks to a little brain trauma and some shady surgical slight-of-hand, doesn't even have a cup of coffee in the minor leagues before he's hitting ropes for the Texas Rangers. Mike's bases are loaded with a zany collection of teenaged girls, villains of every stripe and magical friends, all poised for the hit-and-run sign; meanwhile a crazed designated hitter with an imaginary dog and a bad stutter stalks the hero's nutty family. How it all came about, plus the perils of hitting clean-up on and off the field and insights into why the high, hard one may not be as dangerous to your health as the slider below the belt all make Tickle the Light a hoot to read.

—Dr. Duke Samson, former Head of Neurosurgery at
The University of Texas Health Science Center

CHAPTER 1
THE DUEL

NINETEEN thousand plus change jammed the cozy Omaha stadium. Beneath an intoxicating late spring sky, a dry breeze pushed the scent of mustard and anticipation throughout stands nearly rocking on their foundation. Banners draped the ballpark's railings, their bright multi-colored messages bragging on the condition of amateur baseball in the Lone Star State. Above the centerfield bleachers, a giant black scoreboard read *1985 College World Series Championship Texas State University vs. Texas College.*

Bouncing along his slender neck, Joe Donley's thick, straight hair extended below the red batting helmet as he strode to the plate. Despite a gunmetal gray beard, Joe possessed a boyish, lean face, the type that remains young long after its time. He ground his cleats into the red dirt of the batter's box and waved the Hillerich and Bradsby as if it had lived a lifetime in his hands. Indeed, it almost had.

Joe used a light bat by baseball standards. "Ted Williams, the game's greatest hitter, used a light bat," Joe's father always said. "You've got more control with a light bat," George Donley would add in a voice laced with authority. "Without so much timber to lug around, you can wait longer before you commit. Wait, then attack. Wait, then attack," the senior Donley would continue, his voice rising as he warmed to the subject.

Joe's bat extended thirty-four inches and weighed only thirty-two ounces. To Joe, high with adrenaline, it felt even lighter, more like a plastic whiffle bat.

On the mound Walter "Rocket" Nolin was an imposing presence ("the big un's always eat the little un's," Rocket would later say). Joe, along with most everybody else in the crowd, considered Rocket the most intimidating collegiate pitcher ever. Undeniably, he threw the fastest. With eyes as narrow as his frame, Rocket leaned forward to receive his catcher's signal. But the signal didn't really matter. The scouting reports said what would come: one fastball after another and then more fastballs. Only with two strikes would the square-jawed hurler from Texas State possibly attempt a nasty curve. Rocket's curve would buckle any right-handed hitter at the knees before dipping sharply away from the petrified batter's head, sometimes even across the plate for a strike.

Rocket proceeded with the high kick of his left leg. His windup culminated in a hissing blur speeding toward home plate, its impact with the catcher's mitt loud enough to pass for gunfire. Smoke signals clouded the air around home plate.

"No, no, ball one!" bellowed the man in blue.

"Come on, Joe! Smack it!" urged a powerful female voice from the first row behind home plate. Joan Hegeberg wore her long blonde hair pulled back from her cover-girl face, revealing rapt concentration in her blue eyes, her fingers crossed like the long, slender legs stemming from her black mini-skirt.

Without preamble, a noodle-thin male, his stringy brown hair bouncing off his anemic shoulders, sprinted naked across the outfield. In centerfield, he waved his arms and yelled indecipherably, his head bobbing like an irritated cockatiel.

Gasps and laughter erupted from the stands and even from a few of the entrenched combatants. A slow grin creased Rocket's tanned face into familiar laugh lines. He could allow himself the levity. After all, the contest had advanced to the third batter, and Rocket had fanned the first two.

Joe Donley's concentration was unbroken. His unreadable brown eyes stayed glued sixty feet-six inches away, committing every movement of the future legend to memory. This unwavering focus did not escape the watchful eye of his father. George Donley sat next to Joe's mother behind the third base dugout. He had a hero's presence, a face from an old World War II history book. Since Joe's first step, George Donley had prepared him for the life that George left behind on the shores of Normandy.

Mary Donley's intelligent eyes surveyed the scene expectantly. Her faith in prayer and the power of positive thinking was as legendary in her local community back home as the high school coaching career of her husband.

"Never give in to doubt, Joe. Tell yourself, I think I can I think I can," Mary had repeatedly reminded her son. "And remember, Joe, coincidence is the Lord's way of staying invisible. Pray every night for God to take care of your needs."

After several police hauled away the streaker, Rocket Nolin recomposed himself. With the command of a Cy Young winner, the twenty-two-year-old proceeded into his windup.

Rocket's delivery was a work of art, the knee to the forehead, a leg kick so elevated his left foot obscured his face before he released the ball. Rocket's offering, now on its path to the plate, looked small—very, very small. Joe leaned back as the pitch zoomed toward him. He watched in humiliation as the curve ball broke through the strike zone.

"Steeeriike one!" roared the ump, louder than before.

No curve until after the second strike, fumed Joe. So much for the scouting reports. He would not back down again.

"Wait, then attack," Joe mumbled under his breath.

What Joe saw next was a heat-seeking missile on a path for his head. It was no breaking ball; the fastball would not change course at the last possible instant. Joe saw how it would end but could do nothing. He froze. The ball crashed into the left side of Joe's skull. Shock waves bolted through him. He dropped heavily to the batter's box. A moan escaped him, so dark that the catcher and umpire shivered. Spectators gasped and the stadium became as still as a photograph of itself.

A gagging sound, half strangled in Joe's throat, was the only noise; his convulsing body, the only movement.

The elder Donley knew from the hollow sound that the ball had struck his son's head with deadly force. The man who'd abandoned prayer on June 6, 1944, closed his eyes and began a silent supplication. As George continued his fervent barter with God, his wife clutched his arm, unable even to cry out. Though George pressed her fragile hand reassuringly, Mary's normally pale complexion turned ashen.

Joan Hegeberg saw blood trickling from her fiancé's left ear, but her cries strangled in her throat. Joe lay less than twenty yards from her in the fetal position. His batter's helmet lay beside him, shattered.

Between spasms, Joe managed to roll onto his back. As if looking for God Himself, he searched the sky and then became still.

Joe's father and mother stood and started toward their son, George with a limp profound enough to suggest a demonstration of the proper hook slide. Enemy shrapnel does that to a man's gait.

A small mob rushed to home plate. One teammate, built like an oversized fire hydrant, barreled through to Joe's side. The wavy blond mane that hung to his shoulders nearly concealed his warm, open face as he bent over his friend.

"Deep caca, Little Man, deep caca," mumbled Al "Bull" Lee.

But no one felt more concern than Walter "Rocket" Nolin. Rocket didn't know Joe Donley from Joe Namath. When Rocket wasn't pitching, he fished or hunted or tended to cattle at his father's ranch in Olney, Texas. Witnessing what his own strength had done reduced his breath to short gasps. Convinced that he had killed a man, the pitcher neared home plate as though entering a dark morgue. Rocket squinted so hard his eyes closed, and he wished he were the one unconscious.

Joe's scheduled nightly prayer was called off due to darkness.

CHAPTER 2
THE DUKE

"THE ODDS are in our favor," George Donley said with forced conviction. "There's only been one major leaguer killed by a pitch, and that was so long ago the batters didn't even wear helmets."

George sat between his wife and Joan Hegeberg in a far corner at the University of Nebraska Medical Center's emergency room waiting area. Numb from sedatives, Mary and Joan stared like statues. George's nostrils shrank from the sterile hospital smell. He cupped his hand to his chin. "The guy's name was Chapman, I believe."

George felt a galaxy away from the Donley home of Hutchins, Texas, a sleepy country town south of Dallas. Joe's torture was his torture, causing years to flash before him in the blink of an eye. Golly, life had been so good, at least since the war, until today. Shortly before Joe's birth, George and Mary had lived within walking distance of their mutual employer, the local high school. Mary loved her job of teaching English as much as George loved coaching the baseball team. Teaching history suited him just fine too. Heck, at least his students learned a thing of two about World War II. Sure, his day at the beach on June 6 of '44 shattered his dream, but all those years working with Joe insured that Joe would make it for the both of them.

Maybe Joe could recover from today and continue his rightful path to the big leagues. "Whoops!" George mumbled, thinking of his prayer of less than an hour ago, his first communication with God in a long, long time. George's face flinched with something holding no kin to a smile.

Don't renege on your prayer, he thought. No more rhubarbs with the head ump. Joe still had his parents, still had Joan; they would marry someday. Joe still had Bull, the best buddy anyone could ever hope for. Yep, Joe would be fine without baseball. God, just let my son live.

Samuel Duke, the medical center's chief of neurosurgery, stood over the operating room table. He didn't need the ultra-high-beam lights to know the small boy was dead. The eight-year-old lay tomb still, victim of an accidental fall from a second-story window.

The neurosurgeon sank heavily into a folding chair. He felt the assuring hand of his assistant surgeon, Dr. Louis Portera, resting on his broad shoulder.

"We did the best we could, Duke," whispered the bushy-haired co-worker. Lou studied the listless body, the sight tightening his mahogany brown eyes.

"Hell, yeah, we did. We always do the best we can." Though Duke spoke in a taut whisper, his voice managed to sound amplified.

Though smaller than in his gridiron days at Stanford, the surgeon seemed larger than his six-foot-two, two-hundred-ten pounds to those around him. Years ago, after Duke had awakened in the recovery room after his first college knee surgery, he liked the view. Medicine, it seemed to Duke, was a little like playing ball. You brought all your energies to focus on one problem in a fixed period of time, and it was easy to determine fairly quickly whether you'd won or lost. In his scrubs, Duke still resembled a football player. Like a helmet, his cap and mask exposed only his piercing brown eyes.

"Duke's the real life guy John Wayne plays in the movies," colleagues would say. Instead of horses, Duke rode an 1100 cc Yamaha motorcycle. Spying him on his beloved Ruby-Red, someone would always quip, "Here comes The Duke" or "It's fuckin' John Wayne."

"A near sexual experience just to sit on her," Duke would confide to a friend on rare occasions. Publicly, it was a subject he'd rather not discuss. "A neurosurgeon who rides a motorcycle," he had to concede, "is like a preacher who uses hand guns."

A procedure, such as today's, was also a subject he'd rather not discuss. "This one wasn't necessary. That's what makes it so tough," Duke said. Sort of like a quarterback protecting the lead only to throw a needless interception, Duke decided. He tugged at his chin, massaging his perfectly manicured salt and pepper beard. His drawn face wore the fatigue of the near three-hour surgery. He stirred awkwardly in his chair. Four knee surgeries contributed to his mechanical movements. At this moment, Duke looked much older than his thirty-five years.

Initially, the parents thought no serious injury had occurred. After the fall, the child sprang to his feet like a startled cat and ran away to play. But the youngster soon became lethargic, complained of a headache, and started to vomit. Torn by the fall, an artery in the brain's covering was gradually producing a large clot over the brain's surface. Similar to a closed box, the skull possessed no capability to expand. Additional pressure slowly compressed the brain's critical centers that control consciousness, blood pressure, and breathing. By the time the parents rushed him to the emergency room, the child had lapsed into a coma.

Duke had been in his office when he received the emergency call. In less than five minutes, Duke stood at the operating table inspecting the open head of the small child.

Duke needed only seconds to diagnose the tragedy. Beneath the injured site, the skull was bent inward. The dura mater, the thick gray substance that lined the skull's inner part and provided the brain's protection, was ripped away from the middle meningeal artery—the blood vessels that connected the dura mater to the bone. Detached dura mater created a space into which the torn artery was bleeding. With every heartbeat, blood pumped into the space, creating a bigger and bigger clot. The blood clot itself detached more and more dura mater, creating still more room for blood to accumulate—enough blood to compress the underlying brain and cause it to stop functioning. Pressure inside the head became so great that the heart no longer pumped hard enough to continue the necessary blood supply to the brain. Duke and his team removed the clot and closed off the torn artery, but the child's heart rate and blood pressure remained below normal. Swollen brain tissue had compressed and destroyed the normal brain structure. Duke tried everything, looked everywhere for anything he might have missed, but he and his team were too late.

Duke removed his cap; his matted brown hair showed the initial stages of retreat. His sigh sounded like air brakes decompressing on a country school bus. Damn it, the doctor reasoned, the brain had suffered no primary injury, just an injury produced by the blood clot, treatable if detected early. The child's death was a textbook example of a massive epidural hematoma.

Duke's eyes drifted to the floor. He lowered his mask and exposed a narrow jaw chiseled of granite. He sensed Edna, his circulating nurse, moving quietly in the background. "Ask Dr. Portera to close the head." Duke paused, his words hung in dead air. "There is nothing else we can do."

Within seconds, Duke heard the voice of his anesthesiologist, Ted French. "Son of a bitch! Son of a bitch! Son of a bitch!"

With startling quickness for a man with gimpy knees, Duke hobbled into the doorway. Not twice in the same day he thought! An orderly pushed a stretcher frantically toward Duke with the anesthesiologist following in pursuit. Ted wore oversized aviator glasses, and his shiny bald head resembled a crash helmet. A young man in a baseball uniform lay unconscious on the stretcher. Like peeling paint, dried blood clung to the exterior of his left ear.

"He took a son of a bitchin' fastball right to the temple squama!" thundered Ted, his giant ears twitching, his hazel eyes fried-egg wide.

Duke bent forward, to inspect the baseball player's damaged ear. His associate hurriedly guided the stretcher into a small operating room adjacent to the deceased child.

North of six-six and thin as a fungo bat, Ted towered over his colleges. His hands, the size of baseball gloves, belied their dexterity and skill.

"I think he's got a compound brain wound!" Ted declared.

"Why do you say that?" Duke asked. "It's just a little blood around the ear."

"The bone's driven into the brain. I've seen the CT scan. They did it at Methodist before sending him over here. Gladys has it."

"Then where the hell is Gladys?" Duke's fierce eyes darted around the room.

Suddenly, a green-eyed, shapeless woman burst into the room protecting the CT scan under her left arm like a good halfback cradling the pigskin. She handed off the scan to Duke. Gladys wore her sandy hair cropped, and Duke had long suspected the young nurse possessed her share of male chromosomes.

Duke inspected the CT scan—a picture of the brain sliced flat as a soft melon. He analyzed the scalp, the water chambers inside the brain, the brain itself, and then the bone of the ballplayer's skull. Ted was right. The bone of the skull protruded slightly into the brain.

Duke and his associates huddled around the operating table.

"This kid was a darn good player. That's the shame of it all," Gladys lamented while she inspected the operating tools on an adjacent table. "Word is the Rangers were going to take him with their first pick."

"He's going to be a darn good dead man if we don't get our ass in gear," Ted said. His eyes inspected his big IV line with the same intensity his hands fondled it.

"A right-handed hitter with power like Mike Schmidt," Gladys told them sorrowfully.

"Hey, Gladys, remember, I've been telling you to try the right side of the plate," Ted chided gently. Ted's grin pushed open the right side of his mouth and exposed ivory-white teeth.

"Shut up, mad professor. I'm not watching those dirty movies with you," Gladys quickly replied.

"I'm going with a direct stick to the jugular," Ted announced, a fierceness invading his owl-like eyes. He slid a large-bore needle into the massive vein on the left side of the patient's neck.

"Tube him as fast as you can, buddy, and then let's blow him down," Duke said.

Ted inserted a tube through the patient's mouth into his trachea to allow maximum oxygen and to blow off as much carbon dioxide as possible, temporarily reducing the pressure in the patient's head. Duke's goal was to buy precious time.

Edna carefully inserted a thin rubber tube into Joe's bladder. This allowed the bladder to deal with the large volume of fluid the patient would receive during the surgical procedure.

"Want me to shrink him down?" Ted asked. He taped the endotracheal tube to the patient's face to prevent its dislodging under the surgical drapes.

"Yeah, really hit him with the mannitol. He's young; his kidneys can take it."

"Let's go with a gram and a half per kilo. Then let me know what the brain looks like," Ted said. He started the flow of the drug thru the IV line that would deliver the mannitol directly to the patient's heart.

Duke nodded, his mahogany eyes fixed to the ballplayer. An above average dosage, but Duke wanted to shrink the brain by drawing water from it to the blood system.

Dr. Portera used hair clippers to snip the hair in the area of the temple wound. Then with a straight razor, the resident surgeon began to shave the head with the skill of a master barber.

"You can tell a lot about a resident's hands by the way he shaves the head," Duke said with as much pride as he did authority.

Louis heard the compliment.

"Forget it, Edna," Duke snapped suddenly, noticing the indelible pencil in Edna's hand. "He's crashing. Splash on the iodine prep solution and forget the niceties," Duke said without the slightest change in his flat voice.

A surgeon's knife, firmly entrenched in his delicate long fingers, Duke made an incision from in front of the young man's left ear to behind the hairline. Duke folded the skin down and flapped the muscle down in the same way. Fifty minutes had elapsed since the injury.

The high-speed drill Duke used to make a small hole next to the fracture site whined like an electric saw. Then, Duke's rongeurs bit away the bone surrounding the depressed fragment, leaving a sawdust-like residue. Delicately, with forceps, Duke removed bone crushed fine as eggshell. Then with a thin metal suction tube, he extracted a blood clot the size of a fist.

With the dura mater now exposed, the neurosurgeon could see a bleeding meningeal artery. "Coag," Duke said firmly.

Gladys instinctively stepped on the cautery pedal that provided the two-second charge to the electrical bayonet forceps. Duke squeezed the tiny, pliers-like device, delivering the hot surge. The cautery scorched the artery shut, momentarily turning it white; the surrounding blood boiled.

With hypnotic efficiency, Duke and his crew used minuscule surgical stitches to tack back the thick gray mass of dura mater. This delicate procedure exposed the bloody brain. Gladys and Edna rapidly wheeled the towering medical microscope into place. Duke explored the interior of Joe Donley's skull and cringed at the site of the bone driven into the brain. Without immediate attention, this young man would soon die. A big-league hematoma was near the pituitary gland located directly behind the sinuses. Worse, Duke could see bleeding from an undetected source deep at the base of the brain.

"Shit, this kid's hurt a little worse than I thought," Duke said with icy calm.

Duke, his fingers, cradling the small black forceps, continued extracting crushed bone. Blood gushed like a wild river. Located at the base of the brain was the optic nerve, and behind it was the large carotid artery, obviously damaged.

"Son of a bitch, he's gonna stroke!" Duke's pitch escalated with every syllable.

After only two heartbeats, blood filled the space at the brain's base. Two beats later, the unexpected torrent overflowed from Joe's skull onto the floor.

"Ted!" Duke bellowed. "Find the pulse in his neck and compress the artery!"

Glancing at the monitor, the anesthesiologist reached quickly under the drape. Holding a suction tube in each hand, Duke waited anxiously, but the blood flow didn't abate.

"Damn it, Ted! I said compress it! Push it down!" Samuel Duke felt his sphincter tighten. Unless he could see, the game was lost.

Ted pressed his hand on the patient's pulse hard enough to erupt his own carotid artery. He glanced up to the screen. Finally, thankfully, the bleeding slowed enough for Duke to see.

"Keep the field dry while I find the carotid injury," Duke said, handing one suction tube to Dr. Portera. After a moment, Duke located the laceration site.

"Clips."

Edna handed Duke a nine-inch clip-applier. Black and bayoneted, the applier's two prongs created a mouth that held a tiny temporary clip that Duke desperately hoped would seal off the bleeding.

Looking through the microscope, Duke carefully lowered the applier and released the clip. It closed on one side of the white carotid artery, and the flow of blood slowed to a trickle. Blood, however, returned to the damaged carotid artery from the other direction. Duke promptly placed another clip on the other side of the bleeding artery; it sealed off the blood flow, at least, for a while.

Duke stood erect and exhaled so heavily his mask fluttered. Now came the tricky part. With the flow of the blood arrested to that part of the brain, the brain cells would quickly begin to die. He had about fifteen minutes to repair the artery and remove the temporary clips. If he failed, the young man would suffer a massive stroke, leaving him paralyzed on his right side and unable to speak.

"Edna, give me a two-minute count," Duke said.

His tone silenced those around him. Edna started the clock. Tick. Tock. The room became quiet and still as death.

"Open the microvascular set," Duke said. "Let's go with the one-half circle and a nine-o prolene."

Sixty ticks and sixty tocks later, Edna announced, "Two minutes."

Duke retrieved a set of seven-inch jeweler forceps and a tiny knife from the tray next to the operating table. Though magnified sixteen times, the fine instruments looked small under the microscope. Duke began to "freshen" the edges of the arterial wound, converting the jagged arterial hole to a smooth one.

"Two minutes," Edna reminded.

Once Duke trimmed the wound, Gladys handed him the needle driver and suture. Edna gently wiped the perspiration from his forehead with a soft tissue.

"Two minutes," Edna said for the third time.

Duke commenced to sew, tying each stitch with four knots, carefully placing them to close the wound but not narrow the artery. The clock's ticking, dude, Duke reminded himself. Do the job you are trained to do. Don't panic but work fast!

Edna issued her two-minute warning thrice more before Duke completed the repairs. Duke took a long, controlled breath. His apprehensive eyes met with those of his colleagues.

"Nut-cutting time," he declared.

Time to release the temporary clips. If the sutures failed to hold, the party was over. Duke could replace the sutures, but probably not in time to avoid brain death.

Duke finessed the clip-applier down, as if he were diffusing a bomb. The mouth closed on the clip. Duke slowly pulled the clip from the artery. No one else spoke or moved. No blood appeared. One more temporary clip remained.

"This son of a bitch better hold," Duke muttered. He removed the last clip more tentatively than the first.

"Damn sure better," Ted agreed.

"Nice job, no matter what happens," said Dr. Portera, but even he looked doubtful.

Edna said nothing, but she crossed the middle and index fingers of both hands, allowing them to dangle nervously at her side.

"He could run like Mickey Mantle," Gladys whispered. Everyone watched the monitor. No blood. Collectively, they let out their breath.

"They held," Edna said, her voice bright with discovery.

Duke scanned the interior of Joe Donley's skull. He located the sella turcica, the cavity housing the almond-size pituitary gland.

"Shit! Shit! Shit!"

All eyes darted back to the monitor.

The microscope revealed a pulpy pituitary gland, destroyed from the in-driven bone. Joe Donley's injury had sentenced him, at best, to the life of an invalid. He could look forward to an existence dependent on daily medications for every hormonal function—metabolism, energy, growth, sex drive, appetite, and so on. Duke felt like a pilot who, after a mission on a stormy night, returned to the aircraft carrier, his tank empty, only to discover a live bomb stuck in the rack.

Duke's heart raced like the engine of his Ruby Red, his eyes darting as if rescanning all the medical literature he'd ever read.

"Louis," Duke wheeled in the direction of the other operating room. "Did you close up the little boy's head?"

"Duke, I was going to, but . . ."

Duke held up his hand, his eyes beseeching, his tone demanding. "Louis, you and Gladys go cut the pituitary stalk and bring me that child's gland."

Duke's words echoed into the silence of his shocked audience. His associates faced him the way they would face a review board prepared to take away their medical license.

"We gotta college athlete here, whose life in essence is going to be over unless we do something pretty fucking amazing," Duke said, suddenly unafraid of the consequences. "This is the one chance to give this kid back some of what he's lost."

"We've never done a pituitary gland transplant before," reminded Gladys.

"Duh, Gladys! Nobody's ever done one before," Ted said.

"I don't have a lot of time to go through some goddamn committee! Fuck protocol. Fuck the consequences. We can give this kid a shot at a decent life and make that child's life count. Louis, will you please go pull that kid's fuckin' pituitary gland, or do I need to go do it myself?"

Duke fired a look at Louis like a poisonous arrow.

Ted's eyes locked on Duke's. "Hell yeah. We could do it. Louis, a fuckin' pituitary gland transplant. It could work." Ted rubbed his hands together with glee.

Dr. Portera, with Gladys right behind him, wheeled out of the room.

Louis Portera's hands guided forceps and fine scissors into the open skull of the deceased child. He carefully plucked the boy's pituitary gland from the sella turcica and placed it gently in the sterile cup held by the veteran nurse's unsteady hand.

"Do you think Duke's lost it?" Gladys nervously whispered, referring to her boss's emotional stability, not Joe Donley's pituitary gland.

Dr. Portera managed a grin and raised his thick dark eyebrows. "Who's going to tell him if he has?" he asked, his whisper softer than hers.

Two hours later, the surgical team huddled around the operating table. They marveled at their work in silence. Joe's head was closed. He lay on his back, his eyes shut. He appeared to rest comfortably, offering a hint of a snore.

"Anybody ever tell a soul about this, and I'll cut their nuts out. . . without anesthesia" warned Duke, his laser stare scanning the room.

Only Gladys instinctively dropped her hands, strategically in front of her crotch.

CHAPTER 3
IT WAS TWENTY YEARS AGO TODAY OR YOU SAY IT'S YOUR BIRTHDAY

"Do you think we'll get there before it starts?" Sitting front seat shotgun, George Donley's voice easily cleared the hum of the silver mini-van's air conditioner. "I'm sorry for making us late," offered the old timer, now referred to by friends and family as "Grampa George."

George wore his dress Army uniform from World War II. With bushy white eyebrows advancing up his forehead, he had almost as much hair above his eyes as on his head.

Beneath the white hair was the face of a loving husband, father, and grandfather. Though he'd developed wattles under his chin, the old coach's jaw remained square. If his brown eyes were any measure of strength, he could still do fifty push-ups on command.

"We'll make it, Grampa George, don't worry," answered the van's driver, Cheryl Lee.

Cheryl's glance caught Joe's father through the corner of her eye. He seemed to be looking for something or someone. During the ten-mile drive from Hutchins to Dallas for his son's softball game, George had gotten lost. Coach Donley still enjoyed good health, but occasionally his memory faded like a long foul ball.

Twenty minutes earlier, George had speed dialed his Christmas present from Joe, but there was no answer at his son's house. He then called next door to the home of Alvin "Bull" Lee, his son's childhood buddy and college teammate. Bull's wife, Cheryl, picked up on the first ring and naturally agreed to rescue Joe's father.

"I'm by some railroad tracks and a school," said Grampa George.

"Sit tight; I'll be right there. I was just getting ready to leave. Somebody will take you back to your car after the game," Cheryl had promised.

In recent years, George's body had retreated to its boyish physique; his dress olives fit perfectly. His disposition had become even more youthful, pleasing his wife immensely. "Unless you change and become like children, you will never enter the kingdom of heaven," Mary Donley would quote from Matthew.

"It's Joe's fortieth birthday," George announced.

"Are we going to open presents?" Cheryl's five-year-old daughter Sara asked from the back seat.

"Has Joe seemed a little distant lately, or is it just my imagination?" George asked, his tone weighted with concern as his eyes took in the ancient three-story red brick high school on his left, the school's vacant football practice field on the right.

Sara sighed heavily.

"Oh, maybe a little. Real estate's in a slump; that could be part of it. Or maybe it's just that forty-year-old thing men go through. He'll be all right," Cheryl said unconvincingly.

"I guess Joan's handling things okay."

"I wouldn't worry, Grampa George. I think after all these years, Joan knows how to deal with Joe's moods."

"As far back as I can remember, Joan was always over at our house. She and that husband of yours," Grampa George said, his face breaking into a revealing smile. "Course, things weren't always so good at her house, and that's one of the reasons she liked hanging around our place so much. I sort of feel like I raised that girl."

"I've picked up bits and pieces over the years that Joan's childhood was pretty rough," Cheryl said. "But you know Joan; she'd never talk about it. What happened?"

George smiled at Sara in the back seat before lowering his voice several decibels. "Where do you want to start? Her dad's plastic molding business had problems, and he started to hit the bottle. He never came to any of the kid's functions, like Joan's school plays or when she was cheerleading, things like that. Joan's mom would have to send her into bars to bring him home. That kind of humiliation, I suppose, a kid never forgets. Oh, he wasn't a bad guy. I just think he got so depressed after he chopped off his finger."

"Chopped off his finger?" Cheryl said in a hushed tone, her upper lip contorted.

"Yeah, after he lost his business, he took work as a butcher and chopped off his finger. To make matters worse, he loved playing his banjo. Hard to do without a left index finger."

"Oh my gosh! You're not kidding, are you?"

"Nope. That's when he really started hitting the gin."

"What was Joan's mom like? I never really got to know her."

Joe's father smiled. "Dorothy Hegeberg. Good woman. First generation Norwegian. Always had trouble with the English language though. My wife was an English teacher, you know. Tried to help her, but it didn't do any good. Sometimes when I listen to my youngest granddaughter, I still hear that lady."

Cheryl chuckled at the mention of Joe and Joan's youngest. "For instance?"

"Once, I heard her tell Joan to 'shit damn,' instead of sit down. Sick kids were 'barking.' Dogs were always 'barfing.' If the kids were tired, Dorothy would tell them, 'You should have stood in bed earlier.' 'Are you bald?' meant 'Are you deaf?'" said Grandpa George, his eyes dancing.

"I guess she's been gone almost two years now."

Grampa George nodded. "Doctors said it was a stroke, but I think she died of a broken heart. I guess dealing with her husband's problems and then Patrick, too."

"Oh yeah, Joan's younger brother. I forgot about him. He ran away, didn't he?"

Grampa George glanced at Cheryl's daughter, who was preoccupied with her latest doll, before replying. "He must have been about seventeen. Took off in Luke Brunner's brand new pickup, but not before getting pretty rough with a lady of the night. I don't know who was more upset, the girl or Brunner. Not that anybody could have done anything about it if they'd caught him."

Grampa George's head shook in amazement. "Golly, that boy must have been six-six and weighed 275. Biggest kid I've ever seen. Anyway, one of the ways Brunner identified his truck was a bumper sticker on the back that said: 'If you don't like my driving, dial 1-800-EAT...'"

Grampa George chuckled. "Well, you can guess what it said. Ol' Brunner's neck was as red as the paint job on his new truck. Nobody's seen Patrick since. That was at least fifteen years ago, right after his dad died."

Grampa George cocked his head a bit sideways and pointed his right index finger skyward. "See, that's why Joan gave up her modeling and acting career to stay home as soon as Joe could support them. Sorta like baseball. Sometimes you have to sacrifice for the sake of the team. Lay down a bunt to advance the runner," Grampa George said, raising his hands parallel and chest high in a fist as if about to lay down a bunt. "She doesn't want her kids to go through what she did. She looks after Joe the same way. That woman looks after Joe and those three kids like a female tiger protecting her cubs," Grampa George said proudly.

"I understand the way she feels," he sighed. "I g-u-a-r-a-n-t-e-e you that I've been through a couple of days I wouldn't want my family to have to go through."

"Whatever happened to Joan's father? Bull just said he got real sick."

A troubled look visited Grampa George's face and decided to stay awhile. "Well," he said and then kept the rest to himself.

The van stopped at a railroad track. A crossing gate blocked passage. The ground began to vibrate in warning of the approaching locomotive.

"Grampa George, you look nice in your army uniform," said Cheryl after a weighted silence. "Any particular reason you're wearing it?"

Grampa George briefly inspected his clothing, and then his youthful grin reappeared.

"I had to make a movie today," he winked conspiratorially. "No time to change. Besides, it's D-Day, a good day to show a little patriotism."

Turning to quiz Grampa George about his movie career, Cheryl Lee's glance became super glued to her rearview mirror. Hurtling toward the rear of her stationary van was an ancient red pickup truck.

The train's thunder muffled the wail of a nearby police siren. The warm scent of locomotive steel invaded the mini-van through the air vents. Before Cheryl could react, the pickup was so close upon them that she could see it was more rust colored from age than red. Above the steering wheel loomed a massive Viking head.

The truck punted the van through the railroad crossing barrier, scissoring the yellow warning sign skyward. Cheryl's van landed on the railroad tracks. The racing train pushed the van twenty yards down the tracks before it tumbled off on its side and slid to a halt on a grassy knoll, the yellow sign proclaiming "Stay Off the Tracks" crashing down on top of it. Tiny earth particles erupted in countless formations, like minuscule balloons jitterbugging in midair. The sweet smell of daffodils, white iris, and sunflowers surrendered to the stench of hot steel and engine smoke. Relatively undamaged, the pickup changed directions, effectively eluding the pursuing police car.

After an ambulance removed the bodies, police searched the crumpled van. They discovered Bull's softball uniform (Bull played the game in street clothes, expecting his wife and child to appear any instant), a tennis racket, three Barbie dolls, a PTA directory, a stapler, and an unmarked Maxell video cassette. Police delivered the items to an overcome and inconsolable Bull, who stored them delicately out of sight. Had Bull pulled the cassette from its badly scuffed sleeve, he would have discovered a small white card, scribbled in Grampa George's hand. It read "To Joe, I hope they are few, but on a bad day, maybe this will help. Happy Birthday. Love, GWD."

CHAPTER 4
MY DAD WAS A COACH

IN a week already laden with services that wrenched their hearts, a stricken community crowded the small chapel for Grampa George. Pain-stamped faces, more than their thick frames and uneven strides, branded many in attendance as Coach's past disciples.

Sitting on the first row and sandwiched between Bull and family, Joe simply stared off some place only he could see. Tethered by their loss, the principal mourners had moved through the past few days as parts of a single anatomy. Joe could not imagine how the world could hold any more grief.

"Don't be sad, Daddy," Joe's oldest daughter, Liz, age fourteen, reminded him. "Grampa George isn't dead; he has eternal life."

"Grampa George is in heaven, and I know what he's doing," said the youngest daughter, six-year-old K. C. "He's meeting Mommy's daddy and momma and Mrs. Lee and Sara . . . and Babe Ruth."

The mourners stood for "My Country 'Tis of Thee." Grampa George's fellow deacons then sang one of his favorite hymns: "When the darkness I see will be waiting for me, I won't have to cross Jordan alone."

Dr. Anderson, the Baptist preacher, approached the pulpit. The chapel became as still as the American flag that draped the coffin before them. A man of medium build, Dr. Anderson looked no older than Joe. His hazel eyes peered over the crowd through wire-rimmed glasses.

"Truth is, I love George Donley," announced the fair-haired preacher, his voice breaking. "If I were to share with you everything that needs to be said about George, we'd be here for days. Then it would be your turn." He let his eyes fall to the memorial service program.

"A minor league baseball player with a promising future before World War II," Dr. Anderson read. "A captain in the 196th field artillery battalion during the war. An acclaimed high school coach right here in Hutchins until he retired. A deacon for practically twenty years in this very church."

The preacher's eyes returned to his congregation. His voice rose to a crescendo. His hands gripped the sides of the pulpit.

"George Donley was more than what's printed in your program—more than what we will say about him today. He was friend, father, husband, grandfather, as good a man as I've ever known. We're here today to celebrate a life lived honorably and a faith lived eternally—to celebrate George's victory over death." Dr. Anderson paused and then continued. "George Donley was a hero, the kind of hero who saved this country. In World War II, he won five bronze service stars, a bronze star, an oak leaf cluster, and a silver star."

Mary Donley, her eyes shimmering, laid her hand gently on her son's.

"The apostle Paul said, 'The time has come for my departure. I have fought the good fight,'" the preacher said, sounding very capable of leading men in a good fight. "'I have finished the race. I have kept the faith.' Paul's second letter to Timothy says, 'There is in store for me the crown for righteousness.' Yes, there's one more medal for George. It is not a medal for his uniform, but a crown on his head. It is conferred not by his military commander, but by the God of the universe. It is the greatest reward of all: eternal life in the presence of a God pleased with this man's life."

Dr. Anderson looked intensely at the congregation.

"It is fitting that one of George's own family has said it best," he said. "His twelve-year-old granddaughter, Kate Donley, wrote this to her father on the night of her grandfather's death." Dr. Anderson took in a deep breath. His eyes seemed to touch each and every person in the room before he started to read, 'Dad, I hope you feel better soon. I miss him a lot too! But now he's in heaven with God. I think it's a better place for him. Heaven is twice as good as earth is! He will always be in our hearts deep inside, just like Sara and Mrs. Lee. I will pray for our family and Bull's family and for you every night! Love, Tater.'

"Precious in the sight of the Lord is the death of his servants," the pastor concluded.

At the gravesite, as George was lowered into the earth, Dr. Anderson leaned close to Joe. "Your dad kept a pretty low profile, but man, he plowed real deep."

Heads solemnly nodded their agreement, but only Joe heard his father's familiar authoritative voice. "Nice poke yesterday, Son."

Twice, Joe ducked his own head in thank you. Only those standing closest heard him whisper, "Bye, Coach." Others pressed Joe's hand and offered condolences, but his father's words had already carried Joe back to the previous day when he found temporary refuge at his favorite place--the ballfield.

Thin, scorched grass resembled a parched cow pasture more than the outfield of a softball diamond. The Texas sun left the dirt infield cracked and peeling like a thirsty riverbank in high summer. A dry breeze fanned the faint fragrance of honey suckles blooming behind the backstop. Invisible cicadas chirped. Every so often, a commercial jet's roar muffled the sound of hurried two-way traffic.

Human chatter drifted across from the parking lot of the Methodist church next door. The cemetery across the way seemed distanced as much by context as by the busy four-lane highway that separated it from the diamond and its adjacent park.

Large old oak and birch trees sheltered the complex and the young children who thronged its slide, swing set, and merry-go-round.

Somberly, Joe and Bull's teammates prepared for their weekly slow pitch softball game without them. Some wore jeans; other men had on shorts that revealed legs long deprived of the sun. Baseball caps in every color of the rainbow shielded receding hairlines from the sun's glare. Heat waves rose visibly from the parking lot, but the image they yielded was no mirage. Walking deliberately, Joe crossed the asphalt toward the dusty ball diamond. Bull, nearly paralyzed with grief, moved like a mechanical man and followed closely behind Joe. Though thicker than his college days, Bull's gaunt face housed dark and hollow eyes as if he'd fasted since the accident. His former curly blond locks were now cropped short enough to stand attention at random intervals across his head.

Through his John Lennon glasses, Joe saw the bewildered expressions on the faces of his teammates who stopped playing catch. No one knew what to say.

After reaching the diamond Joe simply said, "My dad was a coach."

Thirty minutes later, Joe stood poised at the plate, holding the blue aluminum bat above his shoulders, a bright red cap bearing the Rangers' white script **T** on his head. Though Duke ordered a life without hardball twenty years ago, Joe, trim as his college days, still looked capable of a one hundred sixty-two game season.

The pitcher's soft toss crawled to home plate but left the infield like a white sputnik. High above the outfield grass, it picked up speed, as though an afterburner kicked in, before landing across the highway in the cemetery where his dad would soon be buried.

The ballfield was still the one place where Joe could tune out everything else, where no circumstance or burden could disrupt his concentration. This was the lesson of his youth.

CHAPTER 5
THIS IS THE BIG TIME

It was the first softball game of the new year, eight months after Joe and Bull's worst nightmare. Their team wore white T-shirts with black block lettering across the front that read *BIOYA Brothers*. The thin jerseys swelled to the shape of the players' expanding stomachs.

Though still mostly brown, the outfield grass sparkled like a dress shirt. The hint of spring approaching perfumed the air. Families filled the small bleacher section behind home plate; others entertained themselves in the park. Children clambered on the swing sets, slides, and monkey bars. Some families picnicked; others lay on blankets, basking in the glorious sunny day. A father hurled a frisbee toward his young son; a miniature collie chased the airborne disk.

"Here we are at the ballpark." From her fourth-row bleacher seat, Liz Donley discreetly lowered her chin to a tiny black recorder. She spoke softly, but with such self-assurance she seemed disarmingly older than her age, fourteen. "Lately, I don't think Dad's doing too well. Mom and I are kind of worried."

A woman of forty, but looking a decade younger, cheered loudly from her seat beside Liz. Joan Hegeberg Donley's once lengthy hair stopped just short of her shoulders, framing a mature but even lovelier face and still naturally full lips. Faded Ralph Lauren blue jeans covered legs as long and slender as outfield light poles. Her starched long-sleeved white shirt matched her size-ten tennis shoes.

Joan watched her husband proceed toward the on-deck circle. "Come on, Joe! Smack it!" she hollered. While flailing her long Nordic arms and elegant fingers, Joan accidentally nudged her oldest daughter in the mouth.

"Mama! Get a grip! You almost knocked me off the bench," Liz said in a defiant tone that reinforced her father's notion of like mother, like oldest daughter.

Liz's shoulder length, light brown hair framed her cherubic bronze face perfectly. Though not quite five-five, Liz was rock solid physically and emotionally. If not the tallest in her class, she was the longest on beauty—a young Grace Kelly, her father was given to declare.

"Don't be so grumpy," her mother said. "Where's your spirit?"

Ignoring her mother, Liz whispered testily into her recorder. "Mom's such a spaz sometimes. I can't believe that she every made it down the runway without tripping over herself. "She always wanted to act anyway, but she made so much money modeling, she never got around to it. We needed the money back then too. I guess neither Mom nor Dad got the career they wanted," Liz added with a shrug.

A baggy BIOYA T-shirt hung almost to the thighs of her bright red sweat pants. Liz had dressed to play ball, hoping to sub if one of her dad's teammates failed to appear. To her disappointment, the diamond now boasted a full roster.

Denied the opportunity for her first adult softball action, Liz focused instead on her second passion. Loving the written word as much as her paternal grandmother, Liz longed to write a book. Unfortunately, no subject matter came to mind.

"Don't be discouraged," Grandma Mary Donley had said. "It's a common malady among writers. Keep a diary. Something will come up."

Liz, by default and only for practice, had decided to write about her family, hence her copious recorded notes.

"Hey, Liz, Mom's right. Where's your spirit? You're just mad cause you're not getting to play," Kate "Tater" Donley said sardonically, reminding Liz of another irritant . . . her middle sister.

With sizzling brown eyes, Liz fired a shrapnel look at her blue-eyed, tow-headed sibling, who sat to the right of their mom. "Tater, you are so immature and a wuss too."

"Not!" Tater's suddenly indignant but angelic pale face and lanky frame bespoke a more fragile child, both emotionally and physically, than her older sister.

"Oh yeah, if you're not a wuss, how come you're the one with allergies and the one that's always getting sick or hurt or getting those gross fever blisters on your lips. You're twelve years old and can't even eat cheese or drink milk without getting a stomach ache."

"Dr. Duke says I'm lactose intolerant," Tater replied. Remorse bled into the blue in her eyes, for she loved cheese almost as much as she loved potatoes.

"K. C. calls it cheese-toast intolerant," Liz said, referring to their youngest sister in a tone too harsh to pass for humor. If Liz inherited her mother's temper, Tater inherited Joan's Norwegian features—the color of her eyes and hair, her stick frame, her feet—especially her feet. Contained by high top red roller skates, the most rapidly growing part of Tater's body dangled in midair. Tater's musical preferences ranged from Christian—she sang in the children's church choir—to rock-n-roll to even opera. In truth, everything Tater sang sounded kin to opera. Her high, perfectly pitched voice lapsed into silence only when she slept.

Liz had long considered her middle sister the family's resident space cadet. One incident, especially, reinforced Liz's suspicion. One evening, mother and daughters were watching a Hepburn/Tracy movie on television. "Kate," Joan exclaimed to Tater, "there's Katherine Hepburn; that's who you were named after!"

"Momma," Tater replied, confusion clouding her expression, "I didn't know my name was Hepburn."

Tater's choice of fashion reinforced Liz's opinion of her sister.

Despite the seventy-degree temperature, Tater wore a red and black checkered skirt over a dancer's black leotard. Concealed beneath the leotard, her favorite blue and yellow one-piece bathing suit hugged her body. Tater's dress habits had rattled more than one cage. When a child psychiatrist speaking to the PTA warned parents that dressing in layers might indicate sexual abuse, Joan's blue eyes flew open. If confronted, the psychiatrist went on to say, the abused child would likely refuse to discuss the issue.

After the meeting, Joan rushed home to quiz Tater in the manner recommended by the doctor. "Has anyone tried to touch your private parts?"

"Ooh la la, Mom. Tell me more," promptly replied Tater, her sky-blue eyes sparkling with playful curiosity. Exhaling a huge sigh of relief, it was Joan who refused to discuss the issue further.

But today, Liz was no more likely than her younger sister to resist a loaded discussion. "Hey, how many pairs of underwear do you have on today?" Liz asked louder than she intended.

Tater looked at Liz through expanded eyes, stuck out her tongue, and farted with her lips.

"That's enough, girls," warned their mom. Joan never took her eyes off Joe, who had left the dugout for the on-deck circle.

Liz turned her back and pushed the ON button of her recorder. "Tater's a real wuss sometimes," Liz reiterated. "The kind that keep their eyes closed the whole time on a good ride at the fair." Liz glared across her shoulder as her sister launched into Pavarotti. "Tater's singing's driving me nuts."

Kent-Claire Donley chattered as much as her middle sister sang. The freckle-faced smallest Donley was far too occupied with her Barbie dolls to be distracted by her two older sisters. Tucked inside her blue-jean overalls, she wore a black T-shirt that stated in blue letters *I've got the blues*. Across K. C.'s chest, no advertisement could have been more false. K. C. never had a bad day. When Grandpa George died, it was K. C.

who'd asked wistfully, "Can't we just bring him back to life?"

Lost in Barbieland, K. C. sat on the other end of the row from Liz. Bright orange hair, cut like her sisters, fell just above her shoulders. Her red and white high-top Converse tennis shoes swung rhythmically in midair. Glancing up with innocent hazel eyes, K. C. noticed her dad ambling toward the batter's box.

"There's my daddy! There's my daddy! Avery, see our daddy."

Liz recorded in her softest voice yet. "That's my six-year- old sister, KC, talking to our invisible brother." Liz's coffee bean eyes glanced about to verify her privacy. Liz could hardly afford to acknowledge an invisible brother publicly. Actually, Liz wished Avery would disappear, but since he was already invisible, this appeared a difficult proposition.

"We have no idea where Avery came from," Liz continued. "He was just with us one day. K. C. can be as much a pain as Tater, especially when she won't let you in your own bathroom because Avery's inside."

If Avery's constant occupancy of the children's upstairs bathroom irritated Liz, it irked their mother even more. Often, Joan demanded of her youngest child, "Go sit on the pot; you haven't gone in a week!"

Invariably, the little redhead replied, "I can't Mom. Avery's using it." Or "It hurts, Mom, like a corn cube's stuck."

"That's corn cob," Liz would hastily reply. All this seemed to support Liz's claim "that KC was full of more crap than any six-year-old in history."

Whistling and hollering encouragement, Joan and the Donley girls watched Joe step into the batter's box. Joe eyed his fan club, offering a brief smile that bordered on the self-conscious. His manner was guarded but not aloof. Before his injury, Joe had seldom displayed much gaiety, anger, or tremendous effort. Out of the limelight, he had become even more reserved, yet the injury hadn't seemed to compromise Joe's easy gracefulness at the plate or in the field.

Outwardly, Joe never betrayed the punishing self-doubt he so painfully confided to Bull: "To take a fastball to the head—for my reflexes and hand-eye coordination to be so piss-poor."

Despite his thwarted chances for a baseball career, Joe knew how much he had to be grateful for. He knew that many of his own teammates envied him the many blessings he was the first to count: his lovely wife, beautiful children, successful business—the list when on and on, right down to the BMW sedan he drove and his five handicap. Yet here he stood coiled at the plate and inwardly recoiling at "a damn girls' game."

Liz hunkered over the small recorder with her chin down, apparently in her continued quest for privacy.

"Dad was a cinch to make the major leagues. In Dad's mind, the only question was whether he'd win a batting title. Since he was a little boy, that was his goal. Mom says that, since the day he got hurt and couldn't play baseball anymore, he only smiles little smiles. Dad said getting beaned in college was the first time he realized people don't necessarily live happily ever after. He said this was his 'first true adult thought.'"

Just then, a short woman in her early twenties, her tattered and faded blue-jean cutoffs exposing the curve of her buttocks, strolled between the bleachers and the backstop. A tight, brief halter top accentuated the swell of her breasts and exposed a firm abdomen and deep-cut navel. Peroxided hair surrounded an overly pink face.

Stopping directly behind home plate, the woman paused to study Joe, her overglossed and collagened lips parted. Joan's impulse was to gaze into the white toes of her own sneakers, but Liz, like many of those behind her, could only stare openly.

"Liz! Daddy's up," whispered Joan, a little too loudly.

"Is that your dad?" the woman asked, turning opal eyes to Liz, who could only nod, her own mouth a little open in awe.

"He's cute," the woman said.

Joan felt her own color heighten as the woman sauntered off, confident of male eyes that trailed her.

It would not surprise a male streaker of twenty years ago to know that Joe's focus never left the mound. The pitcher recomposed himself and gently underhanded the softball to home plate. Joe swung effortlessly and delivered a long laser streak of white down the third baseline, fouling it nearly into his own bench.

One voice bellowed above the rest. "Come on, Little Man! Straighten it out!"

"Bull" Lee now looked neckless, wristless, and ankleless. Like Joe, Bull wore an authentic Texas Rangers ball cap but its crown tilted to the right of center. A slight paunch had settled around his mid-section.

Yet two decades past his heyday and less than a year since he lost his family, not everything had changed with the rambunctious Bull. He still wept during *Cool Hand Luke* and jeered at bad calls by the ump. He still allowed the grease to run down his face when eating a hamburger. Most important, he remained Joe's best friend.

Liz glanced toward Bull and spoke louder than before. "Dad says Bull's the type of guy to come over in the middle of the night and fix your furnace." Liz's dark eyes shifted back to her dad, who took the pitch for a ball. Liz whispered to the black box in hushed confidentiality. "My dad thinks Bull's the toughest man alive, but I'm not so sure. I saw Bull cry after he ran over one of the neighbor's dogs."

Joe passed on another balloon-ball.

In the dugout, the BIOYAs were on their feet. None were more anxious though than a pear-shaped man standing beside Bull.

"Get em, Joe!" the man exhorted.

Bull wrapped a warm arm around the man.

"Don't worry, Big Jim; Little Man is waiting on the one he wants."

Early thirtyish, Big Jim had a hairless oval face and a body just as round and childlike. He always wore a soiled grey filling-station uniform; red script letters spelled *Esso* above the shirt pocket. His thin, oily hair was in a crew cut, hidden by an equally worn red ball cap. The odor of the garage clung to him.

"Joe coulda made it to the pro's, couldn't he, Bull?" Jim asked, shifting his weight from foot to foot. He spoke in a halting high-pitched voice.

"You know it, pal."

Both men's eyes followed the arch of the next pitch. Ball three.

"Bull, tell me one more time what happened?" Big Jim's off-center smile exposed teeth the color of the infield dirt.

"Little Man got beaned in the head by Rocket Nolin, no less, in a college World Series game a long time ago," Bull said, noticing a dog on the field had temporarily suspended play.

"Rocket still throws hard, doesn't he, Bull?" Big Jim quizzed. His eyes followed the duel between Joe and the pot-bellied pitcher with the reverence due a World Series contest.

"I guess, pal. Rocket's the all-time major league strike-out king. He throws so hard the ball disintegrates on the way to home plate, and the catcher puts it back together again. When it passes the plate, you can't see anything but spit."

With the dog removed, Joe delivered another hard foul ball along the left field line. Under slow pitch softball rules, any foul after two strikes means strike three. With the count full, Bull knew Joe would walk or hit the ball in play, and a walk was the last thing Joe wanted.

"Rocket hurt Joe, didn't he, Bull?" the simple man asked, as if hearing the bad part of his otherwise favorite story.

"Yep. Joe had headaches and vision problems for years. Duke never let Joe play anymore hardball. Joe's lucky to be alive, pal." Privately, Bull believed that with the passage of time, Joe no longer considered himself so lucky. "Hurt Rocket, too. He's never backed hitters off the plate like he should. I think he's afraid he'd hurt somebody again."

"Get 'em, Joe!" Big Jim whooped as the throw approached home plate.

Whack! The ball vaulted from Joe's bat and raced across the sky like a shooting star. Team members and family supporters erupted as the BIOYA base runners took off. Joe ran so fluidly past first base his hat flew off, exposing a full head of dark hair streaked with gray.

He slowed after passing second base and was walking by the time he reached third. The runner he'd moved off first had easily crossed the plate to win the game.

Joe's teammates congratulated themselves on their victory and proceeded to the middle of the diamond for post-game handshakes.

One of the opposition eyed the letters on Bull's jersey. "What does BIOYA stand for?" he asked.

"Blow it out your ass . . . pal," Bull said with that "I was hoping you'd ask" grin.

Bull's gregarious nature so disarmed the player that he began to laugh. But Joe didn't join in the banter. Big Jim shuffled toward him.

"That was exciting, wasn't it, Joe?" Big Jim grinned widely. Joe stared searchingly at Big Jim and seemed to consider the question gravely. Big Jim's soft, disproportionately wide chest and protruding stomach looked as if connected to the legs of an exotic bird. Carefully, Joe placed his arm around Big Jim. Just as carefully, his face surrendered to a haunted smile.

"Yeah, this is the big time, Big Jim."

CHAPTER 6
A WILL AND A PRAYER

MARY Donley sat in the middle of her bed surrounded by books. She glanced over to the nightstand, taking note of the contrast between two photos of her late husband. One was an old black-and-white of a youthful George in his Army uniform. Below George's officer's cap shone dark brown sideburns. A seriousness emanated from his eyes. In the other more recent color photo, George was fuller in the face; his jowls sagged a bit, and his white hair was vanishing. But the most striking difference centered in his big brown eyes. Enough warmth radiated from those eyes to heat a ball diamond in early spring. Only eight months since the loss of her husband, but they seemed like eight lifetimes.

Thinking of Joe, she shuddered still at how close she'd come to losing him. Whenever Mary gazed at her handsome, healthy, but somewhat absent son, she couldn't help yearning for what she believed could make him whole again. Only minutes before, her face betrayed fatigue, but now a twinge of excitement flushed her faint cheeks and brightened her eyes.

What had roused Mary's attention was an article from a medical journal entitled "The Pituitary," edited by Shlomo Melmed. Certain passages bounced from the page like one of her favorite Bible passages.

"The pituitary gland is considered the master gland for the regulation of endocrine function. The pituitary not only integrates but also amplifies the signals it receives and any dysfunction of the pituitary gland can have profound effects on adrenal, reproductive, thyroid, and metabolic functions as well as on development and growth.

Over the past twenty-five years, there have been major advances in research on the pituitary, in particular, a better understanding of cell biology and molecular regulation of the synthesis and release of pituitary hormones."

Her mind raced back to a conversation with Duke years ago. "I don't believe in miracles, and I would damn sure hate to be dependent on one," Duke had said. "I believe in a logical explanation, if not a scientific one, for everything. Any faith dependent on a miracle contains more holes than a murder defendant's alibi."

"Well, Duke," Mary had replied, "I guess we're on opposite sides of the checkerboard on that one."

Now, Mary decided to lay her faith on the line, to settle her one issue with God. Turning in her Bible to Paul's letter to the Philippians, she read: "Have no anxiety about anything, but in everything by prayer and supplication with thanksgiving let your request be known to God."

Pressing the open Bible to her breastbone, Mary dropped her chin, closed her eyes, and began to pray fervently.

Back at Joe's residence, and only shortly after Mary Donley finished her prayer of all prayers, Bull stood on the top step of a ten-foot ladder leaning into the Donley's backyard pecan tree. He handed a flood lamp to Joe, who was perched on a limb. Both men still wore their softball attire. They hoped to install an outdoor lighting system before sundown. Big Jim stood at the base of the ladder, doing his best to stabilize it.

Owing to the shade thrown off by the huge tree, little sunlight made it to the Donley's backyard. A black iron fence surrounded the swimming pool. A wooden picnic table and chairs took up about half of the pool's deck. In the far corner of the wood-fenced yard, a cedar playhouse piggybacked a slide, behind which stretched a trampoline and a mini-basketball court. Tree limbs from Bull's yard next door invaded the Donley's yard, completing a natural green dome. In effect, the Donley playground lay nestled in a jungle.

In her backyard, Joan felt insulated from the world's problems. Her daughters loved it. The Cleavers would have loved it. Joe should have loved it.

Liz and Tater were playing catch with a hard ball: no "damn girls' game" for Joe Donley's daughters. After each throw, Tater, who also wore big league sunglasses, would spit disgustedly to the ground.

Like her mother, Tater aspired to become an actress and was now playing the role of a baseball player. Her relentless singing undermined her effort to enact the part faithfully. Tater's errant throws reinforced the notion that cleats provide better footing than roller skates. Her lack of pinpoint control gradually infuriated Liz, who repeatedly had to fight Hershey, the Donleys' beloved chocolate lab, for the ball.

"Like father, like daughter," Bull said.

Offering no reply, Joe continued working on the lighting system.

"Hershey can sure stink up a backyard." Bull turned up his nose at the smell of Hershey's droppings that created a constant minefield of the backyard.

Still no response from Joe.

"I guess we're the only nuts in the tree this year," Bull said, his eyes scanning the barren limbs.

A few feet from the tree, K. C. played in a portable plastic green sandbox while chattering non-stop with Avery, her invisible brother.

"Hey! Little Man, you gonna talk today or what?" Bull said sharply. Hershey stopped quickly in his tracks, as if Bull had demanded that the stunned chocolate lab talk.

Joe smiled tolerantly at Bull.

Joan appeared from the back door. "When do you think you'll finish?" she asked. "I sure would like this backyard lit up before you two leave town, especially with that crazy man running around," she said, referring to recent assaults on several women in the neighborhood.

"Trip?" Big Jim said, sounding concerned.

"Haven't they told you?" Joan asked.

"Joe and I are going to the Rangers' fantasy camp in Arizona week after next." Bull could see the perplexity mounting on Big Jim's face. "For a week, guys like Joe and me get to play ball with a bunch of ex-major leaguers. It'll be a blast, pal."

Big Jim's shoulders relaxed.

"I'd better stay home with this pervert on the loose." Joe spoke in a voice past tiredness. It was the voice of a man acutely depressed.

"Little Man speaks!" Bull cried.

"With these lights, this place will be lit up like Yankee Stadium," Joan said. "Besides, the neighbors will keep an eye on us."

"I'm your neighbor," reminded Bull.

Rolling her eyes, Joan said, "The other neighbors. Both of you need a break."

"I'm not going," Joe announced calmly, staring stone cold at the people in his midst.

"Come on, Little Man. We've been talking about going for years," Bull urged. "Maybe we'll get Big Jim and the girls some autographs."

"Wow!" Big Jim said.

K. C. popped out of her sandbox and ran to the tree.

"Everybody, look! I got a J. C. Penney! Is he a good player?" she cried, proudly waving a baseball card high in the air.

Everyone laughed, though Joe's reaction would hardly qualify as a hardy guffaw, especially in comparison to Big Jim's. Consumed with hearty laughter, Big Jim deserted his post at the ladder and clasped both hands to his swollen cheeks.

Without warning, the house alarm went off loud enough to signal opening day of World War III. Startled, K. C. brushed against the ladder, and the ladder came tumbling down.

Bull bailed out of the tree. His exit catapulted Joe like a man on the high diving board. Bull landed feet first then rolled onto his shoulder unharmed. Joe's flight took on the perspective of an air raid attack from the bomb's point of view.

"Look out for K. C.!" Joan yelled, seeing the child frozen below him.

Joe twisted to avoid landing on K. C., but even Joe could not avoid the ground and landed head first.

Everyone rushed to Joe's side. Bull's eyes locked onto Joan's, their faces whitening. Each knew the other's thoughts. Once again, Joe lay in the fetal position, blood trickling from his left ear. Joan dropped to her knees and cradled his head to her bosom. Her movements jolted the others from their trance.

"Da's head is broke! Momma, fix Da's head!" K. C. screamed. Wailing hysterically, she started to run figure eights in the backyard.

"Is he dead?" Tater asked in a high and bird-like voice. Tater closed her eyes the way she would "on a good ride at the fair."

"Great, Mom! Now we don't have a dad!" Liz's quivering voice stirred anger with fear. "You shouldn't have made him get in that tree." "Liz, go turn off that alarm!" Joan snapped.

Wisely, Liz ran inside.

"I forgot to get it fixed," Joe moaned.

Deep caca, Little Man, deep caca, thought Bull, hovering over Joe like two decades before.

Big Jim turned into a statue, too scared to talk or move. He thought the accident was his fault—the way children often feel when anything goes amiss.

Abruptly, Joe opened his eyes, alert as a squirrel. He rolled on his back, at first blinking slowly but then more rapidly. His glasses, though terribly bent, remained on his face. K. C.'s panic showed few indicators of winding down.

Joan's powerful voice carried over the alarm. "K. C., stop it! Your dad's okay. Are you okay?" she asked Joe.

"Yeah, Little Man. Are you okay?" Bull echoed.

"I can't see," Joe said, his voice calm.

"What?" Joan gasped.

"Everything's out of focus—bad out of focus."

"Aw, Little Man, don't tell me that," Bull almost roared. Bull remembered the countless hours of intense therapy that Joe had endured with his help. Bull dreaded a repeat of that torment. And if he felt this way, how must Joe feel. The deafening noise from the alarm stopped.

Liz returned to the backyard. "K. C., be quiet!" she yelled, taking note of K. C.'s frenetic commotion. K. C. promptly obeyed, stopped running, and joined the others surrounding Joe.

"His head's not broken; his eyes are broken," Liz said.

"His eyes are broke?" K. C. lamented. "Da's eyes are broke?"

"They don't look broke," Tater said, finally opening her eyes to see for herself. "The glasses look sort of broke."

"Joe's eyes aren't broken. It's just his glasses," Big Jim managed to say.

"Everybody hush up! Everything's going to be all right," Joan declared. "Maybe," she added under her breath.

Bull and Big Jim carefully helped Joe to his feet. With Joe's arms draped around both men, they slowly started to walk. Joan and the girls remained close behind, without talking.

"Easy, Little Man. Easy," Bull cautioned.

Joe's mangled glasses fell to the ground. Bull retrieved the eyewear, handing them to Joe, who returned them to his face.

While Joe's face bore not the slightest hint of expression, his eyes darted all about the backyard. After a weighty pause, he announced, "I'm okay."

"You're okay?" Joan asked.

"I'm okay," Joe reiterated evenly.

"Little Man," said Bull, inspecting the trickle of blood around Joe's ear, "Let's go see Duke and make sure you're okay."

"I know my body. There's no need to go see Duke," Joe said, somewhat testily. "I'm fine."

"See, Daddy's okay," Joan said, raising her shoulders apprehensively. "He's as good as ever."

"My daddy's okay?" Tater and K. C. chimed in simultaneously. Tater hit the high notes, K. C. the low.

"My daddy's okay?" Big Jim followed in soprano style.

K. C., in her innocence, would rapidly sink that lofty thought. "Big Jim, your daddy's dead, just like my grandpa," K. C. said. "You can't bring them back to life. I already asked."

K. C. looked at Big Jim most caringly, visibly sorry for shattering his brief hope with such a harsh fact. Even Bull looked stricken, surely reminded of his longest day by the words of K. C. Bull understood all too well that no amount of praying, hoping, or grieving would "bring them to life."

At that precise instant, Mary Donley, newly impregnated with hope and inspiration, entered the backyard. Despite the balmy weather, she wore a gray wool overcoat and a navy blue scarf. This recent burst of optimism provided the closest thing to a tan ever seen on the face of a woman who habitually avoided the sun.

"Momma, what are you doing here?" Joe asked. He looked and sounded more embarrassed than injured.

"I wanted to come by and check on things. Looks like it wasn't a bad idea," Joe's mother said, noticing Joe's disheveled appearance.

Bull gave a brief synopsis. During his recount, Mary's face displayed little surprise. The herd of Donleys and Bull moved toward the back door.

"Mrs. Donley, I think Joe's gonna be okay, but maybe you better say one of your special prayers just in case," Bull suggested with a grin. "Oh, I just said a very special prayer not long ago, and I do think he will be okay." With thin slits for eyes, Mary continued to inspect her son from head to toe.

"Was it a Lutheran prayer or Baptist prayer?" K. C. asked.

"Baptist," Mary replied without hesitation. "All the best prayers are Baptist prayers," Mary said, her eyes cutting toward Joan.

"Mary, this isn't the time for a theological debate," Joan said, raising her eyes to the sky. "Joe doesn't mind going to a Lutheran church."

"Speaking of prayers, have all of you girls been saying your prayers?"

"Yes, Grandma," the Donley daughters replied in perfect unison.

"Baptist prayers, I hope," she mumbled under her breath as they all filed into the house.

With dusk near, Hershey roamed the backyard. Bored in his solitude, the dog noticed something on the ground. A closer inspection revealed a small picture of a tanned, round face. Piercing brown eyes had stared hard at the camera. Tiny squint lines streaked from one side and underneath the baseball player's eyes. Sunlight had not penetrated these thin crevices and looked like white war paint. Revealing a shiny near-hairless crown, a baseball hat sat high atop his head.

Hershey couldn't read any better than he could talk, or the dog would have known it was not a baseball card of J. C. Penney but the player who started all the commotion twenty years ago. Hershey continued to bury his nose in the baseball card of Walter "Rocket" Nolin.

CHAPTER 7
I'VE BEEN AWAY TOO LONG

One week later, Joe and Bull were in the backyard finishing their work on the lighting system when Joe's mangled glasses again dropped off his face. He caught them in midair.

"Nice catch," Bull said admiringly.

Joe blinked rapidly; his eyes danced all around the backyard.

"My vision's been sort of blurry the last few days, but now I can see perfectly," he finally said, still holding his glasses in one hand.

"If you can see without your glasses, wouldn't wearing them make your vision blurry?" Bull asked, his eyes narrowing.

Joe returned the wire rims to his eyes but only for an instant. "Yep," Joe said, his tone flatter than a weak curveball.

"Yep, what? Little Man."

"Yep, it's blurry with my glasses on. Yep, I can see just fine without them," Joe confirmed with a slight chuckle.

And off Joe and Bull went to see Duke.

Secretly elated to relocate so near his prize patient, Samuel Duke left his position at the University of Nebraska Medical Center and accepted the prestigious Dallas position as Head of Neurosurgery at the University of Texas Health Science Center shortly after Joe's transplant. In confidence, Duke half-kiddingly commented to his scrub nurse, Gladys, who followed him to Texas, "We've potentially created a hormonal time bomb."

Twenty years ago, Duke had recommended, "At least three hours of speech therapy and three of physical therapy per week. But if you've got the resources, he can use all the therapy possible."

"You mean, if I can find the people to help, give him all he can stand?" replied George Donley.

"Yep."

Joe's father quickly arranged for amateur therapists to appear at the Donley home five times daily—6:30, 9:30, and 3:00 in the day, then 7:00 and 9:00 at night. Five people manned every session, four for each limb and one for Joe's head.

Initially, Joe could barely speak. Duke explained, "The brain normally uses only ten percent of its brains cells and the unused cells need to be taught new functions." Joe's progress, however, stunned even Duke. After dropping out of college for only one semester, Joe re-enrolled and finished his degree. Regrettably, Duke saw Joe last while attending George Donley's funeral. Now, he anxiously awaited Joe's arrival to his office.

Within an hour of taking Joan's call, Joe and Bull sat before Duke on a maroon cloth couch. Duke's tiny office resembled a mini-library with books, videotapes, and papers everywhere. In one corner, a color TV allowed Duke to study surgeries with the scrutiny of a coach studying game film. Along with a Stanford University pennant, educational and medical degrees decorated the white walls. Pictures of his family were on the credenza behind his desk.

Though more salt than pepper now invaded his full beard, aging agreed well with Duke. Only on close inspection would the strain of attempting to save lives show in his deep-set eyes.

After taking Joe's blood pressure and skull x-rays and conducting an eye exam, Duke listened as Bull explained what happened in the Donley backyard.

"Little Man snagged those glasses out of midair faster than a Rocket Nolin fastball," Bull said and then tried to swallow his words back. "Sorry, Joe."

Grilling Joe with a barrage of questions, Duke learned about the previous week's fall. Joe also admitted to sleeping less, yet noticing increased energy—an indicator that Joe's transplanted gland had suddenly become hyperactive.

"Yeah," agreed Bull. "I didn't think we were ever going to quit working in that backyard."

Without warning, a large bald man wearing a white coat entered the room. Ted French looked more like an escapee from the top floor psycho-ward than a doctor. The mad professor had also remained with Duke's team and joined him in Texas. After the proper introductions, Ted whispered in Duke's ear. Duke excused himself, and the two physicians left the room.

"Bela fuckin' Lugosi," Bull uttered from the side of his mouth. Joe sat still as a stone.

A few minutes later, Duke returned and lowered himself carefully into his chair.

"Your reflexes are obviously in good shape, and your eyesight tested better than 20/20." His words sounded deliberate and measured.

Gladys entered the room holding a set of x-rays. She caught a quick glimpse of Joe and Bull on the couch. Her full womanliness was quite striking. She possessed a smooth, inviting face with a mouth as wide as her cheekbones. Two decades and a bit of surgery had transformed the round-faced nurse into a woman that men might like to touch, but only with her permission.

Accepting the x-rays, Duke walked to his office window and held them up to the light. Though Duke had once described Joe's beaning as equivalent to a rear end auto accident at high speed, he detected no sign of the original injury; the bone remained healed.

"Looks like your skull was up to the stress of the fall," Duke said, his eyes devouring every inch of the x-ray. "But that fall must have done something," he mumbled.

Joe was still testing his flawless vision, his eyes surveying all directions.

He wore the look of what might have been if it all happened sooner.

Gladys wheeled to leave the room. On the way out, she tossed a brief glance at Joe and then fired a longer flirtatious look Bull's way.

Duke's question disrupted Joe from his throbbing erection.

"How's your sex drive?" Duke asked Joe, wondering if Joe's sperm count was high enough to take on a stable of Quaalude-stuffed topless dancers.

Only after the two had left Duke's office and were walking in the hospital parking lot did Joe's erection subside.

"Bull, I'm not going to any fantasy camp," Joe reiterated. "Business is bad; we've got work to do. Not to mention, a deviate is terrorizing our neighborhood."

"With your mystery reflexes and clean bill of health, I'm thinking you might make the team," Bull said.

Joe, then Bull, stopped abruptly.

"Bull, it's a fantasy camp for dilapidated old farts." Joe rolled his eyes to the blue-grey sky as if preparing to pray for Bull's return to his senses. "Everybody makes the team."

"Don't you get it, Little Man? I'm talking the real team." Bull flailed his arms like a preacher on Sunday morning. "Your injury's gone. Maybe Ranger management will see you at the fantasy camp."

"Are you nuts? Just because a guy can see without glasses doesn't mean jack shit!" In a rare display of emotion, Joe waved his own arms. "Do you realize how ridiculous you sound? I'm forty years old, be forty-one in June! I've been away too long. Besides, I'm not going to some old man's camp with a bunch of has-beens and never-beens."

CHAPTER 8
A DAY IN THE LIFE

A BROWN leather sofa took up much of the small reception area of Joe and Bull's office space. A dark, wood-framed print of DiMaggio, Gehrig, Ruth, and Mantle, kneeling in Yankee pinstripes concealed much of the beige wall above the couch. Industrial carpet, green as the painting's outfield grass, covered the floor. The toasty aroma of coffee infiltrated the reception area. Behind a burgundy oak desk, Shirley Knight, long time receptionist of Walrus Real Estate, skillfully fielded the steady barrage of phone calls. White-haired and anorexic, Shirley looked like a flag pole with a snowball on top.

"She's so skinny from answering all those damn phone calls," Bull always said. On a day like today Joe would agree. One apartment tenant needed a plumber; another's air conditioner was broken. All the electricity had gone out in one retail complex. The bank called—two tenants' rent checks had bounced.

In Joe's office, a framed poster announcing the Beatles 1965 invasion of Shea Stadium hung on the wall facing him. A huge map of the metroplex covered much of the wall to his left. Joe's desk was identical to Shirley's. Pictures of Joan and the girls were on the matching credenza behind him. On an adjacent book shelf, oldies but goodies played at a soft volume from a small CD player.

An expensive, bright-colored tie split the middle of Joe's starched white shirt. Pleated, navy-blue pants completed what Bull described as Joe's "G. Q. look." Joe was speaking seriously on the phone, renewing a worrisome subject with his banker.

"Sorry, Joe, but Sam Lucian's on line two." Shirley's voice interrupted on the intercom. "He insisted I break in. He's upset about not being paid for the landscaping at the Blue Sky Apartments."

Joe excused himself and put the banker on hold. The landscaper complained about the nonpayment with a whinny of self-pity, but not for long.

"Sam," Joe interrupted, "you won't get paid until you do the job right. Go look at your work."

Before he could return to his banker, Shirley interrupted again. "Joe, the dry cleaners moved out of MacArthur Place in the middle of the night. They left the space in bad shape."

"Get our leasing people on it pronto," Joe sighed, scattering a stack of papers on his desk. Several floated to the floor.

Feeling defeated but determined not to show it, Joe returned to the banker. "Charles, if your appraisals call for a large principal reduction, you'd better get some new appraisals. We're not—"

Shirley stood in the doorway, her face ashen. "Somebody robbed the restaurant at our McKinney center," she whispered. "Their attorney's on the phone. He says he warned us about the lack of security. He sounds mad."

"No principal reduction!" Joe barked harshly and then cut off the banker to take the attorney's call.

"Donley," he said, his voice barely avoiding a tone of resignation.

The attorney's shrill voice spit from the receiver at a lethal clip. Joe kept the phone to his ear but gently laid his head on the desktop.

The CD player was currently playing a Steve Forbert song entitled "Responsibility," an uncharacteristically unruly rocker from the folk singer. Sing it, Steve:

"Poor ol' surrendered Mimosa,
Finally burnt out by the heat
I feel pretty burnt out myself

When I make that old turn down our street.
Summertime's long been my favorite
Now I can't grab it no more
Can't find no time for a fish on the line
Or that swing in the old sycamore.
I'm in such a hurry now
It starts to worry me
Stop and smell the roses?
Baby, I can't hardly see
No, I ain't forgotten just how good it all can be
But I've got so much responsibility."

Joe closed his eyes and, while longing for a swing in the old Sycamore, he tumbled head first into a dream that provided passage to his youth.

Chewing violently on Milk Duds, Joe lay in his bed scrutinizing a handful of baseball cards. Major league pennants, pictures of big-leaguers, and other baseball paraphernalia smothered all four bedroom walls.

Suddenly, his mother called from the adjacent bedroom, "Joseph Donley. Lights out! It's bedtime."

"Yes, Mom."

Joe gulped his last tasty chocolate, turned off the lamp, and crawled under the covers.

"And don't forget to say your prayers," Mary added.

There was silence in honor of his mother's immense knowledge concerning prayers.

"Yes, Mom."

Ten-year-old Joe Donley began to pray: "Dear Lord, thank you for this day. Also, please don't let those Russians drop the bomb." He took a deep breath and squeezed his eyes shut, as if that might connect him directly to heaven. "I know you're probably getting tired of this part, but could you please help me win the batting title after I get to the big leagues?"

"Joe, wake up."

The voice sounded so faint, Joe wondered if it was in his dream. If so, Big Jim had invaded Joe's childhood and stood by his bed.

"Big Jim? What are you doing here?"

Fighting the cobwebs in his brain, Joe realized he had fallen asleep at his desk and Big Jim was now waving a handful of green paper bills in his face.

"Momma sent me to pay the rent. 'Cept we don't have enough. Momma's social security check got shrunk."

Joe stared at the money until the brain cloud cleared. He accepted the wad of green from Big Jim's meaty hand.

"We can . . . can pay half," Big Jim continued with a nervous stutter.

"No need," Joe said, standing. Joe stuffed the cash in the shirt pocket of Big Jim's ancient Esso shirt. "We'll get even when your mom's social security check unshrinks." He wrapped a big brother arm around Big Jim and walked him toward the lobby.

"Momma says an angel was watching over us when we moved into your apartments."

"So that's where the angels have been hanging out," Joe said under his breath.

"I was hoping Bull was here so we could wrestle," Big Jim said, grinding a toe into the carpet.

Bull and Big Jim's horseplay sometimes annoyed Joe. "We're going to have to buy this building if you two don't quit it," he'd griped more than once.

It had to happen—Bull stepped off the elevator as Big Jim prepared to enter.

"Bull!" Big Jim cried.

Bursting into Joe's office, Bull found Joe with his feet propped on his desk, staring at the overhead light.

"I pinned the big ox," the big man huffed triumphantly. Bull's blue denim shirt escaped his khaki pants; his tie, a brilliant display of Disney characters, dangled from his unbuttoned collar.

"Lady across the hall with the mortgage company complained about us wrestling again," he said, as he dropped heavily into the padded chair that faced Joe's desk. Bull followed Joe's lead, crossed his size thirteen loafers onto the desktop, and clasped his hands behind his head. "That lady's got no sense of humor. She must need to get laid." He snorted. "Hell, I need to get laid, but I don't act like I've got a corn cob stuck up my buetox all the time." said Bull, who was forever expanding his vocabulary. ("That's corn cube," K. C. would have corrected.)

"How did it go with the oil company?"

"Well, Little Man, they're going Mickey Mantle."

Joe flinched internally at Bull's mention of the Yankee great, Number Seven. It was Bull's way of saying Chapter Seven, going out of business.

"Our building will be practically vacant." Joe spoke in a drab tone, like a man accepting unhappy endings.

"It'll work out." Bull didn't sound convinced. "We'll find a tenant." He helped Joe stare at the ceiling.

"Is this all there is?" Joe asked.

"To what?" Bull replied.

"To life." A don't-give-a-shit tone consumed Joe's voice. "We fight this all day, every day, then go home at night, come back, and do it again." Joe paused. "Something's missing. I feel all used up."

"So, we're having a bad day."

Bull preferred to keep life simple. If hungry, eat; tired, rest; punish the bad, reward the good. Bull had seen worse days. A train mauling a vehicle with family inside. Now, that qualified as a bad day.

"They're all this way, Bull," Joe said slowly enough to taste his words, a bitter taste at that.

"What's all this way?" asked Bull, his mind still down at the railroad tracks.

"Here! The days here," Joe said irritably. After all, Joe often ignored Bull, not vice versa.

"Oh, here. We do the best we can for ourselves and our..." Bull's voice softened. He would have said "families." The word painfully reminded him of those missing. "Every now and then, we help somebody like Big Jim and his mom," he added, his voice returning to full strength.

"Who's the guy that said, 'Most men lead quiet lives of desperation'?" Joe's voice sounded more burnt out than an old spark plug.

"Emerson? Lake? Palmer?" Bull displayed his best deadpan expression before his eyes lit up. "Hey, you still don't need your glasses. Damndest thing I've ever seen. Man falls out of a tree and becomes Superman."

Joe continued to stare hard at the ceiling as if searching for new spark plugs.

"Bull, we may as well go to that horseshit fantasy camp," he finally said.

Sing on, Steve Forbert:

"Baby, you know I'm working, sorry I'm busy so much
Sorry those days when the world went our way
Are so hard to return to an' touch.
Maybe our future looks brighter, maybe our ship will come in,
Maybe these years an' these mule-train careers
Will be things we won't think about then."
Don't wish for something too much, Joe; you might get it.

CHAPTER 9
KING DAVID

WITH his legs extended straight, Joe propped his back against the headboard of the hotel bed. He was immersed in a black and white *Andy Griffith* rerun on the TV. Though the sound was on mute, Joe knew every episode by heart. Andy was insisting that Opie stop playing with imaginary friends. Joe, thinking of K. C. and Avery, understood Andy's concern.

Joe took a sip of beer from the can on his night stand, the bittersweet dampness tickling the back of his throat. Bull's open suitcase lay on the other bed. Unpacking, Bull danced between his bed and the chest of drawers. With each thrust, a mysterious electrical charge appeared to invade Bull's big body.

"This is a man's world," Bull hollered in imitation of James Brown and tossed his underwear into a bottom open drawer. Dictated by his happy feet, he eventually returned to his suitcase. "Well, tomorrow we're ballplayers again."

From the corner of his eye, Joe noticed Bull had thrust his barrel chest proudly forward, like a thicker Barney Fife.

Without warning, Bull picked up the lamp stand, dropped to one knee and slung the head over his shoulder. "Please! Please! Please me!" he squealed passionately, the godfather of soul again. Bull twirled his microphone like James Brown tripping on psychedelics.

Joe ignored Bull's performance in favor of Opie's. Opie was telling Andy about Mr. McBebe, a mysterious man Opie had met in the woods.

The man supposedly wore a shiny hard hat, clanked when he moved, and went from tree top to tree top. Incredibly, Mr. McBebe could make smoke come out of his ears! Andy reluctantly told an emotional Opie that he believed him—that Mr. McBebe was real.

"You afraid of dying?" Joe asked flippantly.

Joe's question yanked Bull out of performing mode. "I can't say I'm pointin' to the day," he answered, soberly returning the lamp stand to the floor.

"I know why people fear death," Joe announced as if he had solved life's greatest riddle. "You know what King David said before he died?"

"Yeah. Whoa, Amos." Bull flopped onto his bed.

Joe's eyes shot toward the ceiling in disgust.

"Okay, okay, maybe that was Kingfish," Bull said, who also knew a thing or two about old television programs. He held a beer can above his open mouth and poured a mini-waterfall down his throat.

"King David said, 'May your tongue cleave to the roof of your mouth if you don't remember me.'" Joe's tone was flat.

"Little Man, where on God's earth did you hear that?"

Joe shrugged.

"That's why most people fear death." He paused deliberately. "They're afraid they're gonna die without ever doing anything worth being remembered for anything special."

"Is that the way you feel?" Joe's words had clearly concerned the big man.

"All I know is I gotta do something more than just own a few vacant buildings before I die."

"At least, you've got your family. If I could be the next Ted Williams, I'd give it up to have my family back," Bull said.

If not for George Donley, Bull's wife would have never gone near the railroad tracks. It was an issue that could have put decades between friends of a lesser magnitude.

Joe's eyes never left the television. A tough moment for this friendship, he thought. Joe could see it was a tough time for Andy and Opie's relationship too. Andy traipsed dejectedly through the woods, near the area Opie had claimed to meet Mr. McBebe.

The men remained quiet for a long time.

"Bull," Joe finally said, searching for words carefully, "you think you'll ever remarry?"

"Beats me, but if I do, I'm gonna marry a lesbian," Bull announced assuredly.

"What?"

"You heard me."

"Why do you say that?"

"It makes perfect sense. We can go to ball games together, shoot pool together, drink beer together, and then go out and chase some pussy."

Joe began to spit beer through his contained laughter and looked incredulously at Bull. He failed to see that Andy, still in the woods, called out in frustration, "Mr. McBebe."

"Yes," replied a friendly voice from the skies.

Andy looked up to see a man with a shiny hard hat, who clanked when he walked and moved among the trees. Mr. McBebe was real, a telephone linesman! And yes, when he puffed on a cigarette, smoke came out of his ears! A smile wider than Mayberry spread across Andy's face. Joe missed it all; he remained too preoccupied attempting to control his laughter. But wasn't that like Joe Donley, to miss the good part?

CHAPTER 10
FANTASY CAMP

ALONG with about twenty other middle-aged men of all shapes and sizes, Joe and Bull admired the plush locker room. With thick carpet, wide individual stalls for each player, a massive leather couch in front of the big-screen TV, it was like no locker room any of them had seen before. Except for the expensive uniforms, the men could have passed for the BIOYAs. Navy block letters sewn across the white tops spelled **Rangers**; each participant's name and number were written on the backs. The wannabe players were in Surprise, Arizona, spring training home of the Texas Rangers.

Bull inhaled dramatically. A medicinal odor permeated the locker room, its future need as inevitable as a fastball on three and 0.

"Aaah," he sighed, "I love the fresh smell of A-balm in the morning." Bull's nostrils flared, and his thick frame stretched toward the ceiling. "Fresh towels, too," he sniffed.

A steady drone of men's chatter stopped when a big-eared, big-nosed little man, also in full uniform, stormed into the room. Sacks under each brown eye contained more baggage than Joe's duffel. Narrow and hard as marbles, these eyes maintained a rambunctious purpose about them.

Marty Williams, manager of the Texas Rangers, looked countless six packs beyond his fifty-four years. His commanding presence, in direct contrast to his diminutive size, further embellished his image and reputation, which bordered on that of a human crab.

"You only live once, but if you live right, once is enough," the Ranger manager often said. "Even if it's only for a short period of time," he would add, scowling.

"For the next week," he said without introduction, "you men will train and compare with some fossil players in the confines of one of the finest spring training baseball complexities in western civility. Our major and minor league roosters expedite here every spring before reputing for summer deployment."

"We're going to ignite a special refreshment right off the bat." Marty's voice rolled like thunder, and his bloodshot eyes scanned the blank faces for a response. "One of our current pitchers is in camp today, and all of you will have the apparatus to facilitate him in a game simulcast."

Like an army of bees, the players began to buzz. Joe's stomach surged. He asked himself what he wanted to ask Bull: What if the player was Rocket?

"What if it's Rocket?" Bull asked loud enough for all to hear.

Joe and Bull stepped onto the playing surface from the dugout steps, their cleats sinking into the Hushpuppy-soft grass; both gawked at their surroundings. Red dirt base paths, smooth as glass, divided the sea of green. Multi-colored advertisements covered the outfield walls. Empty grandstands sparkled under the bright sun.

"It's like being in a green cathedral," Bull said.

Hearing cowhide meet timber, Joe pointed to a complex of manicured diamonds that lacked only the grandstands of the main diamond.

"Minor leaguers in camp early," Joe said with authority.

"Let's check it out. Nothing's gonna happen here for a while," Bull suggested.

"May as well."

The two started toward the minor league diamond.

"What if it is Rocket? It would be interesting, you facing him after all these years."

"Why is that?" Joe tried to sound uninterested.

"You know, you being a neurological wonder and all."

"Jesus, Bull!" said Joe, stopping dead in his tracks. "It's a fantasy camp for businessmen, not a tryout camp! Why do you care if I play ball again?"

"Beats me, Little Man. I just had this feeling ever since we went to see Duke."

They discovered two lean hard-bodies at the diamond. Both youngsters possessed faces that submit to a shave once a week, whether needed or not. One player stood a head taller than the other and occupied the batter's box; with each whack, he stirred a breeze. The shorter player fed baseballs to a pitching machine.

"Hey, I bet you young pups a hundred bucks the old-timer here can out hit either of you against that machine," Bull blurted.

Both youngsters wheeled to face Bull, who wore the mischievous smirk of the class cut-up. Joe could only stare at Bull as if he had spoken in the absence of sufficient oxygen.

"Did you hear that, Pete?" said the taller player. His voice sounded cocky.

"He's all yours, Scotty."

Pete placed a ball into the pitching machine; it sped immediately toward home plate. Crack! A solid line drive darted to the outfield. Joe shut his eyes, the crisp sound as soothing as a favorite tune. The ball stopped just short of the 335-ft. sign in left field.

The gloating batter handed Joe the bat and batting helmet. Joe fired a malignant glare at Bull and took a few warm-up swings. An air of youthful superiority so blinded the two young pups, neither noticed the poetry in Joe's practice cuts. It resembled the stroke of Ted Williams. Joe swung like a man who had practiced swinging until mastering the craft and then never needed to practice again.

Pete loaded another ball into the mechanical hurler.

"Careful, Gramps," he said menacingly. "It's throwing eighty-five miles an hour."

"Wait, then attack," Joe murmured intensely.

Joe could almost read the ball's markings as it raced toward the plate. CRACK! The sound of ash spanking a baseball echoed like an ax chopping wood in a vast, deserted forest. Joe's blast seemed to stay in the air forever before it landed beyond the fence in left center field, some four hundred feet away.

"I haven't seen you smile like that in twenty years," Bull declared.

Both young ballplayers looked unsure whether to flee or apologize. Bull, grinning from ear to ear, rubbed his thumb and index finger together in the symbolic gesture for cash.

"Uh, we haven't got a paycheck yet," said Scotty.

"I'll wrestle either one of you for double or nothing," Bull declared, his dark blond eyebrows rising dramatically.

Only a cry from the main diamond requesting Joe and Bull's return saved the two ballplayers from that unenviable fate.

Marty stood in the first-base dugout with his back to the unoccupied infield. He inspected his troops with mock seriousness.

"Ced forth control is better now, so don't sweat it. Allow me to introduce the man who could throw a cream puff through a battlefield, the man who symbolizes everything good about the gregarious game of baseball—Walter 'Rocket' Nolin!"

"Rocket," Bull whispered.

The expressions of the other players registered a combination of anticipation and dread.

"Now, men, I'll gravitate you if we had tried this when he was younger, there would be dead bodies all over the place." Marty sounded like a military leader attempting to sell his men on the merit of an upcoming battle. "His control is better now, so don't sweat it. Allow me to introduce the man who could throw a cream puff through a battlefield, the man who symbolizes everything good about the gregarious game of baseball—Walter 'Rocket' Nolin!"

Marty motioned to the opposite dugout. A man in full uniform stepped out of the shadow of the dugout and methodically proceeded to the mound. All eyes locked on Rocket Nolin, a carved-in-granite, heat-throwing pitcher with a heart as big as Texas.

Rocket no longer maintained a slender youthful body. Age, plus twenty years in the exercise room, had added thirty pounds of muscle to his six-foot frame; he looked larger than his two hundred pounds. King of the hill, the legend soon stood on the mound massaging a baseball and staring holes through his amateur opposition who sat bug-eyed in the first base dugout.

Rocket went into his windup and grunted loudly as the ball raced to the plate. Rocket's delivery did not vary from one pitch to the next; it was like watching a mechanical man. The ball exploded loudly into the catcher's mitt of Pete, the shorter player from the other diamond.

"All right, everybody's going to hit alphabetically, according to your number," growled Marty.

"Old fart can still heat it up there," Bull said.

Joe fired Bull a "no shit" look, rose, and walked to the dugout exit leading to the dressing room.

"Hey! Where are you going?"

Joe ignored Bull and ducked out of sight.

A half hour later, Bull entered the dressing room to find Joe sitting alone in a portable metal chair.

"We're almost finished batting. Aren't you going to hit?"

"I think I'll pass. It just brings back some bad memories. It doesn't mean jack shit anyway," Joe said, staring at the floor.

"If it doesn't mean jack shit, then why don't you bat?"

Bull pulled up a chair beside Joe. After an awkward silence, Bull finally began to lose his considerable patience.

"Little Man, you're not the first man to meet a few bumps in the road. It's how you get over the bumps that matters," Bull said, his voice rising to clear the bumps. Then Bull was gone.

CHAPTER 11
JOE AND ROCKET MEET AGAIN

MARTY, standing in the third base on-deck circle, held a clipboard containing a list of the camp's participants. "Donley, grab a stick! You're the last victim!" Marty roared, noticing Joe re-enter the playing surface.

Still tipsy from facing Rocket, Joe's teammates were chattering among themselves. While selecting a wooden bat from the rack in the dugout, Joe felt Bull's comforting hand on his shoulder.

"How did you do?" Joe asked.

"Fouled one off," Bull answered enthusiastically. "No one else even did that."

Joe raised his eyebrows and, burdened with dread, made his way to home plate.

Arizona's late afternoon sun sliced through the stands, spotlighting Rocket on the mound. His eyes bore down on the last batter of the day. During the last twenty minutes, he'd struggled to maintain his Black Bart persona, but Marty had reminded him: "Boss man said to put on a show."

But who was this guy standing so poised in the batter's box? During his warm up swings, he swung fluidly and with little strain. The batter leaned in slightly over the plate, stance closed, back elbow parallel to the ground, and knees slightly bent; he cocked his bat more assuredly than the others, holding it above the strike zone. Son of a buck! At least one guy today looked like a hitter. From habit, Rocket's memory shifted into automatic pilot. His eyes began to dart about as if recollecting all the batters he ever faced. Rocket's mouth turned down at the corners, causing crow's feet to jet from both eyes. Who was this guy?

Joe dug in the batter's box like an infantryman in a foxhole. Looking toward the pitcher's mound, he saw Rocket walking slowly toward home plate! Joe saw sweat on his high forehead, traces of silver in his sideburns. The ballyard became so quiet that Joe could hear his own cleats shuffling in the loose dirt around home plate. His saliva suddenly felt thick, making it difficult to swallow.

"Walter Nolin," the fire-baller said warmly and extended his firm hand. He spoke in a slow West Texas drawl.

"Joe Donley," Joe replied with uncertainty, returning the shake.

"You look familiar," said Rocket, cocking his head sideways, his memory still searching. "Have we met?"

"I don't think so." Joe's voice was weak.

Rocket shrugged his broad shoulders and ambled back to the mound. Before Joe could blink, the pitcher started into his windup.

The pounding of Joe's heart deafened him to the boisterous encouragement from the bench and to Pete's respectful warning: "Get ready, sir. He throws a shitload harder than that machine."

Rocket let loose with his familiar grunt, and the baseball raced savagely toward Joe. Joe, determined to hit the ball as if finally resolving some unfinished business, delivered a frozen rope to dead center field. His teammate's cheers made him feel like a real baseball player again, and a substantial look of relief sprinted across his face. Joe glanced up to the sky, relief sneaking through his expression like sunlight through a dark cloud. He was looking more to his paternal than Heavenly father.

Using light-as-air, childlike steps, Marty reluctantly approached the franchise's treasure on the mound.

"You see the boss man?" Marty asked just as reluctantly.

"How can I miss him?" Rocket answered. "He's about to blind me, wearing all that damn jewelry."

Rocket briefly glared at the "boss man" and team owner, Tex Maris. Trying to look important, Tex stood in foul territory, his arms folded across his chest. He wore a dark western business suit with alligator cowboy boots and a dress felt cowboy hat. Enough gold jewelry dangled from his wrists and hands to set off an airport alarm. Sunspots flashed off the gold like the blinking of Morse code.

"He just sent one of his goonies over to inform me that you're supposed to blow this guy away on the next pitch," said Marty. The "goonies" were bodyguards who constantly flanked the Ranger owner.

"Blow this guy away, huh?" Rocket said in disgust, his glance shooting to Joe at the plate. Actually, anything concerning Tex disgusted Rocket. Rocket turned, faced center field, and began to massage the baseball hard enough to rub off the cowhide. "That's what I was trying to do."

"Geez, don't tell me that!" Marty said, suddenly looking as if diagnosed with a life-threatening disease.

"What's the big deal?"

"Some Dallas media is here," Marty explained. "Boss man doesn't want the press reporting that some amateur is knocking you around like a stepchild." Marty swallowed hard. "Tex thinks it might hurt ticket sales."

"Bull crap!" Rocket snapped. "Our cheap owner won't sign any sticks. That's what hurts ticket sales. Think about it!"

"I know. I know." Marty placed his hand on Rocket's shoulder. "Now, bend one. Buckle him at his knees."

Marty referred to the same pitch Joe had expected twenty years ago—the curve that would track for the hitter's head before slashing wickedly across the plate.

As Rocket released the ball, the volume of his grunt plainly indicated the zenith of his effort. Joe stood rock steady in the batter's box and ripped at the breaking ball, the ball darting from his bat straight for the pitcher's mound. Rocket never had a chance, taking a direct hit to the forehead. Rocket dropped to the ground so heavily that dust rose from the pitcher's mound and surfed airwaves in the sunlight.

For a tiny instant, the earth stopped turning. Everyone except Joe rushed to the mound. Joe moved toward the plate more apprehensively. Corpse still, Rocket lay on his back. No one talked or moved. Finally, mercifully, Rocket opened his eyes; his look almost immediately located Joe, who by now was standing in the crowd hovering over him.

"Hey, I remember who you are," he drawled. "Nice piece of hitting," the legend said. Grinning slightly, he managed to add, "I wish this made us even."

CHAPTER 12
M. V. P.

Officials rushed Rocket to the hospital, preventing Joe the chance to explore Rocket's surprising remarks further. Due to the minor concussion, doctors recommended that Rocket refrain from flying for a few days. After one night in the hospital and signing enough autographs for the hospital staff to cause writer's cramp, Rocket rented a Chevy pickup and drove home to Olney.

With the current team still ten days from camp and little else to report, the press dragged Joe's past to the present.

"Payback time for Rocket" ran the headlines of an Arizona newspaper. A Dallas newspaper's headline reported, "Dallas businessman evens the score."

Joe called home to tell Joan and the girls the news. One by one, he talked to the women in his life.

"Did you meet J. C. Penney?" K. C. asked.

"Get some autographs," Tater said.

"Dad, you've got to come home!" Liz said, grabbing the phone. "Tater won't quit singing!"

"I feel good," Tater wailed in the background, imitating Bull imitating James Brown.

"I can't even use our bathroom because K. C. says Avery's in there all the time," Liz continued.

"Avery's real sick, Dad," Joe could hear K. C. yelling. "He's upchucking out the front because he's so stopped up in the rear!"

Joan finally seized control of the phone. "K. C.'s the one stopped up in the rear. Big Jim can't wait for you and Bull to get home. He'll probably think you hit Rocket on purpose." Joan took a deep breath. "I guess this is the most excitement we'll see around here for a while. maybe ever."

During the next week, Joe constantly dealt out laser shots against ex-big league pitchers, most of whom were younger than Rocket. At the camp's closing night dinner, Joe and Bull sat together in the banquet room of their hotel. The sounds of alcohol-induced laughter, rattling glasses, and clanging silverware blended nicely with the aroma of prime rib. Tex and Marty occupied the dais, which faced the tables of casually dressed camp participants. Drenched in misery, Tex's burly bodyguards stood off to one side.

With the charm of a tax auditor, Marty took the podium at center stage and tapped a glass with a knife to quiet the crowd.

"Marty, you're looking cool tonight," a half-tipsy camper called out, noticing Marty's shiny Hawaiian-style shirt.

"You don't look so hot yourself," Marty growled into the microphone.

The laughter combined with his hangover fueled Marty's surliness. During fantasy camp, Marty drank enough booze to keep a twenty-five man roster happy.

"Gentlemen," Marty said irritably, while emphasizing the word *gentle*. "May I have your attraction? These old-timer camps and airplane landings are a lot alike. If you can walk away from them, they're a success." He swallowed a belch. "Without further relapse, our owner, Mr. Tex Maris, will present the camp's Most Valuable Player award."

Tex, wearing one of his thousand dollar cowboy suits, took the stand.

Bull leaned in close to Joe. "Ol' Tex inherited a wad. I heard he's slicker than an airport runway on a snowy night. Big-time gambler, too."

"Did you boys get your money's worth this week?" Tex asked.

The crowd erupted into a sea of rambunctious joviality as Tex displayed his best artificial smile. Tex told a few bad jokes and rattled on about nothing until time came to present the camp's Most Valuable Player award.

"Joe Donley, come up here and get your award!" Tex boomed. Amid respectful applause, Joe displayed no emotion while making his way to the podium; he derived little satisfaction from pummeling a few worn-out pitchers. After Joe accepted the obligatory handshake and congratulations, Tex's right hand disappeared into his coat pocket.

"Joe, you broke every hitting record in the history of our camp. We thought that warranted something more than a plaque. No sir, boys, this is no plaque! This is a player's contract, and, Joe, it's got your name on it!"

Tex whipped the contract from his coat pocket. Joe, fearing a joke, reluctantly accepted the paper. Cameramen surrounded him like infielders at the pitcher's mound and snapped pictures rapid fire.

Waving his arms, Tex cried, "Gentlemen, welcome the oldest rookie in baseball history!"

"Kiss my big fat butt!" Bull said.

"What kind of Trigger shit is this?" Marty wondered aloud.

Joe looked at Tex as though the man's hair was on fire. Joe couldn't speak, or move, or swallow. But he could think.

CHAPTER 13
LIFE AT HOME

THE next morning started with the chaos that normally accompanied the Donley family's preparation for school. Joan, still in her brown terry cloth bathrobe, stood barefoot by the stove. Her eyes split time between the newspaper on the kitchen counter and the frying pan loaded with bacon. She was reading about the continued attacks on local women.

Joan ignored Chester, the Donley's pet cockatiel, who zoomed into the kitchen with the recklessness of a Japanese dive bomber, fully capable of great speeds and maneuverability. The white-winged Chester looked the part with its gray fuselage and yellow cockpit of a head, which had red circles stamped on each side. Chirping "Chester, Chester, here kitty, kitty, kitty, kitteee," the mad bird circled Joan's head. "Pretty boy, pretty boy," he continued.

Chester's airspeed stalled the instant his path crossed the Donley's refrigerator as if to read Joan's favorite Bible verse she kept taped to the refrigerator wall. It read "Do everything possible on your part to live in peace with everybody. Never take revenge, my friends, but instead let God's anger do it." Chester's attention to the refrigerator was not uncommon and caused K. C. to joke, "Chester can talk and Chester can read and he's a Christian too!"

While Chester romped through the kitchen, Liz was testily storming through the upstairs hallway in her hated private school uniform. Yuck! The same white shirt with a dark green and black plaid skirt every day.

Liz's inability to access the girls' upstairs hall bathroom increased her surly disposition. K. C., also in uniform, sat dejectedly in front of the closed bathroom door.

"Don't tell me: Avery?" Liz said, planting her hands firmly to each side.

"Sorry. His stomach hurts," K. C. said.

Liz, weary of K. C. and drawn by the crisp odor of bacon, went downstairs. Reaching the kitchen, her mother's paralysis so amazed Liz that she overlooked the thick smoke rising from the frying pan. Her mother tried to speak, but managed only a garbled sound usually heard in the dentist's chair.

Liz's eyes trailed those of her mother to the newspaper. Liz promptly read aloud: "In an unprecedented move, the Ranger's signed local forty-year-old businessman Joe Donley to a contract as a result of Donley's phenomenal showing in the Ranger fantasy camp."

The smoke cloud finally triggered the house alarm. Joan and Liz shrieked like startled birds.

"That blasted alarm goes off at nothing!" Joan cried. "Your dad was supposed to have it fixed before he left!"

Joan turned off the burner and rapidly left the kitchen to silence the alarm. The shrill noise brought Tater on roller skates and K. C. screaming into the kitchen.

K. C. eyed the frying pan disaster. "Mom makes bad bacon," she said loudly.

"Dad's famous!" Liz cried.

"Did that make the alarm go off?" Tater yelled.

"Dork! The smoke made the alarm go off!" snapped Liz.

"What's *famous* mean?" K. C. screamed.

"Dork! Everybody knows that!" snapped Tater. "It's people on TV."

"Like Barney? Dad's going to be like Barney?" She meant Barney Fife, not the dinosaur.

The phone rang and none too soon, thought Liz. Her frustration with her sisters caused her to answer the phone with clenched teeth.

"Dad!" she yelled into the phone. "It's the alarm, Dad. Burnt bacon made it go off. Mom says you were supposed to get it fixed." She paused to listen and then said, "We've already seen the paper, Dad."

"Does he know Barney Fife yet?" K. C. asked.

"Ask him if he's really famous," Tater said, her brows rising with thought.

Joe asked to speak to Joan. "Handle this gently, Dad," recommended Liz.

The alarm went silent, and Joan soon entered the kitchen. Liz handed her the phone. With Joan's children huddled around her, Joan listened to her husband's unlikely story.

"It's a long shot," he explained, "but if I make the team, I'll travel about half the time from April through September." Too stunned to speak, Joan remained silent.

"Joan, are you there?"

"I'm here. I think it's great, Joe," she lied. "We miss you and love you, Joe. We'll see you tonight. Tell Bull, we said hi."

Joan hung up the phone and stood still, facing the prospect of Joe's potential new career. After a weighty pause, she announced, "He's coming home for a few days, and then it's back to Arizona."

Joan felt a sense of guilt growing like crabgrass in the summertime; she wanted her husband to come home and stay home. The doorbell rang, and Liz left to answer it.

"Mom, I think you might want to see this," Liz soon called.

Within seconds, Joan and her daughters stood comatose in the front doorway. None of them could believe what they saw. Their front yard resembled kids' day at the old ballyard. No less than twenty children, mostly boys, occupied the front lawn, clamoring so loudly no one could understand the other. Some had ball hats, others bats, some gloves; a few held baseballs, and others waved baseball cards.

"What's going on?" Joan asked with polite concern.

The juvenile army began to move forward in unison, the relentless chatter increasing.

"Everybody pipe down!" Joan roared, her hands on her hips.

Liz stood beside her mother, her own hands planted in exactly the same manner. In the brisk morning air, Joan's breath steamed like diesel exhaust.

"Shut up!" Joan yelled.

The children turned quiet and rigid.

"Noah, why don't you tell us what this commotion is all about," said Joan, eyeing the leader of the pack.

Noah, age fourteen, stepped forward with the assurance of a soldier in a minefield. He wore black, sharp-angled glasses and kept his dark hair slicked back, which exposed a brief forehead painted with zits. An oversized Rangers' red sweatshirt hung loosely from Noah's frail frame, while his tattered jeans looked baggy enough to carry a load of concrete in the seat. In a sort of nerd revenge, Noah owned the most extensive sports memorabilia collection in the neighborhood.

"Mrs. Donley," he said, choosing his words carefully, "uh, well, we were wondering if Mr. Donley could get some things autographed by some of the Ranger players? Shoot, I'll even take Mr. Donley's autograph!"

"What's that Mormon talking about?" K. C. whispered.

Tater leaned close to K. C. "It's moron, not Mormon," she mumbled testily, like she had reminded K. C. a thousand times before.

"Autographs?" Joan briefly shut her eyes and saw her family's life turn into a looney bin.

"They saw the newspaper," Liz said. "Autographs are big business, Mom."

"Could Dad get J. C. Penny's autograph or maybe Barney's?" K. C. asked from behind her mother.

"Take a look, girls; this is your new life." Joan spoke with dull resignation. "Let's hope it won't last long," she mumbled two decibels above a whisper.

Joan and Liz frowned at the young crowd, which once again started to clamor feverishly. Thoughtful grins spread across the faces of Tater and K. C. Tater, especially, appeared in deep concentration; she had even quit humming. As Joan wheeled and stormed toward her front door, she heard the voice of K. C. hang in midair. "Mom, is Noah's last name Ark?"

CHAPTER 14
DAD COMES HOME

Later that day, Joe entered his home to a hero's reception—confetti, streamers, multi-colored papier mâché and the works. "Take me out to the ballgame" blared over the living room stereo speakers. After Joan recovered from her initial shock, she decided to focus on the bright side. This unique opportunity for Joe, regardless of success or failure, would hopefully lighten his emotional outlook.

Joe, conditioned to restricting his emotions to a very thin band of expression, felt plenty, but showed little. On his return, however, he hugged each family member a little harder than usual and almost broke into a full smile.

Not that the night didn't produce its own dark moments. Chester entered the dining room during K. C.'s "God is good, God is great" portion of the blessing, which seemed to torpedo K. C.'s theory of the bird's spirituality. As customary, the cockatiel's pre-attack, high-pitched cries of "Chester, Chester" provided Joe ample time to avoid the direct hit. Reinforcing Joe's "Chester's out to get me" theory, only Joe felt the wind from Chester's orbit. Everyone but Joe, who fired the bird a heat-seeking missile glance, ignored Chester's high energy exit from the room.

"Dad, we can't get a Keller's burger on Saturday for a long time if you go to play baseball," said K. C., matter of factly. "We always go to Keller's on Saturday."

"Dad, you did say this wasn't going to change anything," Liz announced, sounding too grown up for fourteen.

"Yeah, grown-ups aren't supposed to lie," Tater said between chomps of mashed potatoes.

How could Tater know that grown-ups often lied the most? A mouth full of food prevented Joe from speaking—a good thing, for he could think of nothing to say.

"Girls, this is your dad's chance . . . well, I guess this is his second chance," Joan said, breaking the silence but not the tension.

"Hear that, Avery?" K. C. calmly said, eyeing the one vacant dining chair reserved for Avery. "No Keller's next Saturday. That's life. Life is life. You just have to make the most of it." She paused, as if to listen, and then added, "Avery says maybe Bull will take us."

"Girls, this is my chance to do something special."

"You're special to me," Tater said.

Annoyed with Tater's mush, Liz poked her finger down her throat. "Yech!"

"Look! Liz is barking," K. C. cried.

Joan and K.C.'s sisters broke out laughing.

"Girls, nobody's ever done what I am trying to do," Joe said through his own half smile. "I'll probably get cut in a few weeks, and things will be back to normal."

Clad only in Joe's silk pajama top, Joan sat in bed, propped against the headboard with her knees up, clearly exposing her model's runway legs. Earlier in the day, while packing away some of her mother's things, Joan had discovered a letter she'd never seen before. Spellbound, she silently read:

Dear Joan:

I guess you're surprised to hear from me. I don't know where you live, so I am sending this to our old address. But since I don't know if Mom lives there anymore, who knows if you will ever read this.

Do you remember the time when we were little, and Mom made us take a bath together? And when she left the room you got the flashlight so we could check out each other's butt hole to see what color it was. Just as you were looking, Mom walked in.

That's the most pissed I have ever seen our Mom. Gross, huh? Well, something happened to me that was even grosser. Recently I met a young girl and just as I was preparing to enter the promised land, so to speak, I noticed a small gold ring on each side of her vulva. Pierced just like an earring.

Can you believe it? I had no idea what purpose those rings served, and I didn't ask. I just rolled her over on her stomach before I lost the mood, but then what I saw next wasn't so hot either.

When I spread her buns apart, you are not going to believe what I saw. She had a black lightning bolt tattooed on the middle of her butt, pointing down to the promised land, so to speak. About now was when I thought of you and me in the bathtub.

And then, of course, I lost the mood. I'll have to admit it made me mad, and I did something I wish I had not done. But heck, she had already mentioned maybe tying me up with duct tape and beating me with a spatula, which I am proud to say I was having no part of. I mean what does she think I am, a sicko? I don't know what to

think of young girls these days. What if I had something tattooed on my hooter and when it got hard the tattoo would look real scary like a fire-eating dragon or something? I mean how would a woman like that? Not too good I bet. I have been working my way to Dallas. Maybe I will see you soon.

Love,

Patrick

P. S. Didn't you say purple?

Joan located a pencil and scribbled so passionately, it's a wonder the pencil didn't break. "It *was* purple," she wrote.

"What are you reading?" Joe's voice broke Joan's trance. He stood by the bed, wearing only his boxers.

"I got a call-back for a commercial," Joan answered truthfully.

"Why didn't you tell me? I think it's great that you're getting back into acting."

"I was going to, but your news stole the show. Joe, maybe you should read this."

Joan lowered the script to her knees, which contained the letter inside. Her glance fell to the bulge in Joe's boxer shorts.

Joan could feel Joe's desire as unexpectedly, as unrestrainedly, as feverishly as she had ever felt anything in her life. Quicker than Chester's aerial attacks, Joe grabbed the script from Joan, tossed it to the floor, and embraced his wife; their lips touched with the passion of their teenage days at the drive-in.

Joan started to move slowly beneath Joe—to roll her hips and to moan softly. As Joe buried his head between her breasts, Joan's long legs scissored around his waist and touched down gently on Joe's bottom. Unlike Joe, the master of self-control who had lost control, Joan rapidly came to her senses and started to wiggle beneath him in a respectful lover's protest.

"Joe!" Joan murmured intensely. "It's only 9:30. The kids are still awake."

Too late. Tater was pounding on the door.

"Mom! Dad! Help! Pickles has got Chester! In his mouth!" cried Tater, in reference to the Donley tabby cat that presumably held the mad bird hostage.

Joe and Joan separated violently, as though a hostile had come between them. The door flew open, and Tater stood in the doorway staring.

"That damned bird probably got caught on purpose to spite me!" Joe muttered.

Pickles darted into the bedroom, with Chester dangling helplessly from her mouth, and sprinted under the same bed.

"What's Pickles doing in the house?" Joan screamed. She scrambled to the floor and poked her head under the bed.

"Tater, let him in!" Liz cried, arriving on the scene with K. C. following behind.

"Not!" Tater screamed.

"I'm going under the bed!" Joan said with the inspiration of a military leader called to combat. "Somebody catch Pickles if she comes out."

"Dad, is that your tail?" K. C. asked evenly, staring at the fly of his shorts.

Pickles made a mad dash from under the bed to the open doorway.

"Avery, grab Pickles!" K. C. demanded with rising volume. All four Donley females dove to the floor but without success.

"You idiot!" Liz yelled angrily at the cat.

"Don't hurt him," Tater cried fearfully.

"Ouch!" K. C. yelled.

"He got away!" Joan roared, her arms flapping in the frenzied take-off motion of Chester himself.

"I got him," Joe's reassuring voice announced.

"I'm dying," K. C. announced calmly.

"Damn cat," snapped Joan.

Joan rushed toward Joe, who held the cat, who held the bird. "Uh-oh, Mom. You said a bad word! You're gonna get the hot sauce?" After only a slight pause, K. C. repeated, "I'm dying."

"Oh, Chester!" Joan said, taking the cat from Joe.

Pickles' face displayed a victorious smirk that plainly said, "I've heard 'Here Kitty, Kitty, Kitty, Kitteeee' one time too many." Without resistance, Pickles relinquished the bird and scurried from the room.

Caressing the limp cockatiel, Joan asked, "Are you okay?"

Liz grumbled, "Way to go, Tater."

"Mom, I forgot. Maybe he will be able to see better, like Dad . . . after his accident," Tater said, her voice laced with hope and fear.

Chester blinked groggily, rustled his feathers, and flew away.

Before anyone could breathe a sigh of relief, Joan noticed K. C. "K. C.!"

Her youngest daughter sat dejectedly in the middle of the floor; a small stream of blood trickled from her nose.

"Liz's knee hit me in the nose. I bet she did it on purpose."

"She's okay," Liz said.

With all the fireworks presumably over, Liz then strutted from the room with that oldest sister strut.

Joan knelt at K. C.'s side, inspecting the minor wound.

"Mom, did you know Dad has a tail?" K. C. asked.

"Mom!" Liz's panicked voice rang loudly from down the hall. "Pickles has got one of the goldfish!"

A day in the life at the Donley house. In the Donley family, chaos brought familiarity, like an old comfortable piece of clothing.

CHAPTER 15
AN UNEXPECTED VISITOR

Later that night, with the children finally asleep and all the Donley pets presumably safe, Joan lay nestled in her husband's arms. A burning candle on the nightstand cast off the only light, its spirit circling the room in perfect rhythm with the ceiling fan. Outside, a Texas shower gently pelted the red tile roof, sounding as peaceful and serene as the cooing of a dove. From the considerable branches of the front yard oak, wind chimes tinkled soothingly. An occasional gust of wind propelled the chimes into double time.

"You do have a tail," Joan commented, peering under the covers. Her hand vanished beneath the sheets and traveled lightly along Joe's leg. "And it grows. How nice," Joan said through a playful giggle.

Without preamble, fat raindrops started to assault the Donley roof. Dramatic lightning flashes momentarily transformed night into day. Sonic booms of thunder soon followed. Joe and Joan sat up as straight and rigid as headstones. It thundered again, louder.

"That'll do it," Joe said calmly.

Next came the recognizable pattern of children's feet pounding hardwood. The girls rapidly entered and vaulted onto the bed. K. C. crashed on her mother's tummy. Liz and Tater landed between their parents, nearly causing Joe to fall off the bed. A half-hour later, the children slept soundly.

"Joan, are you awake?" Joe whispered.

"How could I sleep?"

"When was the last time we made love?" he asked.

"I don't know, but I think my boobs were larger and my butt smaller."

Joan pushed Tater's feet from underneath her nose. Tater lay perpendicular between her parents, her body serving as a human conduit. Liz now lay on the outside of the bed, cradled in Joe's arms, likewise K. C. with Joan.

"Maybe tomorrow night," Joan said.

"Yeah, maybe tomorrow night," Joe replied. "Joan, what was that you wanted me to read?"

"Oh, nothing."

"You know what I miss most about my father," Joe said after a short but heavy silence.

"His smile. His goodness," Joan replied after her own reflective pause.

"That's what I was going to say. How did you know?"

"Joe, I miss him too." Joan's hand found Joe's and gave him a firm comforting squeeze. "Good night, Joe."

"Good night."

Like a cornered animal, a man of Goliath proportions crouched behind the Donley front yard shrubs. Beneath the mystery man's black ball cap, low paranoid eyes cut all around. As lightning suddenly lit up the sky, the man watched the upstairs bedroom through these disturbed eyes.

Since his twenty-first birthday, he had answered to the name Steel Claw. This "Steel Claw," the giant's right hand, if applied to his opponent's forehead, reportedly spelled not only defeat but also potential nightmares, increased risk of stroke, shrillness of voice, diarrhea, blindness, impotency, loss of memory, and so on.

He removed the soaked hat, exposing a shaved dome the size of a football helmet. Little grooves and scars marked his skull like imprints in a stark wasteland. Heavy raindrops rapidly overflowed these crevices and spilled down his bloated face. Earlier, as the mystery man heaved his massive bulk toward the Donley front yard, he had heard an unforgettably powerful voice. Only one female possessed a set of pipes like that.

During the drive over, the visitor cruised neighborhoods with the scrutiny of an animal shelter employee searching for strays; regretfully; he saw none. When the man occasionally thought of his previous victims, he did so without guilt. Was his father responsible for this state of mind? After all, his old man never attended his little league games or his high school football games, and never visited his school on parent night. This rage, as consistent as the roadmap-red in his eyes, did not overlook Joan. Where was Joan when his father came home too drunk to stand, tearing up the house, and cussing like a madman. Where had Joan been when he needed her? With the Donleys, that's where.

The man studied the pitch black upstairs window. The lightning had stopped, but heavy raindrops continued to ring in the second story gutter. His tiny eyes grew larger and became wet, more from sadness than the storm. Oh, a thin line separated love and hate— which one was it tonight? He decided to return until he better knew the answer himself.

CHAPTER 16
ROCKET PAYS A VISIT

WHEN Joan said Duke was on the phone, Joe considered not taking the call. Duke was surely calling to try to persuade Joe to nix spring training. Fantasy camp was one thing, but major league hard ball another.

To Joe's immense relief, Duke blessed Joe's tryout. "The cat scan looks good," he said. "One thing you should know is this could all be temporary."

"Any guess as to how long?" Joe asked, registering this bit of information with a tightly lipped grimace.

"Not really. Another shock to your body might do it. I'd like you to come in for a few more tests before you go back to Arizona," Duke said with the same precise manner he employed when performing surgery.

Joe never found time to visit Duke before returning to Arizona. What if Duke changed his mind? The night Joe arrived in Surprise, he found Rocket standing at the door of his hotel room. A straw cowboy hat and lizard cowboy boots had replaced his ball cap and cleats. Wrangler jeans struggled to contain the bulging muscles in Rocket's tree trunk legs, and a white western shirt with Indian-head nickels for buttons concealed baseball's most famous right arm. Out of uniform, Rocket still looked like a gunslinger capable of blasting a hole in a silver dollar from sixty paces.

Rocket's grin exposed craggy smile lines around both cheeks, causing the famous pitcher to look deceptively older than dirt. It was an expression so warm, any notion Joe harbored of holding a grudge vanished as quickly as Joe invited Rocket into his room. After Joe ordered a six-pack of Lone Star longnecks from room service, both men took a seat. Rocket removed his hat, exposing a hair line receding as rapidly as Rocket's best fastball.

A room-service waitress delivered the beer within minutes, and Joe's look latched onto the young lady's fine upstanding breasts. An immediate tingling sensation below Joe's belt caused him to squirm uncomfortably in his chair. Joe's desire did not escape Rocket as the shapely lady left the room.

"That, my friend, will get you in trouble," Rocket warned, only half-kidding.

An embarrassed grin crept onto Joe's face. "I know," he said sheepishly.

The beer moved along the men's conversation like a hit and run advances the runner, but then Rocket threw a change-up. "How come you didn't play anymore?" His voice was full of concern. "I kept hoping I'd hear you were making a comeback, but it's like you vanished from earth."

Joe wanted to say *that's how I felt—like I vanished from earth.* "I just decided not to," Joe said.

Joe resisted the urge to inspect his nose for any sudden growth. He easily read the guilt in Rocket's eyes.

"I tried to visit you in the hospital, but security was tighter than good old Tex's checkbook."

"So Tex is as cheap as I've read?" Joe said, grasping the opportunity to change the subject.

"Yep. That's one time you can believe the papers. Compared to Tex, Scrooge threw money around like paper airplanes. That's why we've been losing all these years. Tex won't pay anybody. Hell, he knows I'll play for less than market value to stay close to my family and ranch. He's just a lucky sperm bank member," Rocket said in disgust. "He inherited the team, and he inherited those oil wells. You know how, don't you? His old man's favorite hooker caught him with another hooker, and she shot him deader than Abe Lincoln. Shot him right in the balls. Those guys with the 'work for food' signs have worked more honest days than Tex. It's a damn good thing Will Rogers never met Tex Maris. Think about it."

"You've been his meal ticket for a long time."

"Nineteen years," Rocket sighed.

"What about the rumor that Tex siphons all the money from the team to pay for gambling losses?"

"I ain't touching that with Babe Ruth's bat."

"How do you get along with Marty?" Joe asked, after a thoughtful pause.

"Marty's okay. Little surly at times, but he's all right."

"It must bother him when the crowd boos every time he takes you out of the game?"

"Funny you should mention that." Rocket flashed a school boy grin.

"Why is that?"

"One time, I'm gassed; it's obvious I'm done, and Marty comes to the mound. He signals for the relief pitcher, and I start for the dugout, but Marty's got an idea. He says, 'Rocket wait; those fans are gonna quit booing just long enough to give you a standing o when you walk off, right?'

"I said, 'Yes, Skip, I guess you're right.'

"'Then as soon as Scotty gets here, and I head to the dugout, they're gonna start booing again, right?'

"I said, 'Yes Skip, I guess you're right again.'

"'Well,' Marty says, 'why don't you wait here until Scotty gets here? They won't boo if we walk off together.'"

"What did you do?"

Rocket's smile brightened the room.

"I stared a hole through those little beady eyes of his and walked off the mound."

Tickle the Light · 95

Rocket slapped his knee and burst out laughing.

"I guess you don't mess with Rocket's walk," Joe said, with reverence in his tone and a nod of his head.

"Ah, I was just havin' a little fun," Rocket said, waving his hands as if shooing away flies. "We ain't been havin' a lot of that around here."

"At least you got to play on a winner in New York."

Rocket shook his head.

"Worst two years of my life. Those Yankee fans treated me fine, but I just got so dadgum homesick. I felt like a caged animal in the Bronx Zoo. I guess I should be thankful to Tex for bringing me back, but man, I've played on too many losing teams in Texas. The groundskeeper crosses home plate more than some of our hitters. It's the bottom of the ninth for me. I'd trade my strikeout records and throw in my Cy Young award to boot if I could go out a winner. I guess you read the other day where that kid for the Yankees was criticizing my won-lost record."

"Jackson? He's just jealous 'cause you broke his old man's strike-out records. Maybe this year you ought to put one in Jackson's e—"

Joe's voice, previously light and playful, vanished in midair.

"Hey, let's talk about something good," Rocket said, his speech more rapid than usual. "You gotta tickle the light sometimes. The dark'll take care of itself."

Joe soon learned that Rocket's baseball career happened in the opposite fashion of his own. Rocket spent his early childhood working and playing on his dad's ranch in Olney. The first hint of his bionic arm occurred at a local egg toss.

"I was about thirteen, and I guess I threw that darned egg about the length of a football field." Rocket grinned. "Only God and Elvis was as popular as baseball in our town in the summer time. The coaches lassoed me to practice the next day."

"How did you do?"

Rocket grinned wider than before.

"Threw over ninety miles an hour, but I was wilder than a baby jackrabbit. It was two years before anybody would face me in batting practice."

Rocket was also a family man with four children: his sons were seventeen and thirteen; the daughters, fifteen and eleven. Rocket and his family still lived on his ranch in Olney. With school in session, his family traveled to Arlington for the weekend home games. In the summer, Rocket's family stayed with him in a house near the stadium for the home stands.

"I miss 'em when we're on the road," Rocket said in a paternal tone. "Funny, you think after all these years, it would get easier, but it don't. It's not natural for a man to live without his family." Rocket swept his broad hand across the top of his shiny head. "On the road, loneliness crowds you, especially so the last few years. Strange things happen to a man when he's away from home. Think about it."

Long a prisoner of his colossal fame, Rocket, Joe learned, would usually stay in his hotel room while the younger players went out. The age difference and communication gap between Rocket and his teammates were totally exasperating to the old ballplayer.

"I don't know what the hell they're talking about most of the time, and I'm sure they feel the same way about me," Rocket lamented through sips of Lone Star. "Hell, some of them have those same funny looking roller skates my kids have." Joe eventually determined Rocket meant roller blades. "Joe, you gotta make the team so I've got somebody around close to my age," he added, with a nod of his head and a West Texas chuckle.

The two men failed to connect only on music; Rocket preferred Waylon and Willie, while Joe loved his old Beatles tunes. When Joe really wanted to rock and roll, he preferred the darling of Woodstock, Ten Years After.

"Ten Years After!" The rancher-flame thrower said. Rocket's face broke into a shark's smile, and he waved his arms all about. "What in the hell's that?" Then, Rocket's expression turned serious. "Are you sure you just decided not to play anymore?"

CHAPTER 17
FROTHIN GREEN

THE following day, Joe and Rocket were playing catch on the same diamond of Joe's earlier triumph. Every toss by Rocket produced a crisp pop in Joe's glove. Joe could not hide his anxiety as he admired the younger players gradually migrating to the diamond for the first day of spring training. No BIOYAs here.

"Impressed?" Rocket asked.

"Sure. I've been following you guys for lots of years . . . well, you for a lot of years," admitted Joe.

"Hey, now, don't show your age," Rocket said, a wide smile dividing his suede face.

As Joe began to absorb the sights and sounds of the baseball diamond, a sight so unforgettable appeared he wondered if his new vision wasn't faltering. A cement-bodied ballplayer of huge proportions stepped onto the ballfield. Joe saw little sign of intelligence in the giant, unless his bulging forehead and turned-up nose somehow transmitted brain power. A dog's leash dangled from one hand, but the leash contained no dog! As if on a leisurely stroll with man's best friend, the ballplayer was slowly moving toward Joe and Rocket.

"Duren Green?" Joe asked.

"Yep. Frothin Green to us ballplayers," Rocket said, receiving a soft toss from Joe.

"He's not the easiest thing to look at, is he?" Joe said, but not loud enough for the others to hear.

"Ugly enough to wrinkle a dress shirt at close range," Rocket said. He moved closer, lowering his chin and then his voice. "Frothin was put here to make guys like me look good."

"What in the hell's he doing?"

Rocket held onto the baseball and moved in another step. "Ain't it obvious? He's walking his dog."

"I don't see any dog." Experienced with invisible companions, Joe maintained an unruffled tone.

"It's a bad sign," Rocket said.

"That I can't see any dog?"

Rocket's head shook; his lips briefly pressed together.

"He only seems to bring the mutt around when something's wrong. It's like he's stressed out," Rocket said. "And when he's really on the edge, he starts stuttering."

"Why's he stressed?"

"Bad shoulder, for one. He had surgery on it this winter, but the team doc thinks his bat will be too slow." Rocket aimed a look directly at Joe. "You ain't helping matters any."

"Me?" asked Joe. It was almost a whisper.

"You're competition for the designated hitter's spot," said Rocket. "What if you lost your job to a forty-year-old rookie real estate man?"

Joe could only shake his head and wonder. "Think about it," he said, taking the words right out of Rocket's mouth.

Frothin now stood within spitting distance.

"How's it going, Duren?" Rocket asked warmly, while extending a firm hand to his teammate of three years.

"Hey, Rocket. I'm fine." Frothin spoke in a stiff mumble as if words represented a minefield which he tiptoed around carefully.

After shaking Rocket's hand, Frothin readjusted his ball cap, briefly disclosing a burr haircut. Joe immediately concluded the man was almost as intellectually handicapped as Big Jim.

"What did you do this winter?" Rocket asked.

"Had surgery," Frothin said to the ground. "Bought a house last week."

"Really? Where?" asked Rocket. His eyes strayed briefly to the empty dog leash, but he brought them back.

"Dallas...Lakewood area."

Joe's heart skipped a beat. Most of the ballplayers lived in Arlington, close to the ball park. Lakewood was more than forty minutes away. Why would Duren Green move to Lakewood?

"Joe lives in Lakewood," said Rocket.

For the first time, Frothin's uneasy glance acknowledged Joe. A look crossed Frothin's face so nasty, Joe hoped it would pass as quickly as major league heat. No such luck.

"How's the dog?" Rocket asked.

Frothin remained mute, apparently considering the question.

"Duren! Get that damn dog out of here!" Marty bellowed from close by.

"Y-y-y-yes sir!"

It was Frothin who exhibited the manners of a well-trained dog as he started to the clubhouse. He moved like a two-legged insect traversing over hot steel.

"That's a big clog in our machine," Marty said gruffly to a coach as Frothin crossed his path.

Watching Frothin disappear into the dugout, Joe asked Rocket, "Do you think he's all right?"

"Nope. My guess is this is the year his corkscrew brain twists off completely." Rocket shook his head sadly. "Tex knows something's wrong, but Frothin's got one year left on a fat contract. Tex is just trying to get his money's worth."

"Tex sounds like a sweetheart."

"Prince of a fellow. He'd cut your heart out if he could sell it for a profit."

"Why do you call him Frothin?"

"When he gets upset, he has these attacks. He starts frothin' at the mouth. Saliva starts drippin' down the side of his face." Rocket ran his powerful long fingers down his chin as if wiping away excess drool. "Word is, he bit off a guy's ear once in the minors." Rocket's upper lip curled to the sky in disgust.

"So, my competition is a foaming-at-the-mouth psycho-Goliath who occasionally bites off somebody's ear," Joe muttered. And my new neighbor, he thought.

CHAPTER 18
BACK AT THE OFFICE

BULL, his blue denim shirttail flapping like the tail of a kite, stormed through the halls of Walrus Real Estate with files under both arms. His customary Disney necktie hung as loose as his demeanor. As Bull raced by Shirley Knight, the anemic receptionist, he blurted out, "Two for four," referring to Joe's two hits in yesterday's exhibition game.

Entering his office, Bull flopped into his brown leather chair and glared with contempt at his cluttered desk. On the credenza behind him, he kept a picture of his family and another of himself and Joe in their college baseball uniforms. With long hair and wide smiles, the two stood leaning on baseball bats. Joe had never smiled as broadly since.

From spring training's first pitch, the media and baseball fans everywhere had followed Joe's every at bat as if he were chasing DiMaggio's fifty-six game hitting streak. More proud than infatuated, Bull kept a small TV on his desk that currently played the local news at low volume.

"Bull, Charles Stengel from the bank is on the phone," Shirley's voice rose through the phone's intercom.

Bull pressed the phone's speaker button.

"Hey, Chuckie-poo," he said, propping his big broad feet onto the desktop.

"How are you, Bull?" Stengel spoke in a deliberate tone.

"I'll be doing fine if our property's appraised okay." Bull's tone indicated what bothered him most about the banker was his occupation. Bull heard the banker take a deep pause, holding his breath too long before finally exhaling. Sensing trouble, Bull returned his feet to the floor, slumped over his desk, and began to tap his pencil on the mahogany desk top to a silent rhythm.

"Sorry, Bull," Stengel finally said. "It's the regulators. They're making us ask you for a principal reduction."

Though he had anticipated the response, Bull pondered a bit, rubbing one hand through his closely cropped golden hair that darted and curled in multiple cowlicks.

"How much?" he finally asked, sighing.

"One million."

"Damn it!" A spasm engulfed Bull so involuntarily that he broke his pencil on the desktop.

The TV caught Bull's attention: Tex Maris filled the screen. Bull tweaked the volume.

With one ear, Bull listened to the bank's conditions and demands. The television newscast captured his curious eyes and remaining ear.

"Tex, what a satisfying spring training this must be," the reporter's voice said. "The ageless Texas wonder, Rocket Nolin, looks fit for another season. But the spring training story is your miracle rookie, Joe Donley. Only one week left and he's leading the Grapefruit circuit in hitting with a .389 average! Season ticket sales are up. You've got to be excited."

"Yes, sir!" Tex grinned into the camera. "This is the year we finally bring that championship home!" Self-centered joy consumed Tex's voice.

"I've got ninety days, right?" Bull said to the phone, his eyes latched to the television. "Yeah, no problem, Chuckie-poo. Find another partner in this down market. Good idea, pal."

Bull punched off the phone. The banker's words had given Bull an idea. His index finger smacked the intercom button.

"Shirley, call the Rangers' executive offices. Tell them Joe Donley's business partner wants to talk to Tex Maris."

On the television, the interviewer was still talking to Tex. "Duren Green's hitting below .200, an all-time low. How's he handling his demotion?"

"He'll be okay," Tex answered flippantly and waved a hand dismissively in a fitting motion of non-concern.

CHAPTER 19
SPRING TRAINING

All alone, Frothin's massive rear end dwarfed the stool by his locker. He held a baseball bat high above his head and brought it violently to the clubhouse floor, shattering it into toothpicks. Drawn by the noise, a young clubhouse attendant entered the locker room and fearfully approached the ballplayer. "Mr. Green, are you okay?"

Duren glared in the general direction of the voice, but his glazed eyes produced vision as cloudy as his brain. Frothin could only sit alone and detest the recollection of his childhood and his pathetic mother and bully of a father.

Compared to his schoolmates, Duren was already a high rise in a one-story shopping mall. Word spread fast across the Blue Ridge Mountains of his ability to bash a baseball uncommon distances. Duren's father, Clint Green, worked odd, low-paying jobs. Though he looked of the same gene pool that produced Frothin, the man was not as dumb as he appeared. Clint already considered his son's baseball skills a first class ticket from the North Carolina hills.

If Duren performed below desired standards in Little League games, Clint might require his son to sit in the hot sun or eat raw fish or carve the letter K, the symbol for strikeout, in his flat top haircut.

During one hot summer game, Frothin swung hard enough to fan a breeze for the spectators in the dilapidated wooden bleachers. Duren's bat found only air polluted with the aroma of poverty. The mighty Duren, age twelve, had struck out. Duren stood mortified at home plate, facing his father in the stands as though witnessing his own execution. In a way it was—the execution of a childhood. Previous torment inflicted by his father registered on Duren's face as mandatory silence, hate, pain, and fear. Clint Green, wearing blue overalls that harbored a foul odor, charged onto the playing field with the diplomacy of a Brahma bull.

"Boy, the pros don't like chokers," Clint fumed.

Clint grabbed his son's ear so viciously that the huge kid fell to the ground like deadweight. Pleading with his eyes, Duren tried unsuccessfully to pull away from his father. From the stands, Duren's mother, a large mass of a woman with zippers for eyes, remained idle, thus reiterating Duren's notion of her uselessness.

Due to Clint's unwavering commitment to his son's baseball development, he failed to notice that a Dalmatian dog had suddenly sprinted on the field. The hot sensation of the Dalmatian's teeth sinking far enough into his ankle to draw blood caught Clint by total surprise.

After a speedy recovery, Clint Green drew back his unencumbered leg. Whack! Amid a desperate, lengthy yelp, Duren's best friend and companion sailed end over end before landing half-way to the pitcher's mound.

On the last day of spring training, while Duren "Frothin" Green continued to transform bats into firewood, Joe ambled calmly to home plate. The other team's manager, who resembled an aging Pillsbury doughboy, approached his young pitcher for a conference on the mound. After the bowlegged manager waddled back to the dugout, the pitcher promptly delivered a high, hard aspirin, its path intended to singe the dark stubble from Joe's chin. Joe knew this moment would come. Sooner before later, big league managers would test his courage.

As the ball shot toward his head, Joe dropped heavily to the dirt of the batter's box. His bat, still in one hand, lingered above him. Like a radar missile, the ball found the timber, deflected southbound and bopped Joe squarely on top of his batting helmet. The baseball bounced high into the air and fell harmlessly into foul territory.

Floating specs of dirt surrounded Joe at home plate, swirling like the emotions in his rattled mind. Joe's past now also surrounded him and threatened to swallow him whole. He saw only a pair of white tennis shoes shuffling toward him.

"Donley, are you okay?"

Joe recognized the fatherly voice of Willie, the Rangers' trainer. A heavily lined, sunburned face replaced the shoes in his field of vision.

"If you're hurt bad, don't move," Willie whispered, placing a consoling hand on Joe's shoulder.

Experience had taught Joe that if he was hurt badly, he couldn't move. And why was Willie whispering? With legs of putty, Joe slowly struggled to his feet. Once upright, he felt dizzy.

"Yeah, I'm fine," he lied, and wondered if he sounded to Willie like he did to himself, as if he were under water.

Joe noticed his vision was blurry. Shit! Not again, not before his first real major league game! He forced his legs to stabilize, but the thick interior mist remained unwelcome company.

"You're still at bat," barked the ump. "The ball hit your bat first."

Joe attempted to buy precious time. Calm masking his internal terror, he strolled back to the on-deck circle and retrieved the resin bag.

"Joe," a voice said, "take your time."

Joe turned to see Rocket, whose face registered concern.

"I just got medical clearance," Joe said.

"What?"

"I fell out of a tree a few weeks ago," Joe confessed as if the truth, whole truth, nothing but the truth suddenly occurred to him. "Now, my doctor says I can play ball again." he added softly.

"What?" Rocket repeated.

Before Joe could answer, Rocket held up one hand in a gesture of understanding and then gave Joe a gentle nudge toward home plate. Joe returned to the batter's box with the optimism of a non-swimmer walking off a plank. Wait, then attack. I think I can. He reminded himself . . .

Miraculously, the round blur did crystallize, and Joe smashed a low line drive that hissed its way into the outfield. Barely fair, the ball rolled into the left field corner and caromed off the fence like a spasmodic pinball. Joe rounded second, and while approaching the hot corner, his good fortune continued: the left fielder's throw sailed over third base and ricocheted off the stands. At the passionate insistence of his third base coach, Joe continued his journey to home. Good fortunes can rapidly change: the baseball bounced directly back to the third baseman, who rifled it to his catcher, and Joe was out at home.

Feeling immense relief—out, but still safe—Joe took his seat on the bench and watched Rocket take the mound. What followed was mesmerizing in its efficiency. Into his windup, Rocket's left foot seemed to stretch several stories high; the right arm came whistling over the top, releasing the ball that raced toward home plate. Payback time. The batter dove to the ground, barely avoiding the baseball.

In the opposing dugout, a lean bodied-coach sat beside the wide oval manager. Both men's jaws worked furiously on baseball-size wads of tobacco. It looked like baseball's version of Laurel and Hardy hooked on snuff.

"Did you see that?" the manager asked, his words jumbled due to the mass in his bloated jaw.

"He doesn't pitch inside, does he?" said the coach, his words no more intelligible.

"Must have got away from him," the manager grunted.

When Rocket brushed back the next batter, both men's eyes expanded.

"If that crusty old buzzard pitches tight this year, nobody will hit him," warned the manager. He drew his short, stubby right leg up off the dugout floor, until his chin rested on his right knee, and scratched his wide oval ass the way some people scratch their heads when thinking.

"What if he starts hitting people?" asked the coach, considering this dim prospect for the first time. A worried snort burst through the coach's nose. "Hell, nobody will even step up to the plate!"

All three batters hit the dirt before striking out, and Rocket began his mechanical walk toward, of all places, the opposing dugout! Rocket leaned in to glare at the coach and manager, who returned anemic smiles. They appeared to share one nervous system between them.

"Hello, Rocket," the manager squeaked. He tugged on his jersey collar, as if it were too snug. "Pitching kinda tight today, aren't you?"

"I'm not going to hit anybody." Rocket's tone was as cold as opening day in Chicago. "At least, not on purpose." He stared the grins off the duo's faces before adding, "Unless somebody dusts back our rookie. Pass the word."

The manager gulped down a burp that made his eyes mist. The coach choked on his chewing tobacco.

"Think about it," Rocket said.

After leaving the dugout, he turned back and fired the two men a spaghetti western stare, as if issuing a dare to challenge him and his laser right arm.

As Rocket returned to the Rangers' side of the diamond, his look found Joe. In this look, an understanding passed between them: they were even.

CHAPTER 20
MEANWHILE

Later, Rocket tried to quiz Joe about his baffling reference to falling from a tree.

"What in the hell were you talking about?"

Joe shrugged off the question. "Who knows what I was saying? That damn foul ball stunned me."

Making the team stunned him more. Before a packed opening-day crowd in Arlington, Joe soaked in the pre-game festivities: the vendors' cries of "Hot dogs! Get your fresh peanuts, cold beer here!" Contrasting colors of home team white and road gray contrasted again with every color of the rainbow in the stands. Pre-game fragrances of infield dirt and freshly cut Bermuda grass, foul line chalk and chewing tobacco, and adrenaline-inspired perspiration infiltrated the brisk spring air.

The Donley contingency sat a few rows behind the home team's dugout. Even Mary Donley, privately gloating over her and God's good work, had left the seclusion of home to see the results. Joan, forever the team player, was all smiles. Tater sang all the while, contemplating her first true business venture. Liz furiously made notes for her book. Because of a ticket shortage for opening night, Joe had adamantly refused to secure a spot for Avery. Nevertheless, K. C. and Avery continued their private conversation. Big Jim gleefully clutched Joe's present of a baseball autographed by the entire Ranger team as carefully as if he held a vital body part. Burdened with business, only Bull's face failed to reflect the general good spirits.

Joe stood along the first base line with his teammates as they waited for the National Anthem. His eyes to the sky, he held his ball cap snugly to his heart. Oh, if Daddy could see me now, he lamented. As the first notes floated over a modest breeze, only a few minutes separated Joe from participating in his first true major league game. His moment had finally arrived.

Joe looked damn near content, but unfinished business remained. Joe wanted to win that batting title more than Liz wanted to write, or Tater to sing, or K. C. to play with her imaginary friend, even more than Joan wanted him to stay home.

Both Joe and Rocket took care of business opening night. Concerned batters stood timidly in the batter's box, meekly fanning air at Rocket's heat. Joe's first at bat, a fly ball that stayed in flight longer than an astronaut, caromed off the centerfield wall for a double. Two vicious line drive singles followed.

By June, Joe led the American League in hitting, belting out base hits as frequently as Chester conducted air raids throughout the Donley home. Also in June, Tater raced to the living room waving a magazine.

"Daddy! Daddy! Look! You're on the cover of *Sports Illustrated*!"

"You're kidding," Joe said, his tone prototypically calm. Joan and the girls hurriedly crowded around.

"You're looking pretty good there, Dad," Joan said.

Joe's facial skin looked tighter, like a younger man. His jaw appeared more manly, his already heavy beard thicker. Previous lightning streaks of silver in Joe's hair had vanished.

"What does it say, Dad?"

Liz reached for the magazine, but Joe hid it behind his back. He dropped into an armchair and flipped pages until he found the headline: "Miracle Rookie Helps Rangers Miracle Turnaround." He started to read aloud: "'Thanks in no small part to the efforts of Joe Donley, a man beaned by Rocket Nolin twenty years ago, the Rangers find themselves in foreign territory in the American League West standings—first place.'"

The Donley cheering section promptly erupted, but then came the familiar chirp of "Chester, Chester, Chester."

"Daddy! Duck!" K. C. cried. Sure enough, Chester zoomed perilously close to Joe's head. "He just misses you, Dad."

"Hey Dad, will you sign my homework sheets?" Tater interjected. "I've got a bunch of them."

"Not now," Joe answered. His irritated eyes followed Chester out of the room.

Joe continued reading. "'In baseball's version of Ripley's Believe It Or Not, the Rangers discovered the forty-one-year old rookie in their fantasy camp. Donley currently leads the American League in hitting with a torrid .384 average.'"

Joe's eyes scanned the page. "Listen to this," he said. "'No one deserves to play on a winner more than the game's good-will ambassador, Rocket Nolin. It appears more long-deserved good fortune has finally come Rocket's way. He always seems to pitch when the other team doesn't score,'" Joe read through a grin.

Joe stopped reading aloud, but his eyes continued on the page.

"Keep reading, Dad," K. C. said.

"Oh, this part's really good," Joe announced. "'Word has filtered throughout the league, opposing batters better not crowd the plate and opposing pitchers should avoid dusting Ranger hitters. No one has crossed Rocket's orders to date because the oldest man in the game seems in a real nasty mood. Not to mention, he still throws harder than any man alive.'"

Consistent with Rocket's tickle the light theory, *Sports Illustrated* could not avoid the dark side. The magazine theorized that Duren Green's moodiness, deeper since the loss of his job to Joe, represented the mere tip of Duren's emotional iceberg. Unnamed sources claimed that Duren often sat in the clubhouse, motionless, for hours at a time. The article's author implied that Ranger management should seek psychological help for Duren.

S. I. also hinted of unsubstantiated heavy gambling losses by the Ranger's "eccentric owner."

"Wow. What's Tex going to say about that?" Joan asked.

"Nothing. He'll ignore it." Joe suspected Tex was long immune to such subtlety as the insidious tone of a magazine article.

"Dad, do you have time to sign my homework papers now?" Tater asked, a trickle of conspiracy creeping into her angelic voice.

It took a late-night phone call from an obvious drunk to interest a twenty-three-year-old woman from New York City in the story piece. From the bed of her Manhattan apartment, the woman answered the phone on her nightstand without turning on the light.

"This better be good," she mumbled through her sleep. It was.

"Have I seen the new *Sports Illustrated*? Who is this? You're a doctor? Yeah, right, and I'm Julia Roberts."

But the caller knew her brother's name and that he died from a fall over twenty years ago.

"How did you know about my brother?"

"I have big ears to hear things and big eyes to see things," slurred the mysterious man.

"You were there?"

"I didn't say that."

"How did you find me?"

"Easy. The Internet directory. There's only twenty-six Carla Malones listed in the whole country."

"You called them all?"

"Most of 'em. Why do you think I'm so smashed?" He hiccupped so loudly, the young woman's ear recoiled at the sound.

The caller went on to provide information that made Carla flinch from ear to ear. She listened with disbelieving ears and big eyes of her own as the man told of a medical team's efforts to save her older brother's life.

"But I want you to know something," the man continued. "Your brother didn't die in vain. He helped save somebody else's life, and it's the person on the cover of *Sports Illustrated*."

The phone went silent.

"One more thing," he finally said.

"What's that?"

"Have you ever tried phone sex?" Laughter exploded through the receiver louder than before.

The day after the release of *Sports Illustrated's* article, the Rangers traveled to Chicago. From his office phone, Duke reached Joe at a Chicago hotel under the pretense of congratulating him. Ted French, obviously nursing a hangover, lay listlessly on Duke's office couch.

Joe's voice rose up from Duke's speaker phone. "I've never felt better. I've even gotten stronger. I had to get a bigger batting glove, and my feet have grown half a size."

The fall must have awakened the pituitary gland, Duke theorized. Only a super discharge of pituitary hormones could account for the changes. This hyperstimulation would last only long enough to produce a pituitary adenoma, a small but benign pituitary tumor which, in turn, produced all the secondary effects Joe was experiencing.

"I need to see you," Duke said for good reason.

"What for?" Joe answered.

"Just a routine check," Duke replied, but his face said otherwise.

Before Joe hung up the phone, he assured Duke that he would schedule an appointment when the Rangers returned to Dallas, but Duke knew Joe's track record for following up on doctor appointments was less than stellar. Duke stared at his anesthesiologist sprawled on his couch. Ted lay on his back with his forearm shielding his eyes.

"Routine check my ass," Ted mumbled with difficulty to the ceiling. "Pituitary adenoma?"

"Probably."

"Wow whee!" Ted sprang to life, quickly returning to a prone position on the couch. "Increased strength with motor skills and vision like Superman." Ted flashed a school boy grin and rubbed his hands together with glee. "And a sex drive raging like a herd of rock stars!"

"Not to mention the possibility of hypertension and diabetes or that the tumor could grow and push on the nerve that controls his vision," Duke said soberly. Duke drug his hand down his concerned face. "It's not like we have a lot of case studies to fall back on here."

Though worried, Duke dared not explain to Joe. Only his loyal medical team knew of the transplant, and none of them would ever tell. Besides, his prized patient was finally living a life of distinction.

Duke stared harder at Ted than before. "You've never told anybody, have you?"

"Me?" Ted replied, his voice level dropping several decibels. "Of course not."

CHAPTER 21
FEELING IMPORTANT

IT took a BIOYA softball game for fame to boost Joe's new found feeling of importance to record heights. Bull's wide feet were pawing a minor trench at home plate when he heard a familiar voice from behind.

"Let's go, Big un, base knock."

Bull turned to discover Joe standing behind the backstop and instantly recognized his companion.

"Little Man! Rocket!" Bull roared, flashing a grin as twisted as the ball cap on his head.

Bull dropped his bat and spread his arms as if welcoming long lost relatives. An adoring crowd soon surrounded Joe and Rocket.

"Hey, Joe! You guys gonna beat Oakland tonight?" a voice rang out above the crowd.

"Sure gonna try," Joe said, with more of a veteran's tone than he had a right to.

"Joe, can you hit Rocket in batting practice?" asked another.

Only a special pitcher threw batting practice, but Joe played along. "No way," he said, shaking his head at the ground in playful frustration. "It's like trying to mine coal with a teaspoon."

Everyone but Big Jim howled with laughter. A wall of people now totally encompassed Joe and Rocket, but Big Jim could not bust through.

Joe, preoccupied with the crowd, overlooked Big Jim's desperate lunges.

"Say, Rocket. What's it like having Joe for a teammate?"

"Great! He's darn near as old as me. We put our pictures above our lockers so we can find our way back after the game."

More laughter followed.

After a few more minutes of similar banter, the miniature mob moved progressively closer till Joe expected Rocket was feeling claustrophobic.

"Sorry, fellas," Joe said. "We're supposed to be at the ballpark in an hour."

Joe and Rocket briskly strolled from the diamond and moved toward Joe's late model BMW. Bull broke away from the crowd to walk with Joe.

"Joe," he said in a worried tone, "we need to talk about the properties."

Feeling important obviously impairs the hearing because Joe failed to hear the urgency of Bull's request.

"Just do the best you can," Joe said.

Bull's feelings were evident in the ensuing pause.

"Thanks for your help, old buddy."

Joe and Rocket entered the auto. Big Jim and his underslung chassis waddled dejectedly to Bull, who wrapped his thick arm around Big Jim's broad shoulders.

"Get 'em, Joe," Big Jim wistfully said. He lowered his head like a beaten puppy as the car pulled away.

The instant Joe's car passed a two-story apartment complex, a house-sized blur of a man vaulted clumsily behind a row of waist-high shrubs. The late afternoon sun reflected off the man's head, and then he was gone.

"Did you see that?" Rocket said.

Joe put on the brakes, and his car pulled to a halt, chugging in its own exhaust.

"Was that Duren Green?" Joe asked.

Joe and Rocket stared at the deserted shrubs.

"You want to check it out?" Rocket asked.

Through his rear view mirror, Joe saw a small crowd moving rapidly toward the BMW.

"Guess not," Joe said, his foot returning to the pedal. "You know, I swear I think I've seen him hanging around my neighborhood a couple of times."

"Who?"

"Frothin," Joe said in a manner suggesting the name referred to the messages scribbled on dirty bathroom walls.

"Well, he lives close by, right? He bought a house in your area, remember."

Rocket's attempt at nonchalance came up shorter than a two-hop change-up.

"Yeah, but this guy's always hopping around and hiding. Just like that guy back there."

A shudder went up Joe's spine, and he reached to turn off the air conditioning.

"Better open the windows. It's not hot enough for the AC."

In spite of the sunlight which penetrated the open sun roof, the car's interior mood suddenly turned darker than the entrance to an abandoned cave.

CHAPTER 22
AWAY FROM HOME

THE team bus hissed to a stop in front of New York's Essex House, and Rangers players soon exited single file. Though hotel security provided a clear walkway to the hotel entrance, Rocket stopped to sign autographs along the guarded path. After two decades with a losing team and despicable owner, he still appreciated the privilege of playing in the big leagues. Unlike Joe, when Rocket watched reruns of his favorite old TV show, *Rawhide*, he never missed the good part. Only a few Rangers shared Rocket's attitude and bothered to sign autographs along the way.

But how could anyone appreciate his big league roster spot more than Joe? Joe also gladly obliged the fans, signing his name as legibly as he would sign homework assignments for Tater.

Would Joe react in the same manner today if he had achieved big league status twenty years ago? Exposed to, if not sold on, his mother's spiritual beliefs, Joe also heard another of his father's theories as regularly as he heard his theories on hitting: "If a person treats another person with respect and dignity, even though he knows full well this person can never do a damn thing for him, -now that's a good man." Maybe Joe would have aged in the bigs like a good bottle of port, like Rocket had.

As the Rangers' entourage filed into the Essex House lobby, loud music pulled a group of players directly to the main bar. Once inside, several attractive young ladies promptly served as ornaments for the ballplayers' arms and later, certainly, more strategic anatomy parts.

Spaghetti straps poorly concealed the women's shoulders. Most of their dresses clung to their bodies like spandex and were brief enough to barely cover "the promised land." Though a humid summer night, the women looked the type to avoid an abundance of clothing, regardless of the weather. An aura of sex held its own mixed with the smell of good liquor. From the bar's entrance, Joe and Rocket watched the embraces and greetings.

"Looks kind of hot in there to me," said Rocket, wiping away invisible beads of perspiration. "You going in?"

"No way."

Joe felt the familiar sensation below his belt. Rocket nodded approvingly, and both men moved toward the elevator. On the way, they passed a smaller, more intimate bar. Sinatra replaced hip hop as the night club's musical choice.

A raspy, deep voice came from the direction of the bar's dark opening. "Joe? Joe Donley?"

Joe and Rocket stopped and turned to face a tall silhouette framed in the doorway.

"Do I know you?" Joe asked.

"You're getting ready to."

The mystery woman stepped from the doorway's darkness. She looked like a Miss World competitor, her body ideally covered by a tight one-piece or a revealing bikini or less. The snugness of her black mini-dress emphasized the swell of large, firm breasts. Her nipples, practically escaping the plunging neckline, looked hard as ball bearings. Sex in a slipper, high-heeled sandals enhanced her sculptured voluptuousness, the muscles in her calves, thighs, and tiny waist. The stunning whiteness of her flesh clashed magnificently with the color of her dress. Heavy, dark hair draped past her bare shoulders, exposing only the tip of her pointed nose.

"How about a drink, Joe?"

"I better not," said Joe faintly. How about a respirator? he thought.

Joe glanced at Rocket, who looked relieved that she was asking for Joe. Joe could feel temptation rising like simmering charcoals.

Both men stood less than ten feet from wonder woman. Joe leaned into Rocket.

"What do you think?"

"I think she looks like a high-priced call girl that nobody can afford to buy."

"She doesn't look like a call girl," Joe replied indignantly, as if Rocket had insulted his mother.

"You're right, but she looks too expensive. You know," Rocket said softly, staring hard at the woman, "in Texas, you see a lot of eights and nines, sometimes even tens. But that's a flat dab fifteen."

"Yeah," Joe mumbled.

"Come on, guys; I won't bite."

Each man flinched.

"That woman's got a plan," Rocket whispered. "The women here in New York...sometimes they have a plan. It's like going deer hunting, but the deer's got the rifle."

Moving quietly as her shadow, the woman approached and pushed her jet black hair away from her face. It went well with the rest of her. Faint blusher tinted her ultra-smooth cheeks. Pinkish lipstick shone on her thick, shapely lips, the type of lips wealthy women pay plastic surgeons to duplicate. She moved with self-assurance, but somehow maintained the aura of a wayward soul who would play hard, love harder, and party all night with the gypsies.

"My name's Candice," she announced, now standing close enough for Joe and Rocket to inhale her scent: the smell of lust. "I already know your names."

Joe stood goggle-eyed, mute.

"What's one drink, Joe?"

Joe, a man devoted to a life of self-control, felt less in control with every passing second. Intimidated and self-conscious, he stepped back.

Candice grabbed Joe's hand and pulled him toward the nightclub. She turned back to eye Rocket. "Don't worry. I won't eat him," she said, the ice in her voice matching the ice in eyes dark enough to pass for black. "Yet."

"A flat dab fifteen," Rocket muttered while shaking his near bald head and making his way alone to the elevator. "Strange things seem to happen when a man's on the road."

From across the nightclub's dime-sized table, Joe stared at Candice's high cheekbones and full face. She sat so close that Joe smelled her seductively minty breath. Candice ordered a kamikaze drink, and he somehow managed to order a beer. He told himself he stayed only as a courtesy to a curious fan. Right, and some day he would sell himself Braniff stock, too.

"What makes you so sure I'll have a drink with you?"

Joe's glance fell to his hands, clasped together on the small table top. Fearing she would plainly read his weakness, he wanted to avoid her eyes.

"Easy. I'm what you don't have."

Candice distinctly pronounced every letter in all the words. Her perfect white teeth glowed in the dark. She flashed as cocky a smirk as Joe had ever seen.

"Like what?" Joe asked, then knowing he shouldn't have.

"I'm young. Your wife's not," Candice said with astonishing wickedness. She tossed her long hair away from her face.

"She's not exactly a prune."

Below the table, Joe felt the fire from Candice's hand through the cotton of his summer pants, raising a tingle that nailed him to his seat.

"Joe," Candice said slowly, as if digesting him. "When's someone like myself going to hit on you again? Come on, Joe. You boy. Me girl."

"There's more to a woman than what she looks like," Joe uttered unconvincingly.

Candice leaned in so close their noses touched; her coal black hair moved forward, obscuring her face and brushing gently against Joe's nose and cheeks.

"Exactly." Candice grinned obscenely. "I'm free, uninhibited, delicious," she continued as if announcing the best items on the menu. "Untamed by the responsibilities of raising a family," she added for desert.

Joe felt punch drunk. ("Pugilistica dementia," Duke called it.) Why was the desire for sex so out of whack with everything else? he wondered. And why had she chosen him?

"You're probably wondering why I've picked you. You're baseball's newest darling." She shrugged and pursed her lips. "That appeals to me, and I like having what appeals to me. I like having it all." Candice squeezed his leg. "You can have it all too, Joe. Having it all; it's the key to total fulfillment," she whispered in a voice consumed with more desire than Joe had ever heard before.

Joe, now wondering how to acquire the key, heard his own swallow echo in the bar's emptiness. The waitress brought the drinks, and Candice stirred her kamikaze with her index finger. She lifted the finger, placed it into her mouth and, as if bathing in her own orgasm, began sucking on it. Without foreshadow, she grabbed Joe's chin with her right hand and positioned his face level with hers. Her lips parted, and her sizzling tongue raked the top of his lip, then the bottom, then plunged into Joe's mouth. Abruptly, she stopped, rose, and with the preeminence of a rock star diva, stalked out of the bar.

Joe took her kamikaze and splashed it to the back of his throat. A slow burn eased its way to his queasy gut. He downed the beer in one long swallow. His breath sounded harsh in his own ears. His heart was beating like a jackhammer, which delivered a vibration all the way to his groin. Joe's excessive breathing rate would not leave for several minutes; neither would his pulsating erection.

"Strange things seem to happen when a man's on the road," Joe gasped.

CHAPTER 23
POINT OF NO RETURN

HALF asleep, Joe heard a stir outside his hotel door. Players and women from the main bar still partying, he guessed. Not five minutes earlier, he'd gotten up to investigate a series of loud bangs and discovered golf balls zipping through the halls faster than his best line drive!

"Chill," Joe had ordered, only half-serious. "Us old guys need our sleep."

The tipsy players and their giggling girlfriends had promised to take their clubs and go to bed. Now, the late-night golfers had evidently returned. Outside Joe's door, a human shadow obscured the dim hallway light.

With the dexterity of a cat burglar, Joe tiptoed to the door and jerked it open. Holy shit! The girl from the bar stood in his doorway. She wore the same clothes she'd worn earlier, which is to say she wore little. To Joe, it seemed she wore less than that. Due to her heels, Joe realized that she was slightly taller and must weigh a rock solid hundred and forty pounds. She was no small problem.

Like Chester venturing from his cage, Joe poked his head into the otherwise deserted hallway. He quickly surmised he had two options and little time to choose. He could shut the door, crawl into the bed, pull the covers over his head, and not dare come out until morning. Or he could quickly pull her from the hall's light into his room's darkness and tell her she must leave as soon as possible. Yeah, right, or as Rocket would say, "Think about it," considering that lust has clouded more than one good man's judgement.

He pulled her inside and shut the door. He could see Candice better than she could see him. Despite the noise of Manhattan's late-night activity rising up from the streets below, Joe could hear her breathing. His own heart fluttered at the rate of a hummingbird's wings.

"You're going to have to leave as soon as the coast is clear," Joe blurted.

"Don't be silly. The coast is clear." Candice moved closer. "You were looking for the key," she whispered. "The key to total fulfillment. Well, you found it. Or better yet, it found you."

What now? Should he cooperate in his own seduction? Nothing would ever come of it, Joe told himself. Nothing but a guilty conscience that would torment him until death do us part.

In one flawless motion, Candice reached behind her neck and untied the thin strap that held up her dress. The woman's nakedness meant nothing to her. Her dress dropped to the floor as effortlessly as a bird shedding feathers. Nothing was left to Joe's imagination except the bottoms of her feet; she still wore her high-heeled slippers. The high-rise breasts, her indented belly button and six-pack stomach, her breathtaking firmness, the rose tattooed on her inner thigh—he could see them all. Joe stood still as a night stand. Candice moved so close that he could feel her breasts against his chest.

"Jesus, take off your clothes!" she whispered, louder than before.

Candice didn't wait for Jesus; her hands Braille-read Joe's shirt buttons. His shirt fell to the floor, and he felt the wetness from her lips against his bare chest: first one nipple, then the other. As if to prevent his flight, Candice cupped her left hand around the back of his neck and kissed him long and hard on the mouth.

Joe's stiff arms rose slowly. Another body part had already risen. An interior thought exploded inside Joe like fire into gasoline. These fiery lips, this tongue slashing inside his mouth—this was not Joan.

Joe had never kissed any other woman on the lips.

God almighty! Just this one time, Joe promised silently, his arms now embracing this stranger. Just this one time.

By the time they flopped onto the bed, Candice was wet and warm, and Joe entered the promised land in one mad thrust. Inhaling fiercely, Candice dug her fingernails into Joe's back, rotated her hips, and moaned wantonly. Virgin moves and fresh sounds, he thought. She arched her back until Joe's rump raised to the sky. Above his backside, her legs hung in space.

Maybe he could have it all, Joe decided: fresh passion and playing ball, two of life's pleasures he thought had long ago passed him by.

Joe had no idea how much time had elapsed when Candice's high-heeled shoes crashed sharply at the base of his spine. Joe yelled, and his head snapped sharply toward the night stand. The photo of Joan and the girls on the stand pierced Joe's soul like a hot bolt of lightning.

An erection of Joe's current condition didn't come along every day and did not wilt immediately, but it doesn't take that long either. Candice didn't appear to notice; she continued to moan and writhe beneath her partner. After Candice finally acknowledged her emptiness, she slid out from beneath Joe and snuggled under his left shoulder. They both stared at the ceiling in darkness and quietness.

Her hair tickled Joe's face and neck; he could taste a few strands that gently poked his lips. The overpowering aroma of her fertile sex sickened him now. Everything's going to be okay, he told himself, another illusion he knew adulterous men attempted to fall asleep to. He lay awake all night, his emotional generator supercharged with shame.

"You want to take off your shoes?" Joe said softly.

With the devastation of a Rocket beanball, lust took another good man down.

Twaa-aa-ang! The first note of the electric guitar meandered softly across the alarm clock radio of Joe's hotel room. A rowdier, pulsating bass followed, and then the drums kicked in; rock-n-roll didn't feel right at such low volume. Joe didn't feel quite right either.

Now the Boss, Springsteen, began to wail in that distinctive raspy voice:

> "Well my soul checked out missin' as I sat listenin'
> To the hours and minutes tickin' away
> Yeah just sittin' around waitin' for my life to begin
> While it was all just slippin' away
> I'm tired of waitin' for tomorrow to come
> Or that train to come roarin' around the bend
> I got a new suit of clothes, a pretty red rose,
> And a woman I can call my friend"

But which woman? Joe wondered.

Joe lay in bed, trying to clear his cloudy brain. Maybe he had simply enjoyed a good dream—a harmless fantasy. Better yet, with his outstanding morning erection, maybe he was still dreaming. In this morning version, however, soft moist lips skated gently across his stomach. Moving south, they encompassed Joe. Only after Joe arched his back and heard his own groan did he suspect this was no dream.

The first morning light slanted through the hotel room windows, showcasing a mass of shiny, black hair, bobbing up and down like a well-oiled piston. The dew inside Joe's head rapidly began to evaporate, and he remembered the events of last night. No dream. Maybe a nightmare, but certainly no dream. Like the Boss's wake-up call, Candice maintained her own methods of generating an early rise. Candice's heavy scent continued to dominate the room. The Boss sang on:

> "Now a life of leisure and a pirate's treasure
> Don't make much for tragedy,
> But it's a sad man, my friend, who's livin' in his own skin
> And can't stand the company
> Every fool's got a reason for feelin' sorry for himself
> And turnin' his heart to stone
> Tonight, the fool's halfway to heaven and just a mile
> Outta hell
> And I feel like I'm comin' home."

CHAPTER 24
CANDICE LEAVES SOMETHING BEHIND

JOE lay sprawled across the bed on his stomach, listless and exhausted. His neck tilted upward. He pretended to watch television, but only one eye focused on *Good Morning America;* the other followed Candice, who stood totally nude in front of the bathroom mirror. Candice blew her hair away from her face, and the soft current briefly exposed her nipples. She was totally uninhibited, her nudity as teasing as a no-hitter in the ninth. The familiar tingle did not intoxicate Joe. After Candice's morning attack, the two had made love so long and so intensely that his genitals ached and stung.

Joe felt worse than after a hitless home stand. First, he had betrayed Joan. Worse, Candice was closer to Liz's age than his own.

"Joe, would you get me some things from my room?" Candice asked brightly. "There's a brush and some clothes on the bed. It's unlocked." Earlier, she had told him that she easily convinced a young male desk clerk to rent her the room directly across the hall. "In case you tossed me out," she had coolly volunteered.

Candice's request fell on deaf ears. Joe's mind was at the dinner table with Joan and the girls and skillfully ducking Chester's attacks. At the office, he monitored Bull and Big Jim's wrestling match. He heard his family's cheers at the BIOYA's softball game.

"Joe, are you okay?" Candice asked.

Tickle the Light · 133

"What?" Joe said, sounding as if just awakened from a restless sleep.

Wearing only his brown terry cloth robe, Joe crossed the hall to Candice's room with the care of a teenager arriving home after curfew. He found her hairbrush and a small pile of clothes—a pair of flat leather sandals, light brown pleated cotton jeans, and a brief beige halter top—in the middle of the unruffled queen-sized bed. Joe's head shook at the notion of the garment's futile attempt to cover Candice's chest. There was also a sleeveless denim vest—probably for insurance, Joe thought, in case the police stopped her for indecent exposure. As he prepared to leave, Joe noticed the phone's red message light blinking. After the shortest of moral battles, he picked up the receiver.

"Front desk," answered a man in a thick deep voice.

"Yes, I was checking the message light."

"You have a message from Duren Green in Room 679."

"Dur—en Green?" Joe practically hiccupped.

He hung up the phone like it was hot and then wished he hadn't. His perplexity mounted rapidly into total confusion. Recrossing the hall, Joe's bewilderment shaded toward anger. In his room, Candice sat naked on top of the unmade bed, her legs folded under her. He tossed the clothes to her, but she made no move to dress. Mass production of her smirk would eliminate the concern of global warning.

"Your message light was blinking." Joe's voice was flat.

Candice's left eyebrow edged upward.

"Hmm. Better go check it."

Candice seemed to admire her body as much as any man. Still naked, she left the bed and moved toward the door.

"I already did."

Candice wheeled to face Joe. Surprises lowered her a notch from Rocket's previous fifteen on the rating scale. Her deep, dark eyes narrowed with suspicion; her nose crinkled and turned up at the tip. The thick lips turned thin while the veins in her red neck rose visibly setting off the white in her cheeks.

"How do you know Duren Green?"

"Duren Green!" Candice cried, displaying a look of bored superiority. "That big ugly toad! He asked me my name in the lobby. Then he asked me for a date, but no way am I going out with that moron! ("Mormon," K. C. would have corrected) Why? Are you already jealous?" she asked, with a degree of mock-teasing scorn.

Before Joe could reply, Candice rushed toward him and snuggled close. Her left hand disappeared inside Joe's robe.

"What do you do? I mean...where do you go from here?" asked Joe, trying to ignore her fingers sliding across his chest. After a long pause, she said, "Actually, I have class. I'm working on my master's. Business. Surprised?"

"Kinda."

"My dad ran out on my mom when I was six. Haven't seen him since." Her tone was suddenly frosty enough to fog mirrors. She moved away from Joe and toward the clothes on the bed. "No way am I ever going to be dependent on a man."

"Where's your mom now?"

"Around." Her legs vanished into the legs of her jeans, and the clump of chocolate-colored pubic hair followed. "My mother was in a bad car wreck when I was eighteen." She drew in her stomach slightly and buttoned her pants. "Messed up her mind." Candice tugged on the halter top. "She kicked me out of the house."

Candice dropped to the end of the bed to put on her sandals.

"How do you support yourself until you finish school?" Joe wondered aloud. Would she ask for money?

Candice began to brush her hair, her head tilting a bit with each stroke. With one friendly eye and one not so friendly, she looked up at Joe. He stood motionless in the middle of the room, suffering a relapse of pugilistica dementia.

"You're full of questions. Don't worry about me. And I'm not going to ask you for any money."

Now dressed, she looked like someone going to or leaving an expensive health club. Head high, she stood and stepped over her shoes and revealing black dress. Still loaded with Joe, she moved like a "corn cube" was stuck between her legs.

"Bye," Candice said, walking out the door. She took with her more than Joe's sex, while leaving behind far more than last night's clothes.

CHAPTER 25
IT'S DECEPTIVE

By September, Texas, carried by Rocket's magical right arm and Joe's league leading .379 batting average, led their division by three games. At home, Joe did not perform so well. His dark mood returned. What was the problem now? Joan, experienced with Joe's emotional reclusiveness, concentrated on raising her children.

Not that raising children, and often alone, didn't have its problems. K. C.'s continued constipation worried Joan. Talking long distance to Joe, Joan would joke uncomfortably, "K. C.'s full of more crap than a Christmas turkey."

Liz, in behavior similar to her grandmother, retreated more and more into her world of words by increasingly dictating into her tiny black box. Further concerning Joan, Liz recently hadn't even asked Bull if she could substitute for any AWOL BIOYAs.

An incident with Tater worried Joan the most. Joe returned from a road trip to learn that Tater's principal had requested a meeting with Tater and her parents the next day.

The private school, attached to a Lutheran church, had been in session only a week. The meeting took place in the deserted church sanctuary. Standing a meaty six foot-five inches tall, Doug Moeller, the principal, resembled a giant teddy bear. He lowered himself into the front pew and twisted to face Tater, who sat pale-faced between her parents in the second row.

"It seems Kate has started her own little enterprise," the principal said quietly, looking at Tater with calm analytical scrutiny.

Tater fidgeted in the pew as if his glance made her itchy. The principal intimidated Tater the way large adults often intimidate young children.

"She's been selling Joe's autographs to the other kids. A few are even fakes."

"Tater!" Joan cried. "Autographs! The homework assignments," Joan murmured. Joan knotted her fingers into her lap. "You said some of the autographs were fake?"

"There are some pretty sophisticated copy machines out there." Mr. Moeller's words barely echoed in the emptiness of the sanctuary. "The younger kids evidently couldn't tell the difference. I guess she ran out of originals during the summer." His reproachful stare returned to Tater. "Some children were using their lunch money to pay for them." Moeller's eyes shifted to Joe. "Everybody at Zion is proud of you, Mr. Donley, but we can't have Kate selling your autograph to the kids for their lunch money."

On the chapel's front wall, a multi-colored glass mural of Jesus stretched from floor to ceiling. A shaft of sunlight shone through the stained glass directly on Tater, God's spotlight, Joe thought. Tater attempted a brave front, but her scared eyes and down-turned mouth betrayed her. Her eyes filled, and she sniffled.

Joe had been staring listlessly at his hands, but Tater's tears were acid on his soul. "Jesus!" he blurted, looking upward as if summoning the Man himself.

"How could you do this?" Joan asked, her concerns and worries as visible as K. C.'s freckles.

"It was a mistake," said Tater, pale and trembling. Tater had not yet lived long enough to know it's the mistakes in life that create so much havoc. "It started as fun."

"Fun!" Joan cried, shaking her head at the floor.

"But then Bull told me the business was having money problems," Tater added in a barely audible monotone. "I've been saving the money. I have $315.00."

Silence fell upon the sanctuary like a mortal blow. As inconceivable as it sounded, Joe could imagine Bull sharing business concerns with an eleven-year-old. The man had no secrets, especially from any Donley.

Joan sighed. "It's okay," she said, wrapping an arm around Tater. "But anything we have to hide is usually not right. It's deceptive. We Donleys try to do what's right."

Joe said nothing. How could he counsel his child about right and wrong? He sat looking as if remembering; and, of course, he was—he was remembering his own deception. For Joe to love his wife but lust for another was a dilemma for the most self-controlled of men.

And what money problems? he wondered.

CHAPTER 26

THE HOLY GHOST

WITH a Sunday night game on tap, Joe attended morning church with his family. They occupied the same pew as the day before during the pow wow with Mr. Moeller. As the congregation stood to sing, Joe mutely scanned the crowd. Trapped between adults, adolescent malcontents fidgeted, tolerating their confinement.Some fathers maintained a seriousness, but looked as if their minds were on the golf course. Joe, familiar with the look, expected they attended only for a little peace in the household. When their children became old enough to leave home, these men, himself included, would stay home.

Bad enough he'd been cheated out of twenty years, Joe thought, without the burning fuse of Duke's warning. "This could be temporary" had started to worry him though not as much as his infidelity. And what about his father? How could God have neglected such a God-fearing man? Or Bull's family?

Joan's voice soared high and loud enough to shatter glass; her daughters cringed with embarrassment. She drowned out Tater, and Tater was belting the words out pretty good. Joan sang even louder than Bull, who did everything loud. He sat behind the Donleys on the third row.

The service drifted in and out like a poor cell phone transmittal. The music stopped. Kneeling pads flopped down in unison, reverberating throughout the sanctuary as the congregation dropped to its knees.

Pastor Reese, a man with thick white hair and a comfortable swell over his belt, began to speak. Joe heard only static—something about King David. His mind tuned the dial. No question, he and King David shared similar thoughts on certain points.

"This was King David's prayer after he committed adultery with Bathsheba," the pastor said. Joe cringed. Time for a new station. Oops, the dial was stuck.

"'Create in me a clean heart, O God, and renew a right spirit with me. Cast me not away from thy presence; and take not thy Holy Spirit from me. Restore unto me the joy of thy salvation. Amen.'"

The congregation stood but not for long. A mass of buttocks now moved downward. Visible as wet paint, Joe noticed a bright red whoopee cushion directly underneath Liz and snatched it away an instant before she sank into her seat. While storing away the cushion in his coat pocket, he glowered at K. C., who flashed a caught-in-the-act grin, her freckles dancing with mischievous glee. Joan missed it all. A good thing for K. C., for Joan dealt severely with kids disrespectful in church.

From the pulpit, the pastor continued.

"The subject of our text today, some of us may find terribly unsettling: adultery," the man announced, as if proclaiming the end of all mankind.

The pastor peered over his tiny rectangle-shaped glasses directly at Joe. Joe was sure of it. He changed stations.

Later, the congregation rose to recite the Apostles' Creed. In the middle of the confession of faith, the entire congregation gasped, and Joe felt all eyes on his back. He turned to look and gasped at what he saw. Joan's floor-length white cotton dress looked as if the Holy Ghost had invaded her backside. It was no ghost. Unknown to Joan, K. C. had crawled under her white skirt, and K. C.'s frenetic movements conveyed to the congregation the image of a ghost more restless than holy.

Joe was already feeling a tad skittish, so it should come as no great surprise that his usual self-control so rapidly and completely deserted him. Like the wings of a startled Chester, his elbows flapped involuntarily to his side. His movement triggered a noise from the whoopee cushion that rivaled the fart of a constipated elephant.

Already stunned by the sight of the Holy Ghost, the congregation surely wondered if the day's topic had disturbed their holy visitor enough to pass gas. If so, for the first time in twenty years, Joe and the Holy Ghost had something in common.

Joe expected some comment from Bull; he just didn't know when. It came later, while standing in line for communion.

"That King David got around, huh," Bull whispered into Joe's ear from behind.

Not funny, Joe thought. Bad enough the sermon had nailed him. He didn't need it from Bull, too. He hated standing in line for communion; it made him feel like a fan at an overcrowded turnstile. At the railing, when the pastor passed out the wine, Joe had long wanted to say, "I'll have a double."

Joe favored the Baptist methods of his youth: sit in the pew and communion will come down the aisle just like the offering plate. He really didn't feel strongly about communion one way or another. What was the significance of a cracker and a shot of Mogen David to, if not a non-believer, certainly a faint one? He'd only joined Joan's church to keep her happy. Forms of worship didn't matter much to a man who'd quit worshipping.

Joe did feel strongly about Walrus Real Estate, Inc, a business that he and Bull had devoted practically their entire adult lives to. When the service ended, he walked with Bull to the church parking lot. Joe wanted to know more about the "money problems" Tater had referred to yesterday.

"Come and gone," Bull said.

"You got *who* to take all the empty space in the Stengle building?" Joe asked.

"You heard me, Little Man. The electric company," said Bull, his grin taking up his entire face. Clearly, Walrus Real Estate's new tenant had re-charged the big man. "Now we can get some permanent financing on that building. Get rid of that second lien."

"Second lien?" Joe stopped abruptly, and Bull stopped with him. "What second lien?"

"I've been trying to tell you, but you've been too busy King Davin' it."

"What does that mean?"

"You know. Trying not to get your tongue stuck to the top of your mouth...something like that." After a moderately tense silence, Bull continued. Chuckie-poo demanded a million-dollar principal reduction."

Bull's remark took a sudden and tense hold of Joe.

"Who in the hell lent us a million bucks in this market?" Joe blurted.

"Joe, the kids are starved!" Joan called from the front seat of the mini-van. "Bull, you want to go eat with us?"

"Thanks, but no thanks," Bull said, with a wave of his big hand. He turned back to Joe. "I'll tell you later."

CHAPTER 27

WHACK IT OR WHANK IT?

ONLY the mild rumpus on the other side of the diamond caused Joe and Rocket to pay any attention at all. On a sultry Texas night, less than an hour remained until game time. The two men sat together peacefully in the Rangers' first base dugout. Like a movie star, Candice was majestically making her way down the aisle. Men cheered and clapped and whistled admiringly as she passed by their seats. Obviously braless, she wore another close-fitting, low-cut tank top. Designer denim cut-offs hugged her buns and showed no trace of panty lines. Large, round sunglasses concealed her face. Candice plopped into a front row seat, her sight line level with the third base on-deck circle. Assuming a spread-eagle position, she propped her white tennis shoes on the railing that separated the playing field from the stands. Candice looked directly across the diamond at Joe. Her devious grin broadened with mischief and conspiracy.

"You see that?" Rocket said, staring. "Isn't that the girl we met in New York?"

Joe nodded, his eyes also riveted to Candice.

"How'd she get that seat?" Joe asked. "She'd have to know somebody to get that seat."

"Women like that don't have a lot of trouble getting to know somebody."

Rocket drew one granite leg off the dugout floor, lifted his knee to his chin, propped his heel on the bench beneath him, and clasped both hands around his calf.

"You know, my first year in pro ball, my dad gave me some advice that's helped my marriage last for over twenty years," he said.

Rocket lightly stroked his chin with fingers powerful and large enough to hold multiple baseballs. Rocket knew what happened in New York, reading the guilt in Joe's brown eyes the next day was easier than reading his catcher's signals.

As though attempting to suffocate his conscience, Joe sat on his hands and looked at Rocket with less than his usual detachment. "I'm listening," he said.

"My dad said don't get hung up with all this religious morality stuff. But," he added with heavy emphasis, "if you're gonna fool around, be prepared to trade the one you're with for the one you're messin' with. Think about it."

After an uncomfortable pause, Joe said softly, "I guess your folks been married a long time."

"Shit, no!" Rocket replied, his voice suddenly livelier than his best stuff. "They got divorced when I went to college." A sheepish grin divided his crusty face. "My dad's on his third marriage. Hell," said Rocket, his hands flying up as if trying to stop a baserunner at third, "his present wife's younger than mine. Foxy as all git-out, too." He paused before adding, "Still good advice, though."

Joe stood slowly and glanced over the top of the Rangers' dugout into the stands. About ten rows back, Bull sat with Joan and the girls. Joe waved through a weak smile and returned to his seat beside Rocket.

"How have you stayed faithful to your wife all these years?" he asked. "I mean, there's bound to have been plenty of temptations."

Silence. Rocket appeared to be thinking. He stared at Joe in a manner kin to brotherly wisdom. His machine-steady gaze slowly surrendered to a twinkle as he leaned forward to whisper, "You wait until you get so horny you want to sleep with your wife."

Rocket burst into laughter so hard, he began to cough, reminding Joe of another old television program, *The Red Skelton Show*. No one laughed harder at his own jokes than Red Skelton. "Just kiddin'. Just kiddin'," Rocket said, waving his hand in surrender.

Rocket's laughter was so contagious that Joe almost laughed out loud. The other players in the dugout started to howl along as if infected by the same gas.

All but one: Frothin Green. With sourness radiating from him like curdled milk, Frothin approached Joe, stared him down, and then stalked away.

"Why does he always look like he's about to commit assault and battery?" Joe asked glumly.

"Easy. You've got what he wants."

With Joe soon at bat, he rose and assumed his place in the on-deck circle. While taking his warm-up swings, he heard his family hollering, "Come on, Dad!" and "Whack it, Joe!"

Next, Joe heard the recognizable twang of Rocket from the dugout. "Yeah, whack it, Joe."

Or did Rocket say, "Whank it, Joe"? Marital or hitting advice? Joe wondered.

During the game, Joe's eyes wandered often and unwillingly across the diamond toward Candice who maintained a concentrated look right through him. Joe went three for five, a homer and two doubles. Although Joe's last hit, a low line drive, never rose more than a few feet off the ground, the ball still drilled the right center wall on the fly.

From the dugout, Joe heard Marty boom, "The way he's hitting, they're gonna start walking him in batting practice!"

After the game, Rocket sat on the edge of the dugout closest to home plate. A non-participant in the game, Rocket was enjoying the sight of thirty thousand plus fans filing out of the ballpark. As though requesting his attention, the park's lights beamed in long slashes across the diamond on Candice. Now standing, Candice was staring at the Rangers dugout. Since Joe had already left for the locker room, Rocket, full of intrigue, followed her gaze until it landed directly on Frothin Green. From the opposite end of the dugout from Rocket, the big oaf was waving to Candice the way an overgrown child acknowledges his domineering mother.

Joe was resting on his locker room stool when Tex made his obligatory grand entrance into the locker room. Bull occasionally visited the dressing room after home games and occupied a similar stool beside Joe. Tex's rapid stride plainly displayed his shallowness and arrogance to most humans in general and especially to those of no use to him. With Guido and Rocco at his side, he passed Joe's locker.

"Nice game, Donley," he said, a demented optimism to his voice.

"Let's talk real estate tomorrow, Bull," Tex called back over his shoulder as he strode away.

Joe froze.

"How do you know, Tex?"

Bull squirmed on the small stool.

"He loaned us the money when the bank called the note." His glance alternated between his feet and Joe.

"What? The guy's a piranha! He'll eat us alive!" It was the closest thing to animation in Joe's voice in a long time. "You know that."

"Not as long as he needs you," Bull reasoned.

"How did you get with him?"

Bull sat with his head slightly bowed toward Joe.

"I called him. It was a natural. He doesn't need you worrying about business during the season. I know nothing can distract you, but Tex doesn't."

"I wish I'd known what you were doing. He's bad news. He's—"

Bull brushed aside Joe's concerns with a wave of his big hand.

"Little Man, like I said before, if you'd had some time for the business, I would have told you."

Joe didn't know whether to apologize or object. For sure, feeling important had taken up a lot of time.

"Speaking of time," Bull continued, "Big Jim's feeling down that you haven't been to visit him."

Annoyed, Joe said, "I'll get over there sooner or later." He stared at his hands, which lay folded in his lap. "Bull, did you see that girl on the third base side tonight? The one causing all the stir."

"Are you kidding?" Bull said, his voice warming to the subject. "Be tough to miss that."

"She caught me in a weak moment in New York," Joe said, his voice softening.

Bull flinched. His face turned as white as Joe's home jersey.

"I feel bad about it. Real bad." Joe shook his head. "I don't know why I couldn't resist. It's like it wasn't me." Joe closed his eyes. "She was just so, so—"

"Stacked!" blurted the blond hulk, who maintained great powers of recovery when discussing the opposite sex.

"Stacked," Joe reiterated.

"Wicked," Bull continued, comprehending the situation fully.

"Wicked," Joe repeated. After all, he should know.

"Little Man, you've obviously gotten ahold of some poison poontang." Bull sounded both disgusted and admiring. "What's she doing here?" Bull asked, his eyes growing smaller.

Shoulders hunched, Joe glanced in all directions, as if "here" referred to the locker room. Seeing only the other players, his shoulders relaxed. He expelled air heavily.

"Beats me. She travels on her own."

Bull rose from his seat. Joe buried his head between his hands. He appeared to be rubbing the skin and hair off of his skull.

"The wrong head's doing the thinking," Bull said.

Joe's glance rose to his buddy.

It was a sad, pondering voice that said, "Can you give Joan and the girls a ride home?"

"What'll I tell Joan?"

"Business. Tell her it's business. Say Marty wanted to talk to me."

With a nod of his head, Bull agreed and left Joe to his solitude. Joe did not fully understand his complicated feelings, but he understood that lust packed more of a wallop than a good clean-up hitter.

Bull stepped from the dressing room into a small, protected area where friends and family waited for players after the game. Somehow, a group of idiot autograph seekers always managed to gain access.

Bull immediately noticed a small mob of mostly teenage boys surrounding one unfortunate player like courtiers around royalty. Moving closer, he saw that the subject of all this attention was not a player but Candice. Bull's eyes threw daggers all about. No sign of Joan and the girls, thank goodness! Danger loomed everywhere. Deep caca, Little Man, deep caca.

Bull moved toward Candice. His manner toward her implied admiration on a level equal with the drooling teenagers.

"Ma'am, could I speak to you in private for just a second?" he asked, damn near worshipfully.

His words appeared to startle her, but she recovered quickly. "Sure," she said, smiling widely. Her voice was sensual, mockingly sweet.

Bull pulled Candice away from her fan club and leaned in close enough to smell her perfume. Making no attempt to conceal his actions, Bull's big droopy eyes raced down Candice's neckline into her cleavage.

"Joe's gonna be awhile," he said, but not so loud that the others could hear. A dead-panned expression perfectly accompanied his sudden sternness. "His damn venereal warts are acting up again. Team doc's taking a look at them. One of em's oozing puss—stuff like that."

A sudden chill seemed to attack Bull around his shoulders and his face distorted in disgust.

Candice displayed no emotion, staring through Bull like he wasn't there. But the next voice he heard generated emotion from Bull.

"Bull!"

No mistaking Joan Donley's voice. Bull wheeled around, his wide frame concealing Candice.

"Where's Joe? Is he okay?"

"Joe?" replied Bull, as if he had never heard of the man.

He wrapped his powerful arm around her shoulders and started walking. With prep-school precision, the Donley daughters trailed closely behind. Bull flashed the contented, albeit false, smile of a man in control.

"Joe's fine. He'll be home soon," Bull said, regretting having lied not once but twice today.

CHAPTER 28
PATRICK RETURNS

ATRICK Hegeberg's rear end easily overlapped the commode lid in the tiny downstairs restroom. The john seemed as good a place as any to hide. Patrick lit one of the bathroom candles with his unfiltered Camel cigarette. It was the same brand as his father's. Patrick's shiny dome glowed softly in the light of the flame's dim flicker, and his enormous shadow covered one wall. A pair of pantyhose lay on the floor; they served as Patrick's mask when violent urges overcame him. Nothing materialized during the drive over.

Patrick sucked down the last of his twelve-pack in one long, loud gulp before he was assaulted by a terrible and clear vision. The restroom reminded him of the one back home, where he had discovered his father's body. Patrick's discovery had terrified him more than anything had ever terrified him, and its memory endured horribly unfaded by time. The wall's shadows hurled helter skelter images of his father's death directly at him. He saw an ocean of blood flooding the floor, drowning his father in a wave of red. He heard his father's last sound, a groan still so unnerving Patrick violently bit his lip. He tasted his own salty blood and imagined it was the blood of his father. He started to cry, but it sounded more like the cry of a little boy than the hellish pounding cry of The Iron Claw.

"I found the body," Patrick slurred. "He used the same damn knife that he cut off his finger with." What did you expect? How did you think things would turn out for me?

Through watery eyes, he looked at his watch: 9:30 P.M. Suddenly, feeling trapped, even imprisoned in such a small room, Patrick stood, his balance briefly teetering. His hairless crown almost bumped the room's ceiling. Time for a beer run. Patrick stepped over the pantyhose and stumbled out the bathroom door.

From the dreamy comfort of her bed, Joan bolted rigidly upright and clasped her hands over her ears to stifle the deafening noise. A glimmer of comprehension slowly crept into Joan's sleepy gaze. That damned alarm! Joe said he had it fixed. Her hands slid to the other side of the bed. Joe wasn't home from the game yet.

All three girls ran into the bedroom. Tater and K. C. leaped into the bed, flanking Joan, and jerked the covers over their heads, nearly flattening their mother. With the curiosity of a future writer, Liz ran to the window overlooking the front yard.

"Where's Dad?" Tater asked, her voice muffled and shaky. "I'm scared!"

"I'm not scared," said K. C., her red head poking out from beneath the covers. "It's okay if we die. We'll just go see our great Lord Jesus." Since K. C.'s affiliation with the Holy Ghost, she had become quite spiritual.

"Don't worry," Joan said, her tone crammed with worry. "It's just that stupid alarm messing up again."

"Mom!" Liz whispered fiercely. "There's a truck out front!"

Joan rolled out of bed and crossed to the window. Sure enough, an ancient red pickup truck was in front of the Donley home, its lights off. Light gray clouds hovered near the exhaust pipe; the motor was running.

"Oh, my God! Liz, call 9-1-1! No, call Bull first, then call 9-1-1!" Joan stared at the truck and clutched her fists tightly against her chest.

Joe kept a pistol in the house but Joan's heart was racing faster than her brain could think. Where was the gun? Think, woman, think! She could not remember.

Wait! she cautioned herself. Below, Bull was sneaking up on the truck, a metal baseball bat in hand.

Approaching from the rear, Bull wore only dark, baggy boxer shorts that hung to his kneecaps. With each shoeless step, he raised the bat higher above his head, preparing to strike. Just short of the truck's cab, he stopped.

"What's wrong, Mom?" Liz demanded.

"I don't know, honey. Hush!" Joan whispered. "Go get in bed with your sisters. They're scared." She could not have torn herself away from the window for anything short of fire or blood.

Bull took another step toward the rusted pickup. Was that a head or a motorcycle helmet? Bumps and craters interrupted the slick dome. Must be some tough guy.

Bull moved close to the driver's open window. The body had thick arms, massive shoulders and a neck wider than its unusually large head. Was he dead? No, the giant's breathing came in irregular sucking breaths. Bull cautiously poked his head inside the front window, where his lungs filled with the stench of stale alcohol. Beer bottles and cans littered the cab's floor. Man, this was one large dude, big as that guy Fuckhead, or whatever his name is. He looked like Mr. Clean, blown up with a bicycle pump.

Bull's shoulders sagged, and he exhaled heavily. A massive grin overtook his face as he turned and faced Joan and Liz in the upstairs window.

"Relax!" Bull yelled over the shrill alarm. "It's just a drunk, passed out."

Mother and daughter commenced to jump, clap and yell with delight. Their hugs of one another expressed their emotions more than any spoken words.

"And turn off that blasted alarm!" Bull roared. After the alarm went quiet, Bull grumbled, "I thought you got that darned thing fixed."

CHAPTER 29
LIZ TAKES A RIDE

UNDER Bull's watchful eye, the police hauled away the drunk while a wrecker towed the old pickup. After Bull started for home, Joan and Liz, who had ventured outside, also headed back inside.

"I got to pee—bad," Liz announced.

"Thank you for sharing," her mother said.

Liz ran to the downstairs hall bathroom, only to find the door shut.

"K. C.," she yelled, "you and Avery get out of there pronto! I'm about to wet my pants!" She shifted impatiently from side to side, waiting.

"I'm in here," K. C. called from somewhere. "Avery's with me."

Puzzled, Liz opened the door, which was never closed unless somebody was inside. She found herself staring into the third shirt button of an enormous man with pantyhose over his block head! With his flattened face, he looked like the Monster from the Black Lagoon. Liz's entire body went numb; her jaw hung in midair. She felt a scream escape but heard nothing. Too terrified to move, she felt a trickle of warmth leaking down her legs.

Initially, the giant didn't move either; his head cocked off center. He simply returned Liz's stare. With quick movements for such a big man, he then stepped into the hall and tossed Liz over his shoulder as if she were no heavier than air. Terror and vibration took residence in the young girl's body. She managed a high shriek.

The intruder charged into the kitchen. Joan and her daughters gaped at the giant carrying Liz, who wore a bravely doomed expression. The masked specter darted out the kitchen side door into the yard.

Bull, his front door still open, heard Joan's mad scream and briefly froze into a block of ice. Recovering quickly, he raced across his yard to find Tater and K. C. nestled under Joan's protective arms. All shook like someone rescued from a cold swimming pool. An overpowering scent of fear had smothered all the air around them.

Joan could only point in the direction of the monster's escape. Bull's eyes followed her finger, his eyebrows arched, and he started to run.

Joan released the girls and stumbled after Bull, but her legs had turned to mush.

"Y'all stay here!" Bull yelled over his shoulder.

Joan fainted dead away. "Mama! Mama!" cried the children's voices. Tater and K. C. rushed to their mother's still body. What little that remained of the Donleys' Cleaver-like existence was officially toast.

Bull thundered across the green ribbon of front yards in the warm night air. Due to the brooding clouds that obscured the full moon, only a slab of dull gray light slanted across the neighborhood. Huge branches drooping over the yards enhanced the darkness.

Two-story brick homes, built long before artificial grass and domed stadiums, lined both sides of the street. The outside lights that most of the residents kept on through the night produced the illusion of an airstrip nestled in a residential area.

If Bull ran any faster, he probably would have needed a runway. "Put me down!" Bull clearly recognized Liz's passionate falsetto cry. If he could hear her, he thought, he must be gaining on them.

Seconds later, he narrowed the gap enough to see Liz's ponytail flapping. Her kidnapper was running on the concrete path that connected the front yards. He saw Liz buck on the man's wide shoulders, pound him with her fists, and kick his kidneys. She pulled his hair and bit his shoulder.

No wonder the kidnapper's stride faltered, and Bull could now hear him breathing in buffeted loud gasps. Suddenly, he stopped and confronted Bull, who was less than twenty yards away.

Thank God! Tiny blind spots, brought on by his own shortness of breath, danced in front of Bull's eyes. Sweat drew an army of orbiting gnats around his eyes and forehead. He flinched at his first good look at Liz's captor. Damn! This guy was as big as that guy in the truck! The giant's short-sleeved shirt exposed muscles layered in concrete. Through the pantyhose, his wide eyes glistened with excitement. A smile gradually seeped through the mask, but it was not the type of smile to encourage making friends. The giant's distorted face looked subhuman.

Liz collapsed over his shoulder and the two men glared at each other. Bull held still. Liz's assailant held still. So did the air. So did time itself.

The giant's eyes gradually transformed to angry slits. He twirled Liz around from his back to his chest and held her high above his head as though offering a human sacrifice to some pagan god.

Bull held his hand up like a traffic cop. "Don't!" he blurted. "Not the sidewalk!"

Either the madman was smitten with Liz's beauty or possessed a scrupulous conscience or, like an obedient child, simply responded to Bull's hard command. He tossed Liz lightly to the plush green grass of a nearby yard. From her front yard seat, she looked vulnerable enough to levitate off the ground and drift into the night.

Bull sprang to her side and clasped her to his chest.

Over her whimpers, her kidnapper tried to speak, but danger gripped his throat. "I'll...I'll...be baacck," he finally stuttered and disappeared into the darkness.

Later that night, Liz lay tucked in her bed and dictated into her recorder. "It took a Rocket fastball to my father's head for him to learn life wasn't perfect. My grandfather's death reminded him of that. I found out life wasn't perfect riding the back of a crazy man. I think my childhood left me tonight; it passed right down my legs through the balls of my feet. No kid should ever have to be that scared."

CHAPTER 30
THE THIRD DIMENSION

Joe arrived home to the alarming sight of flashing red lights in his driveway. For the next few minutes, with Joan trying to settle down the girls upstairs, the police and Bull filled Joe in on the night's happenings. During all this explaining, the look on Joe's empty face never changed.

After the police left, Joe spit out questions faster than bullets. Bull, still buzzed on danger, returned the fire.

"Everybody's okay?" Joe asked for the third time.

"Yep. Probably not sleeping too well, but they're okay."

"How did he get in the house?"

"Don't know. He was hiding in the downstairs bathroom."

"The police think it's the same guy that's been terrorizing Lakewood?"

"You heard 'em. The victims all say the guy's huge and wears pantyhose over his head."

"He wore pantyhose over his head? Nobody mentioned that."

"Yep. Biggest son-of-a-bitchin' head I ever saw. Those pantyhose must have belonged to one fat-legged woman," Bull said, nodding thoughtfully.

Now it was Bull's turn to ask questions. "Who's the toughest by-gawd you know?"

"You, Bull."

Bull thrust his chest and chin forward as if daring the assailant to return and take a poke at him. "You ever seen me afraid?"

"No, Bull." Joe strained a bit not to roll his eyes.

"Well, this was the biggest, ugliest, meanest-looking dude I've ever seen. I was not looking forward to tangling with that nasty SOB one bit."

A sound as loud as the Donleys' alarm went off in Joe's head. "Was he big and ugly enough to be Duren Green?"

Bull seemed to stop breathing as his mind shifted to playback mode. "Big enough, for sure. Plenty ugly under that mask." Bull thought further. "I really couldn't get a good look at his face." Before Bull could become suspicious of Joe's suspicions, his own interior alert sounded. "Say, what took you so long to get home?"

Joe pressed his lips together and looked away.

"You were with the poison poontang," Bull blurted, but barely above a whisper. "Little Man, something's not right here. You've changed. You still haven't even been to see Big Jim. All this fame's gone to your head...both heads! Doesn't Joan notice things are different?" Bull asked disgustedly.

"She's too busy doing her thing at the school, the church, her acting lessons...all that stuff. Romance got lost a long time ago. We've just been playing out the schedule," Joe said, with a simple shrug that acknowledged surrender to a situation gone bonkers. "Bull, you ever feel like you're always searching for the right combination of security and adventure? Well, something's pulling me toward adventure these days," he continued, confusion simmering between his words.

"Ah shit!" Bull waved a brusque hand. "Where did you learn that? King David?"

Joe shot Bull a quick, annoyed glare but said nothing. Bull's words cut like a buzz saw, reminding him that his actions might bring repercussions to his family, his best friend, his Maker. Whoops! Was Joe acknowledging a higher being?

Later, with the lights off and the enormous front yard oak blocking the moon's dull glow, Joe carefully navigated the stairwell in total darkness. The night's events had left Joe wondering if he somehow had visited *The Twilight Zone*, another of his old favorite TV shows. Outside his bedroom door, he heard a soft, whimpering sound. Entering, he found Liz sleeping restlessly with her mom. Joe reached down and kissed his wife on the cheek in the same manner he would kiss his children on the cheek.

Earlier Bull told Joe that Joan took a sleeping pill. Now she mumbled groggily, "Joe, is that you?"

"It's me. Everything's okay," Joe whispered.

"Bull said he wouldn't leave until you got home," Joan slurred and then relapsed into unconsciousness.

"He didn't."

Joe leaned across Joan to check Liz's breathing. Irregular and shallow. In her sleep, Liz looked as fragile as a glass doll. For the first time in a long time, she seemed as fragile as her younger sisters.

As he quietly moved to his side of the bed, Joe's foot slipped on something. Joe staggered and then steadied himself, but was still teetering. A low, resonant sound slid across the hardwood floor. Beyond the hope of retaining his balance, he grabbed the side of the bed, bounded to his feet, and darted after the trespasser. He rapidly reached down and grabbed the culprit. Tater's roller skate surrendered without a struggle.

Joe sighed so long he practically gagged on his ironic chuckle which scared away any potential tears. Everybody knows Donley men don't cry.

Joe began to undress. Before his fall from the tree, when he thought life was passing him by, when he considered himself the poster boy for mediocrity, he used to crawl into bed easily as a hand into a glove. Not tonight.

Quack! Something stabbed him in the back! Joe shot straight up in bed, as jumpy as he was rigid.

Joe frowned a small, swift frown after discovering one of K. C.'s hostile toy ducks. A subsequent kick to his groin convinced Joe to sleep elsewhere. He pulled back the covers to find K. C. snuggled against Tater, who was nestled against Liz, who lay in her mother's arms. Oh, how vulnerable were the faces of his children while sleeping. A thought, rapid and sharp, came to Joe. He hoped his daughters would marry better men than he, someone like Grandpa George, Bull, Duke, or Rocket.

Joe went to Tater and K. C.'s bedroom at the other end of the house. Before he could turn on the light, his right foot skidded out from under him. They say (whoever they are) that stinging scorpions travel in pairs; if you see one scorpion, another is close by—ditto with roller skates. This time, Joe wasn't so lucky. He looked like a black-belt trying to kick the ceiling. His head crashed to the hardwood floor, and he went as still as still can be.

During the night, Joe's breathing could have passed for Hershey snoring after a double hit of sleeping pills. Daybreak was skeptically broken with dull rays of sunlight spreading across the room. Outside, under a grey, sickly sky, birds warbled, and squirrels chattered. From the back yard, Hershey's bark carried over the wind chimes, probably at the same squirrels dancing above him in the trees. Fresh morning air smelled of a new day and beginning.

Joe awoke and raised himself with a catcher's weariness after a violent home plate collision. Little ball bats were pounding inside his head.

Fully upright, Joe squinted into the mirror that hung over his children's chest of drawers. He tried to bring his beard into focus. These days it seemed he had a five o'clock shadow before he finished washing the shaving cream off his face. And was he squinting? Shoot! His panicked eyes searched the room. Lord, he could hardly read the Texas Rangers' posters and pennants that covered a good portion of one wall! It was like looking through water. For an instant, Joe didn't breathe. With mindless, automatic accuracy, he remembered Duke's warning: "This could be temporary."

"It's over," Joe mumbled.

He embraced this thought as readily as K. C. embraced the thought of sitting on the john. He gazed at the shadow in the mirror trying to figure out how to reclaim his crisp vision. Christ! He hadn't wakened without an erection since the fall, and now look at him—limp as a noodle! Joe threw himself face down onto the bed and pulled a pillow over his head. Joe's entire life became one rapid instant replay, and he wondered why all the good and all the bad had ever happened.

CHAPTER 31
BURDENED WITH CONCERN

Entering the kitchen, Joan detected nothing out of the ordinary. Joe stood looking out the window. He turned to her quickly, as if she had broken his trance. Joe's eyes caught the morning light, which seemed to magnify his look of grave concern.

"What's wrong?" Joan asked.

"I took another fall last night. Landed on my head." If despair had a voice, this was it.

"On your head! How?"

"Tater's skate," Joe said sheepishly.

"You're kidding!" Joan said, talking with her hands. "Well, of course, you're not kidding. Are you okay?"

"My vision. It's a little…" Joe's voice trailed off into nothingness.

"What about your vision?" Joan practically snapped. "What's wrong?"

The disappointment in Joe's facial expression said it all.

"Oh no, Joe." She rushed to her husband and snuggled her head against his chest. "Maybe it's temporary," Joan said hopefully. "Or maybe everything else is okay; you know…like your coordination, reflexes, all those things."

"We'll find out in tonight's game," Joe said evenly.

Joan rubbed her soft cheeks against his. She could feel her husband's fresh and immediate desire.

"I don't like sharing you like this," she said.

"Sharing me? What do you mean, sharing me?"

Odd, Joan thought. His body'd gone stiff, but his erection—what happened to that?

"With the whole damn country." Joan's tone was actually nice and playful as if she sensed an end to the circus, that normalcy would soon return to the Donley household.

Joe sighed, and his body relaxed.

Nice and playful came and left Joan as quickly as did Joe's erection. "Joe, that monster said he'd come back. Lord, we were so scared. Do you think he really will?"

"Naa, Bull scared him away," Joe said after too long a pause to sound convincing.

Last night's clouds made good on their warning. They suddenly opened up, and the pounding rain sounded capable of penetrating the Spanish tile roof. Joe and Joan Donley, sweethearts too long to remember, stood embraced in each other's arms.

Turbulent Texas weather wrought havoc on the Rangers' homestand, forcing a record five straight days of rainouts. It took a certain pituitary gland about the same time to wreak havoc on Joe. The headaches and sensitivity to light disappeared after a couple of days. Joe's difficulty in focusing also gradually stopped; by week's end, his eyes refused to focus at all. Joe reluctantly took to wearing glasses. After practically a week without baseball, Joe rode to the ballpark with his family and Bull.

"Don't you think you should check with Duke to see if it's okay to play?" Joan begged.

Bull tried to lighten the mood. "Little Man, I forgot how good you looked in glasses," he quipped.

With the temperature dropping to a brisk eighty-eight degrees, Tater wore several layers of clothing. Joe, his affinity for roller-skates at an all-time low, refused to let her wear skates to the game. Tater chirped like a bird, "I feel nice. Like sugar and spice." Thank goodness for the resiliency of children, thought Joe.

Liz, her brows dipped downward, scribbled furiously in her journal. Unexpectedly, life as a Donley was providing enough material for sequels.

Leave it to K. C. to take note of whom she couldn't see. "We forgot Big Jim!" K. C. cried. "Hey, Avery can have a seat tonight!"

Joe, now more burdened with concern than feeling important, had once again overlooked Big Jim.

CHAPTER 32
THEY TURN ON YOU IN A HURRY

During the rainouts, Joe skipped a series of informal workouts that allowed the players to use the Rangers' indoor batting cage and throwing area at random. Upon entering the locker room, Joe's spectacles raised a few eyebrows, but most showed only mild concern.

"Is Joe wearing glasses?" asked one teammate, evidently not seeing all that well himself.

"Don't tell me he's gonna start acting his age," Marty grumbled.

"I didn't know you wore contacts," Rocket commented. During his first at bat, the opposing right-hander's sharp curve almost hit him on the left wrist. Joe Donley, a man intensely devoted to avoiding awkward or embarrassing moments, suddenly found himself in a most precarious situation. The pitch had fooled him.

On the next pitch, at least Joe's ears still worked properly. He recognized the crisp pop of a fastball meeting leather. A heater had split home plate for strike one.

Joe's predicament showed in his eyes. He froze at the next pitch, another breaking ball.

"Steeerikee two!" cried the man in blue.

Joe felt the breeze from the ball as it zipped past his ear back toward the mound.

"Donley, that wasn't even that good a curve," growled a voice from behind.

Joe looked back at Flat Nose Wilson, the crusty veteran catcher and no youngster himself. White glistened in the midst of his unkempt beard. A sarcastic smile deepened the lines that angled from the side of Flat Nose's mouth, and tobacco juice oozed down his chin.

"Are we having a little trouble with the breaking ball today?" Flat Nose mocked. "Maybe we'll try another one until you get it right."

Grandpa George would have reminded Joe: Never trust the enemy when presenting himself as an ally. Joe swung a tad slow at the next offering, a hissing fastball.

"Steeerike three!" loudly informed the umpire.

"You still got a pretty swing," Flat Nose said, his words providing no comfort.

Joe fanned his first three times up. When he stepped into the batter's box for his final at bat, he maintained the aura of a boxer with a glass jaw.

"Man, am I glad to see you," rasped Flat Nose sincerely; sweat ran in an unbroken stream off his bent-wide nose. "It's not often a guy gets a chance to get four Ks in one day."

Wait, then attack. Focus on the positive: ignore the ugly SOB. Voices called to him from the stands:

"You can do it, Joe!"

"Base knock, Joe."

"You're due, Joe!"

"You haven't had this many strike-outs in eight weeks." From his knees, Flat Nose rifled the ball back to the mound. "It's about time you had a bad day."

Joe fouled the pitch off into the right field stands. It was a sure sign of a late swing.

"Way to get around," teased Flat Nose. "Hey, you wearing glasses?"

"Would you shut the fuck up?" Joe practically yelled. "What are you hitting this year? Two-thirty?"

Flat Nose grinned like a thief inside a vault after hours. "I'm the catcher," he continued. "I play good D."

Joe swung. His heart soared with hope as the ball soared in a high arc toward dead center field. His hopes fell with the ball as it vanished into the outfielder's glove. A smattering of boos drifted down from the stands as Joe sheepishly made his way back to the dugout.

Flat Nose's raspy voice bellowed above the crowd's noisy din. "Hey, rook! They turn on you in a hurry."

CHAPTER 33
CONCENTRATE ON WHAT YOU'VE GOT LEFT

Over the next few weeks, Rangers fans worried about the aging rookie's first slump. Fans on the street approached Joe and offered moral support. "Keep your chin up, Joe. I remember Willie Mays going through a hell of a slump his rookie season," said one oldtimer.

Some offered advice. "Joe, I think if you'll get that back elbow up, you'll get around a little better on the fastball." Or "Try to hit the ball up the middle," or "Don't commit too early on the breaking ball," and so on.

Others sacrificed their good luck pieces, such as a lucky coin or a rabbit's foot. One lady tried to give Joe a piece of crystal. "It'll give you strength," she claimed.

Joe turned the crystal down. "Crystals are sacrilegious," his mother always warned.

Neighborhood kids left encouraging notes in the Donley mailbox. The media stayed positive. "Joe Donley represents all men trying to live the impossible dream," a sports journalist wrote.

After one more bad game, Joe asked Rocket, "What if I told you I've lost the edge I've had working for me?"

"I'd say, Concentrate on what you've got left, not what you've lost. Think about it."

Joe knew Rocket was thinking about it, especially that division title Rocket wanted so badly. The gap was closing between the Rangers and second place Seattle.

Predictably, Tex proved less understanding. "Let's don't blow this thing," Tex repeatedly told Joe, his acid tone on full display.

Tex's testy behavior reinforced a whispered theory in the Ranger clubhouse: Due to gambling losses, Tex needed revenue like a TV preacher needs sinners, and no playoffs translated into less revenue.

The strain of the division race was aging Marty by the day. It came with his job description. "This job's making me puke out of both ends," Marty grumbled.

Frothin even lumbered about the clubhouse and ball diamond looking concerned. Probably the anxiety from the anticipation of taking over the DH spot, thought Joe.

And Joe's friends and family worried. "Joe never comes around anymore," Big Jim still complained to Bull.

Bull favored keeping matters uncomplicated, blaming everything on Candice. "It's the dirty legger. She's bringing bad luck," he told Joe. Bull blamed Candice for Liz's kidnapping, Tater's skates, Joe's neurological setback, his slump, Tex's recent discomforting attitude toward Walrus Real Estate, bad weather, the international situation, and spiraling inflation.

"You've got to go see Duke," Joan begged.

"I will, I will," Joe lied. His voice hid his fear more effectively than his eyes.

"I feel like a jet pilot in a hurricane. I'm ready for the ride to end, but with a gentle landing," Joan said.

As Flat Nose had prognosticated, after a few weeks, some of the hecklers began to hurl insults at Joe. These verbal attacks hurt Joe's children more than a Rocket fastball to the gut. Wally and Theodore never had to endure anything like this.

With his lead in the batting race continuing to shrink, nobody worried more than Joe. That's not all that was shrinking. Joe's feet returned to size nine and a half, and he needed a smaller batting glove. Traces of silver lined his hair. Probably from worry, Joe thought. And fear trailed Joe like his shadow. As promised, would the monster return to the Donley household?

Bull tried lifting Joe's spirits. "You can still win the batting title," he said.

"No problem," Joe said too abruptly to pass as a display of self-confidence.

"I bet nobody's pulling for you like Tex Maris."

"That's nice of him," Joe said.

"Oh, I don't think all his concern is for you. When I hit him up for the loan, I mentioned I had some inside info."

"About what?"

"About you winning the batting title. I told him for reasons I was not free to divulge, I thought you'd make a run at the batting title."

"Why did you do that?"

"You know...brown nosing a little," said Bull, raising his shoulders. "I needed a million bucks. Besides, it wasn't bad advice."

"Well, who gives a rat's ass?" Joe said.

"Well," Bull said cautiously, "after I left, I couldn't find my car keys. I was just about to go back in his office, but guess what I heard?"

"Rattling car keys," Joe said, bored stiffer than a cemetery headstone.

"Little Man, I heard Tex placing a ten thousand dollar bet on you to win the American League batting title!"

Joe's eyes turned small but only for an instant. "BFD Bull, everybody knows Tex is a gambler. Ten thousand is chump change to that guy. I don't think he's going to lose much sleep worrying about whether I make his bet good."

"Yeah, I guess you're right." Bull sighed heavily.

"I don't think he's supposed to bet on baseball, though," Joe said, mainly wondering out loud.

CHAPTER 34
CATS ARE CHASIN' DOGS

THE Rangers made their last road trip of the season to New York City. Rocket Nolin would not ordinarily trail a young woman through the streets of Manhattan, but these were not ordinary circumstances.

She moved innocently along a crowded sidewalk. The mass rumble of feet shuffling along concrete drowned out the particular sound of Rocket's own rapid stride. Her unisex attire—loose fitting faded blue denims, red University of Nebraska sweatshirt, and white tennis shoes—created a neutered look; it showed nothing at all. A silk navy blue scarf concealed most of her jet-black hair, and jumbo sunglasses shielded her eyes and much of her face. Those sunglasses sure looked familiar, mused Rocket.

Rocket made a lousy private eye. Wranglers, a white western-style shirt, cowboy boots and hat made him as visible as a pumpkin on the pitcher's mound.

She stopped at a busy intersection, nervously glancing side to side. Without warning, Frothin Green, his head towering above the crowd, approached the woman. He handed her an envelope and disappeared, swept away by a strong current of human mass.

The woman melted into a crowd heading in another direction. Serenaded by the sound of car horns squawking like irritated ducks, Rocket followed the bounce of her blue scarf.

After a few blocks, the scarf took a sharp right and disappeared into a weathered two-story building. A theater? She went into an off-Broadway theater? Rocket proceeded with the caution of a timid child entering a haunted house. Inside, a handful of casually dressed people occupied the first few rows of the wooden theater seats. Several more were rehearsing on a weathered hardwood floor stage.

For a few minutes, Rocket stood in the shadow of the deserted balcony. Like grandpa to a porch swing, he carefully lowered himself in an aisle seat. Above him, a huge chandelier hung from the white plaster ceiling. It had more glass prisms than Rocket had strike-outs. Rows of quaint loge seats, with dark mahogany railings, flanked the stage. The high dollar seats, no doubt. A small forest died to build this place, Rocket surmised. Dim and musty, the old auditorium looked to have staged more performances than Rocket himself.

Rocket's subject walked onto the stage and removed her scarf, exposing slick-as-lacquer hair swept tightly away from her face and clamped in the back. The sunglasses went next. With no make-up, her skin looked pale as shortening in the glare of the spotlight. Rocket began to wonder if he'd trailed the right person. No make-up, neutered clothes, hair in a bun—what's next? A nun in a whorehouse?

Squinting, Rocket leaned toward the stage. She was talking. He tilted one ear toward the front stage, then the other. Sounded like she was apologizing for her tardiness, and meekly, at that. She shuffled uncomfortably from side to side, as if she needed to pee but was afraid to ask.

A reed-thin young man in a Yankee cap bounced down the aisle and plopped into the seat in front of Rocket. Turning around, he said through vicious chomps of gum, "You wouldn't think this girl could act, but once she gets in make-up and wardrobe, she'll surprise you."

"I won't deny that," Rocket said softly.

"Hey! You're Rocket Nolin!" The young man's voice soared in the building's near-emptiness.

All eyes darted toward Rocket.

"What are you doing here?" the kid asked.

"Watching a hell of a performance," Rocket said without turning his eyes from the stage.

The girl looked at Rocket as if he were a Martian that she hoped would return home. Her face and throat turned fire engine red, which served to advertise the dark in her inflated eyes. She turned and said something to a small man who wore a black felt beret angled slightly off center. She left the stage and strode purposefully up the aisle toward Rocket. All the while, she maintained the look of someone preparing for a performance. Sensing the theater's impromptu production of *Gunfight at the O. K. Corral*, the man quickly rose and left his seat. Rocket and the young woman exchanged shrugs and tilts of head.

"Hello, Mr. Nolin."

To Rocket's surprise, she sounded shy.

"Candice?"

"Actually, my name's Carla, Carla Gardner."

Carla took the seat vacated by the kid. She folded her hands in her lap like a little girl caught lying.

"How did you find me?"

"It wasn't hard to get somebody to follow you from the ballpark."

No problem spotting Candice at the game earlier in the day. For a hundred bucks, Rocket had hired a wide-eyed clubhouse attendant to follow her out of Yankee Stadium. After trailing her to a Manhattan apartment, the attendant called the Yankee's locker room and reported her address to Rocket.

"I wasn't sure it was you when you came out of the apartment." Rocket cleared his throat. She did look different, sort of like the female metamorphosis of Superman to Clark Kent. "Carla," said Rocket, wishing that he sounded less parental, "would you please explain what this is all about?"

"Froghead hired me."

"Who?"

"Froghead. You know . . . Duren Green."

Rocket slumped in his chair. His stomach felt queasy.

"Actually, I tricked him into hiring me," Carla volunteered.

"Hired you to do what?"

"Distract Joe Donley. Mess up his game. Blow his mind," replied Carla.

A sly grin flickered across Carla's face. She's reminiscing of blowing more than Joe's mind, thought Rocket.

"But why?"

Carla's words came fast, as if she were afraid to stop.

"Earlier in the season, I read a *Sports Illustrated* article about the Rangers. I knew Froghead was upset about losing his designated hitter spot, so I approached him about helping him get his job back."

By now, Rocket, correctly sensing a long performance, had shut his eyes; his right index finger lay next to his nose.

"By seducing Joe."

"Exactly. Except, until lately, it hasn't worked. Joe could stay up all night, and I do mean up! Then he'd go out the next day and get three hits. I don't know what's wrong with him lately but something's different. Not just a slow bat—he's getting old! Going gray. His skin's sagging. He's wearing those glasses." Her words poured out like jellybeans from a bag. "I think his chin's even shrunk." The grin returned, as if to imply that's not all that had shrunk. "And he doesn't want to stay up all night anymore." She paused to catch her breath.

"You're very observant."

"I'm a professional actress. I majored in drama at the University of Nebraska. Have you ever heard of Ava Gardner?" She lifted her chin.

Before Rocket could answer, Carla kept on puffing the way a steam engine puffs on a cold day. "I read her biography. I patterned my character after her, except the part about my parents. I told Joe my father left my mother, and then my mother kicked me out of the house. Things like that." She flicked a hand. "That part wasn't true. Actually, it is true about one of the other actresses here. She's also a stripper." Carla shrugged. "Anyway, if Ava Gardner could seduce Frank Sinatra and all those other husbands, I figure her character could do the same to a real estate man from Texas."

By this time, Rocket's foot was tapping a rhythm to all this hard and fast rhetoric. His head hurt, and he felt nauseous. There's nothing so discomforting as discovering something's not as it first appeared. The girl's just a dumb little actress who doesn't understand the harm she's done.

Carla's speech slowed, and her hands folded and unfolded in her lap.

"I do feel a little guilty about one thing we did," she said.

"We?" Rocket's mind felt more cluttered than his suitcase after a long road trip.

"Right before Joe's slump, Froghead arranged for the *American Enquirer* to sneak a picture of Joe and me having dinner at a restaurant in Baltimore," said Carla, her words starting to flow rapidly again. "Joe didn't want to, but I told him if he'd meet me, I'd leave him alone." Carla preened slightly and added confidentially, "Until recently, he couldn't really resist me, you know. Anyway, the picture's going to run tomorrow."

Rocket jolted upright in his chair. "How could you do that?" he demanded, waving the index finger of his right hand somewhat threateningly. "Why would you do it?"

"I didn't really want to hurt Joe," Carla said. "I needed the money . . . and I wanted to be closer to my brother."

"Brother?" said Rocket, as if having been summoned from some distant place. He rolled his eyes to the ceiling searching for heavenly help.

"Well," Carla said after a deep pause, and then paused again. "I guess you know Joe Donley has my dead brother's pituitary gland."

Rocket, deservedly known for maintaining control in tight situations, calmly re-swallowed his post-game meal. She and Frothin made an excellent couple. Neither one of them had the sense God gave a groundhog.

Like a long flexible ruler, he stoically unfolded himself from the chair and walked out of the theater more deliberately than he ever walked off a pitcher's mound.

"Cats are chasin' dogs, and it's rainin' sickness," Rocket mumbled, shaking his dazed head.

CHAPTER 35

ILLEGITIMI NON CARBORUNDUM

THE smell of recently applied floor wax and fresh produce dominated the airwaves of Hutchins' only grocery store. Local employees anxiously shuffled about preparing to open for the day. A recently arrived batch of *American Enquirers* provided a morning rush greater than any ten cups of coffee.

Word of the weekly rag's contents spread quickly throughout the store. And everybody knew Mary Donley, an early riser, would enter any minute.

"Better have an ambulance ready," one ex-student declared.

"Here she comes!" said another.

Entering the store, Mary immediately noticed an unusual stillness. They're all holding their breath, she concluded. Why is everyone staring but pretending I'm not here? She saw Johnny Ray, another ex-student standing by the checkout-stand, hiding something.

"Hi, Mrs. Donley," Johnny practically stuttered. "How are you today?"

"The question is how are you and everybody else in here? If everybody doesn't start acting normal, I'm going to make every one of you stay after school," Mary said through a light-hearted chuckle. "Now move away from that stand and let me see what it is you don't want me to see."

Johnny stepped back, exposing the *American Enquirer*. The picture of her son with a...a hussy was enough to transform Mary's eyeballs into a ghostly shade of pale grey. The black and white photo focused on the substantial rise of Candice's bosom. Her low-cut cocktail dress barely concealed her nipples, and her cleavage looked like the opening to a large dark cave. Every eyeball in the store gawked at their ex-teacher gawking at the picture.

"Oh," Mary gasped. She looked in shock but only around the eyes. "I see," she said with a calmness that betrayed her inner feelings. "Thanks for trying, Johnny. You were always a considerate kid."

She kept her chin high and straight and mechanically walked out the door. During the drive home, Mary decided to cut her losses in a manner similar to her husband's at a long-ago college World Series game. She began to pray:

"Lord Jesus, Lord Jesus, I'm so confused. You answered my prayer, and Joe, well, he's all he ever wanted to be and more, but Lord, he's less now, too. Lord, Lord, why do people take your blessings and go to sinning. and forget friends who helped them back when. . . how could he do that adultery thing and hurt his mama so? Lord, I just don't know what to say or pray, but let the Holy Ghost touch his heart, convict him of his sin, and get him out of this mess one more time. Lord, please, I just want my Joe back, better for some things and not worse for others. Lord, Lord, hear me please." Mary Donley could really pray.

Later that day, Joe entered the visitors' dressing room at Yankee Stadium. He quickly sensed the earth was off its axis. All locker room eyes nervously alternated between Joe and their lockers, and solemnly sported that "I know something you don't know" look. A newspaper on the stool by his locker stuck out like bright red socks with a tuxedo. Who put that there?

Joe picked up the tabloid cautiously. A line drive to the eye could not have stung more than the headline: "Baseball Star Cheats on Wife." "At least these rags tell the truth sometimes," Joe said under his breath. Under the headline, he saw his picture with Candice. Stunned, Joe dropped stiffly to the stool, thus allowing a real ass to replace the picture of another.

"It was all a set-up."

Rocket's voice shattered Joe's trance.

"A set-up?" said Joe, as if some harsh reality had suddenly occurred to him for the first time.

"Frothin hired her to distract you. To take your mind off baseball and hurt your game." Rocket moved in close enough for a head shot. "She's as crazy as he is."

Chill bumps the size of Candice's nipples erupted on Joe's forearms. A clubhouse attendant, mobile phone in hand, apprehensively approached Joe's locker.

"It's your buddy in Dallas," he said apologetically, handing the phone to Joe.

"Yeah, Bull, I'm looking at it," Joe said wearily.

"Joan's beyond upset," Joe heard Bull say. "Don't bother to call. Pick up your clothes when you get home. Don't count on seeing the kids anytime soon. Don't even count on seeing pictures of the kids anytime soon. Joe, I've got more bad news," Bull announced.

"There's more bad news?" hiccuped Joe, hoping his ears were malfunctioning. "Tex called the real estate note! We gotta pay up in ten days."

Joe's head snapped violently. "Can he do that?" he cried. Bull didn't need to answer; Joe asking the question had been enough. A thought, accurate and provoking, came to Joe.

"Tex doesn't want the lien paid off. You found too good a tenant. He wants our properties," Joe reasoned, contempt rushing in like a tidal wave.

"We'll be home tomorrow. Keep a close eye on the girls." Joe's voice cracked a little. His brown eyes gave no indication of what he would do next. "Bye," Joe said, his eyes regarding the phone sadly.

"Good old Tex," Rocket said. "'What have you done for me today?'" he whined, imitating the owner. "'Nothing, you say?... Well, I'll take those properties, Joe, old buddy.'" His voice returned to its normal tone. "Tex obviously thinks you're done. Think about it."

Before Joe had time to think about it, Marty tiptoed to his side, looking as if he knew top classified information. "Donley," Marty said, lowering his voice to a confidential tone, "you're sitting today."

Joe, though suffering a relapse of pugilistic dementia, looked serene. "That keeps this day consistent," Joe muttered. "How long?" he asked through lips as grim as the mood around him.

"A week."

Joe's upper body flinched. "That's the rest of the season!" Joe said, bitter resignation in his tone.

"Look, Joe, maybe Tex is just looking out for you. These fans are going to be Brutus after today's news, and I mean Brutus. Especially those loonies from the Honx."

Joe assumed Marty meant the Bronx.

"Yeah. Well, I've already gotten notice once today on how he's looking out for me." To Joe, the surrounding air now seemed dangerous enough to need a catcher's mask.

"You're still ahead in the batting race. If you don't play, you can still win."

Joe so obviously wore the expression of a man needing to burp that Marty patted his shoulder and tiptoed away.

A sinking feeling invaded Joe's gut. "I'm in a mess," he said.

"Yep," Rocket said. "Are you prepared to make the trade we talked about? The one you're with for the one you're messin' with?"

"Nope," sighed Joe. "I've got no idea what got into me. What in the hell do I do now?"

Rocket shrugged.

"Can't help you with your woman problems. You've already ignored me once. As far as Tex goes, only one thing you can do." Rocket squinted his left eye toward Joe. "*Illegitimi non carborundum.*" Rocket accentuated every Latin syllable with his thick Texas accent.

Rocket allowed the statement to dangle in midair. A tape measure blast could not have cleared the silence that followed.

"What the hell does that mean?" Joe finally asked.

"Don't let the bastard grind you down," Rocket answered, his speech slower than a knuckle change-up. Then he walked away.

A slow burn replaced the queasiness in Joe's stomach. His dark eyes were on the verge of erupting from the devastation of the events of the day.

CHAPTER 36
DID SOMEBODY SNEEZE?

Since the night of Liz's abduction, Bull always slept on the Donley's living room sofa during Ranger road trips. Now, Joan sat nuzzled against Bull on the same sofa, wearing a black pant suit worthy of a funeral. To be sure, the *Enquirer* picture had seemed to Joan like the death of an entire family. They were not the Cleavers any more. If life was a TV show, more threatening modern-day dramas had snuffed out programs such as *Leave It to Beaver* and *Andy Griffith*.

"Happiness is like a beam of light, which the least shadow intercepts," Joan announced, answering a question Bull did not ask.

"Where did you hear that?" Bull asked. Before Joan could answer, he raised his hand in a stop-traffic gesture. "Don't tell me... King David."

Without warning, the Donley girls burst through the front door, cradling schoolbooks under their arms. Finding their mother nestled in the protective care of Bull failed to strike the girls as peculiar; but Joan's eyes, empty as a TV preacher's promise, caught Liz's attention.

"What's wrong?" asked Liz.

"Your dad messed up," Joan answered glumly.

"Oh no," said Liz, raising her eyes in frustration. "Oh-for-four again?"

"Dad needs to get a new bat," Tater said.

"On the contrary, it appears his bat is just fine," Joan said. "He needs a new place to live."

"Do we?" K. C. asked.

"No. Just Dad," answered Joan, the worry lines between her eyebrows deep as tunnels.

Puzzled looks surrounded Joan.

"Why, Mom?" Tater asked.

Joan took a deep breath. She pursed her lips. "He slept with another woman."

Liz's mouth dropped open. Tater's head snapped violently. K. C.'s freckles looked as if they lay on virgin snow.

After a moment of shocked silence, K. C., dropping to her knees, pounded her fists on the floor. "Daddy's dying! Daddy's dying!"

Bull reached her first. He scooped her up in his arms and cuddled her against his chest. "It's okay. It's okay," he said soothingly.

"He's not dying," Joan said.

"Don't lie, Momma!" Tater whimpered. "You said that's how you get AIDS: take drugs or go to bed with someone you're not married to."

Still unconvinced, K.C. continued to wail. "Daddy's going to die! "I'm gonna bark!"

"That's barf," Liz corrected K. C. the way she'd corrected her a hundred times before. "Daddy's not dying," she added sternly. "He's just been messin' around."

K. C. stopped her howling. After a thoughtful pause, she and Tater spoke simultaneously. "What's that?"

Weary of the subject before it got started, Joan dismissed further discussions on "messin' around" with the enticement of a family outing to Keller's with Bull. The old-fashioned drive-in served not only the best burgers and shakes in town, but also Tater's favorite cheese tater tots. With dollar bills wrapped around their fingers, carhops wore faded jeans and soiled T-shirts and weaved their way among the cars with loaded trays in their arms. Hand-painted menus covered much of the one-story brick storefront. A tin roof sheltered the cars and their occupants from the Texas weather, a good thing, for Keller's allowed no customers inside.

Visible through glass windows, waitresses and cooks scurried around inside. Cars and pickups regularly lined the storefront to buy beer. The waitresses, many tough enough to wrestle Bull, would toss a case of beer into the autos with no more strain than sacking burgers and fries.

No wonder memories from happier times flooded Joan's mind as she nibbled on her Number Five Special. In spite of her inner wounds, Joan pretended to enjoy her cheeseburger, even offering an occasional chuckle or smile.

Later, with the children in bed, Joan sat with Bull on the living room sofa. Rays of moonlight slanting through the front window landed on the coffee table before them; a ceiling fan gently ruffled the air above.

"What else can go wrong?" she sighed. Her troubled blue eyes assumed that cross-continent expression.

Before Bull could answer, the phone rang. Bull's large paw engulfed the receiver.

"This is Sergeant Banks of the Dallas Police Department," a baritone voice said. "May I speak to Mrs. Donley?"

"Police," Bull said, handing her the receiver.

Joan took the receiver more carefully than usual.

"Sorry to bother you, Mrs. Donley. It's probably nothing," said the policeman. "We had a man in custody, the same guy we arrested in front of your house a while back. We think he's the man that's assaulted several women in your neighborhood. A laundry list of transgressions has kept him in jail," according to Banks.

Joan's heart skipped a beat. Did he say *had in custody*? "He's escaped?"

"No," said the gravelly voice. "He'll never hurt anyone again." Officer Banks cleared his throat as if an announcement was coming. "He's dead now. He got killed in a jail fight tonight. Stabbed by another prisoner," Banks said with a strong voice that seemed to indicate stabbing was a good way to die.

If not a good way, it certainly was a familiar way to Joan. She released a sigh of relief, but immediately drew it back in again.

"What does all this have to do with me?"

"He didn't have any identification to prove it, but he said he was your brother."

"I thought you said he was dead."

"He told us that right before he died. I just needed to check it out." The cop rattled off a physical description: height, weight, coloring, the man's immense shaved head.

"I had a brother," Joan said, "but we haven't heard from him in years. And it can't be him. He's not that big, and he has a full head of hair. It's blond, like mine, and thick."

"Probably just some lunatic that knew about Joe and you because of baseball," the cop agreed. "But he sure said some weird last words."

"Like what?"

"Well, he repeatedly mumbled something like 'I found the body.' And he kept asking, 'Was it purple?'"

Oh my God! Patrick! Joan screamed silently, wondering if this was the moment that she finally went over the edge. The phone went silent, like a long distance call with a poor connection. A look of disbelief smothered Joan's face.

"Will you come down and try to identify him? Just for the record."

"No," she said, her voice turning cold. Joan hung up the phone with more force than she had intended.

"What's wrong?" asked Bull.

Joan remained silent as her mind swirled. Patrick was the one with the purple butthole, the one who found their father's body. The brother who fell prey to the dark, allowing it to encompass him like a cocoon. A cerebral punch floored Joan. If Patrick was on the way to jail when Liz was kidnapped, who in the world took Liz?

"What's wrong?" Bull repeated.

"They caught the Lakewood rapist," she announced, forcing a smile weaker than a number nine hitter.

A darkness thrown off by a gray mood accompanied the darkness of the night as all three Donley children crowded into Tater's and K. C.'s bed. Experts, who supposedly know about these things, claim children harbor two major fears: their parents' splitting and nuclear war. Many divorces appear to accomplish both.

Though she would never admit it, Liz felt as vulnerable as her sisters. K. C., straight from the tub, smelled fresh as country rain. Her red hair, still wet and brushed straight back, glowed in the dark.

Tater's voice was light but her question heavy. "Are Momma and Daddy going to get a divorce?"

"I doubt it," Liz said, but not without skepticism.

Liz looked at Tater. She chose to ignore Tater's several layers of clothing but could not overlook the dual mounds under the covers at the foot of the bed.

"Tater, do you have on your skates?"

"It might not be too bad," Tater said, oblivious to Liz. "We'd have another house to go play at."

"It would be bad," Liz said. "We'd never see Dad. Dads never get custody."

"Yeah," piped in K. C. "Daddies don't know about girls. Daddy doesn't even know the right toothpaste for me to use. He makes bad bacon. He burns the toast worse than Mom. He scratches my freckles off my face with his whiskers. When he brushes my hair, he pulls out my brain. He . . ."

"Shut up, K. C.!" Liz whispered ferociously.

"Huh," K. C. fumed. "This is a fumin' family."

"We're saying our prayer and going to sleep," fumed Liz. "Dear God, protect us from the bad guy that tried to steal me. But if we can only have one thing, don't let our parents get divorced," Liz prayed, fear swirling around her head like June bugs around the porch light.

Liz hesitated briefly, the only opening K. C. needed. "Can we get AIDS?" K. C. asked.

The quiet that followed was lengthy and curious. "Why?" Liz asked, air escaping her in a rush.

"Well, we're sleeping together, and we're not married."

Liz rolled onto her side. Her dark eyes latched onto a life-sized picture on the wall. Her father stood in the batter's position, bat cocked, staring hard and challenging her to deliver the pitch.

If the oldest sister neglected her duty to berate her youngest sister, the middle sister did not.

"You idiot!" admonished Tater, her customary egg-shell tone rivaling thunder. "We can't get AIDS! We're sisters!"

"Huhh!" K. C. repeated. "This is a fumin' family."

"God bless us all," Liz mumbled. "Amen."

"Did somebody sneeze?" wondered K. C.

CHAPTER 37
THE BET

Joe returned to a deserted household. He found only a note from Joan stating that she and the girls would return only after he took his things and left. Joe promptly went next door.

"Well, look what the buzzards drug in they couldn't eat," Bull said when Joe walked dejectedly through his front door.

Bull's indifferent greeting startled Joe, but not as much as the sight of Gladys, Duke's long-time nurse, sitting close to Bull on his living room sofa. She wore a pair of tight black stretch pants and a white T-shirt that hugged her breasts like loving hands.

"What did you expect?" quizzed Bull, his voice more sarcastic than bright. "I couldn't wait for you any longer."

"Cut it out, Bull. She's gonna think we're gay."

"I can assure you I don't think Bull is gay," Gladys announced through an approving grin.

"What are you looking at?" Joe asked Bull.

"Nothin,' Little Man. Nothin' at all."

Bull stared a hardball-sized hole through Joe's chest. Joe felt as if he occupied the batter's box before a hostile road crowd. He longed for the safety of the dugout.

On Joe's way out, he cut a quick glimpse to Gladys. He felt no desire now, but six months ago, he'd risen like a flagpole at the sight of her in her nurse's uniform.

When Joe reached the front door, Bull's voice rang out. "Take a look at the newspaper by the door. I saved it for you. It's on the front page."

Joe's eyes grew as he read about the death of a wrestler known only as "The Claw," the man believed to be responsible for sexual assaults on several women in Lakewood.

Joe, feeling more isolated than important, decided to attend the next day's BIOYA practice. When Big Jim saw Joe, he stopped dead in his tracks and measured Joe carefully. Joe tried to put his arms around Big Jim, but the retarded man shunned Joe like he was radioactive. Whether Big Jim knew of the *American Enquirer* spread or would have understood its implications, Joe did not know. He only knew he was no longer Big Jim's hero.

After the practice, Joe's former teammates migrated to the adjacent public park with their loved ones. Under an ocean-blue sky and a dry September wind, children's laughter pulled Joe toward the park. Husbands and wives and sons and daughters, even a grandparent or two, played on the swings and slides. He watched with eyes that implied his desire to join in with his own family. He wondered if a life of solitude would be a worse fate than a life lived without distinction?

Joe walked toward his car; it was Joe's identical walk after a strikeout. He briefly considered visiting the girls at school but figured that would cause quite a stir, and he'd rather declare a truce with Chester, the Donleys' mad bird, than cause a scene. Besides, with the church next to the school, he'd probably see Pastor Reece, who would certainly offer a few words from his King David sermon on adultery.

At, no further word from Candice, Joe thought. She was, he hoped, preoccupied with her acting career, its modest rise enhanced by publicity from the weekly rag. The magazine said her name was Carla Gardner. What the hell? Her off-Broadway play had opened with decent reviews concerning her performance; Joe could readily testify on her performance skills.

Two days remained in the season as Bull and Joe rode together to the Rangers' ballpark. "What are we going to do about the properties?" Bull wondered, his eyes on Interstate 30. "Tex needs a wad soon, or they're his. Then we're both out of work."

"I haven't gotten around to worrying about that yet," Joe said, though his tone indicated otherwise. "Frothin's hitting worse than me. Why won't Tex let me bat? This isn't exactly the way Ted Williams won his title in '41," Joe grumbled.'

"Yeah, the manager offered to let him sit that last day to protect that .400 average," Bull added.

".39955, which rounds off to .400. Man, I heard my daddy tell that story a hundred times," Joe said wistfully.

"Me too," Bull reminded.

"I can hear him now." Joe's eyes and ears tilted to the sky. "'You know what Ted did, don't you?'" Joe said, trying to imitate his father's voice. "'He played the last day—a doubleheader no less. He went six for eight. Hit a dinger too. Wound up hitting .406. You can look it up,'" said Joe, thrusting his chest forward as if his father had gotten the six hits.

Considering the vast influence of the game's last .400 hitter on George Donley, it's little wonder that Joe could not accept with distinction winning or losing his life-long quest while sitting on the pine.

"Little Man, I still think Tex wants you to win that batting title so he'd win some cash. The papers keep saying he needs money, and the way you were going, you'd lose it for sure. Look at it his way."

"The bet?" Joe said, his mind returning from 1941, from his childhood. "Like I said before, that's no money to Tex." Joe waved his hand as if waving goodbye to Tex's ten grand and the batting title. An idea quietly crept into Joe's brain the way an intruder or two had crept into the Donley home. "Hey, what were the odds on that bet?"

"Beats me," Bull replied with nonchalance, but not so much to disrupt Joe's concentration.

"I was a nobody. What if the odds were, like, a hundred to one?" The wheels of Joe's brain spun, struggling to escape slippery ground.

In deep thought, Bull pushed out his lower lip. He lifted one hand to scribble on an invisible chalkboard. The zeros on Bull's chalkboard glowed like a movie star's diamonds. "It's a million bucks!" he crowed. "One m-i-l-l-i-o-n reasons to keep you on the bench!"

After they reached the ballpark, Bull called a betting service in Vegas to check the odds on opening day of Joe winning the batting title. Bull listened to the bookie's reply from a secluded pay phone, his jaw dropping like an orphan at his first big league game.

"A thousand to one!" Bull roared, his voice ringing out in the ballpark's emptiness.

In the pre-game locker room, Bull privately informed Joe of his findings.

"Ten million dollars!" Joe blurted.

"Little Man, only way you're gonna play is to bribe Tex. We need a picture of him with a sheep," Bull said discreetly. Churn those inner wheels! Did Bull say bribe? Bribe—gambling—bookies—bookies! Aah, the solid ground Joe was searching for. Who knew Tex better than anybody? Longer than anybody? Somebody must know Tex well enough to reach his bookie.

CHAPTER 38
A PLAN

FROTHIN Green still could not hit. That night, the opposing pitcher used the deception of an exaggerated windup to deliver a change-up. Frothin, standing tall and massive but wound tighter than Tex's checkbook, swung before the ball reached home plate, missing so terribly, he practically corkscrewed himself into the batter's box.

"Strike two!" called the man in blue.

Rocket sat by Marty on the bench. Frothin, teeth clenched, burrowed a foxhole in the batter's box. "He's so fidgety, he'd make coffee nervous," Rocket groaned. He pulled the brim of his cap over his eyes and with arms folded against his chest leaned against the dugout wall. "If he don't relax, he couldn't hit with a sackful of bats," he said quietly to his ball hat.

Marty sat on his hands, saying and doing nothing. He merely observed through enough self-induced smoke to sound the Donley alarm.

The next pitch bounced before it reached home plate. No wait in Frothin, only attack. Frothin swung so hard, the bat shattered on impact with his shoulders and back.

"Steerike three!" cried the ump.

The crowd gawked at Frothin the way people gasp at a rare sight such as a batter pissing on home plate. Head down, smoke rising from his helmet, Frothin slowly made his way to the dugout.

"How can anyone that big hit so small?" muttered Marty.

"You can't cover the sun with your finger," Rocket theorized.

To describe the mood in the Ranger clubhouse as only semi-dark would probably qualify as a rather feeble attempt to tickle the light or maybe an argument for an eye exam. The Ranger defeat continued their slide into a long black hole. Another loss on the season finale to the mighty Yankees and a win by second-place Seattle over the Angels would force a playoff.

On the bench and in his solitary confinement, Joe discovered plenty of time to string together several impulses that could be liberally described as a game plan. Phase one consisted of approaching Frothin.

Frothin sat dejectedly on a stool by his locker, his face pasted to the floor. Joe, a specialist in recognizing haunted expressions, approached Frothin gingerly, as if he might explode.

"Duren, if you've got a couple of minutes, I'd like to discuss something with you," Joe said. "I know about you and Candice and…"

Frothin raised his head to face Joe, the sight alarming enough to turn Joe mute. Frothin's beady eyes were ablaze, his glare a blend of misery and shattered dreams. Rising like a mythological figure from the sea, he stood to his full height, then stretched taller. A dark cloud smothered his face. Who knows what stage of insanity his mind was going through? He whirled on Joe, his mammoth head in a disfigured frenzy. Frothin slammed Joe's shoulders against the locker, which about now looked the perfect size for a coffin.

"I, I ought to, to bi… bite your fu… fuckin head ooo… off!" he snarled, inner demons twisting his face as his stutter twisted his speech.

Everyone in the locker room froze.

"You do, and there'll be more brains in your stomach than in your head!" George Donley's son said in a threatening tone. However, it must be duly noted, with Joe's feet dangling in midair, backing down did not currently represent a viable option.

"You, you think I'm I'…m ss-stupid?" stuttered Frothin. The fact Frothin understood the intent of Joe's words would seem to imply he suffered more from derangement than ignorance. Frothin's wild eyes raced up and down Joe as if daring him to reply.

"Let me put it this way. If you put your brains in a hummingbird, it'd still fly backwards." Joe cast a wild eye of his own toward Frothin.

Frothin drew back his granite fist. Joe heard the other players collectively sucking in air. He braced himself and closed his eyes.

"Spot! Come back!" Rocket rushed toward Duren with the good intentions of a fireman drawn to duty's call. "Frothin, look!" he yelled, pointing toward the clubhouse exit. "Spot's running away!"

Frothin dropped Joe and bolted after the invisible canine.

"Whew," Rocket sighed, rubbing his hand across the top of his balding head. "That boy's possessed by the Furies!"

Joe knew his heart was still working because it pounded his ribs with prize fighter force; his nervous system was bathed in a fear-induced rush. His face, suddenly resembling his mother's, looked ridiculously pale. It took a minute before Joe could speak.

"Do you know how to reach Tex's bookie?" Joe asked Rocket with a soft tremble. Like a runner picked off first who somehow reached second, Joe advanced to the second phase of his plan.

CHAPTER 39
THE EXORCIST

THE morning after Joe's run-in with Frothin, he began the dreaded chore of packing. Joe knew, unless he met Joan's demand of leaving home, he would see the Holy Ghost before he saw his family again. As Joe was loading a suitcase onto his bed, he noticed Bull's broad body filling up the bedroom doorway. Bull's complexion was all wrong, like a photograph with too much of the wrong color.

"What's wrong, Bull?"

"Hey, Little Man," Bull said. His stride into the room matched the dread in his voice. "I just found this," Bull said, extending a hand toward Joe.

Joe's eyes strained toward Bull's offering—a videotape? Accepting the tape, confusion dug ditches across Joe's brows.

"There's a note with it. . ." Pausing, Bull's thoughts hung on something private.

George Donley's handwriting leaped off a white index card inside the clear plastic sleeve of the tape. Joe quickly read to himself: "To Joe, I hope they are few, but on a bad day, maybe this will help. Happy Birthday. Love, GWD."

"I guess I've had it since, you know...that day," Bull said softly. "Talk to you later, Little Man." Bull turned and left the room.

Studying the note, Joe managed to chuckle internally. GWD for George Washington Donley. Joe's father had the same birthday, February 22, as George Washington. George Donley's mom, quite a patriot, considered this no coincidence and named her son after the first president of the United States.

Reflecting on his father's message hit Joe like a ton of cerebral TNT. Today was a bad day, a really bad day. Joe gently shoved the tape into the bedroom VCR. Unlike Joe's anxious thoughts, the fuzzy picture soon crystallized.

Grinning like a kid, Joe's father filled the TV screen. . The video displayed the date: June 6, 1:22 p.m.—almost sixteen months ago. It was Joe's birthday, only a few hours before his father's death. Joe wondered if he had managed to cross the dimensions of time, sort of a vision within a vision. "How do I look?" the dead man asked in a mesmerizingly gentle voice. A warm brown eye winked youthfully.

"Good," Joe barely managed to say.

Pretty damn spiffy was more like it. Wearing his Army dress attire, the old man sat in the leather reclining chair in his den. An explosion of multi-colored medals decorated the front of the jacket. George looked as much of a patriot as George Washington himself. Though he'd developed wattles under his chin, the old coach's jaw remained square, his eyes still strong.

"How do you like my new gizmo?" his dad asked, pointing directly at the camera. "Bought it yesterday. Had to call Liz and ask her how to get it going," he said proudly, his pride more for his granddaughter than his ability to operate the new "gizmo."

Joe briefly wondered what newfangled contraptions his grandchildren might someday assist him with. "It sure has a clear picture," Joe answered. He referred to his dad's gizmo, not his general understanding of things. For the first time, Joe noticed a few liver spots around his dad's temples and forehead.

"Are you wondering why I'm wearing my Army uniform? I mean, don't you think it's kind of strange for an old geezer to traipse around in his World War II uniform over fifty years after the war ended?"

"Sort of," Joe answered, his eyes settling into the shape of balloons.

Joe crept close enough to the TV to crawl inside.

"Me too," George said with a sideburn-to-sideburn grin. "Did you know I fought in D-day?" asked the old soldier, his playful eyes suddenly turning serious.

A look of doubt tugged on Joe's face.

"Ah, don't worry about it," George said, waving his hand in grand forgiveness. "If I had wanted to talk about it before now, I would have. What a son-of-a-bitchin' day that was." George's right hand tugged down on both cheeks as if they were rubber. "Was a day of death, killing and being killed. Landed on Omaha Beach." He squeezed the bridge of his nose, shutting his eyes. "Course, swam on would be more like it. Shell fire shattered our landing craft a hundred yards from shore." George squirmed in his leather chair, like he sat on something sharp.

"I could hear machine-gun bullets hitting the water around me. Dead bodies were floating all around. I didn't know if I was going to get shot or drown," Joe's father said with quiet dignity. "It seemed like I was in that damn water forever. When I got to land, everybody was searching for cover, but there wasn't any. There must have been a band of dead Americans seven yards wide on that beach." George's movements and tone were totally and completely reverential; his eyes misted. "I bet we lost nine out of ten men on that first assault. I watched my friends die in every way you could imagine. The head wounds were the worst." Grampa George shivered a little. "I never knew brain tissue was so pink and fluffy," he said, swallowing hard as if suppressing vomit.

Joe shivered a lot and swallowed harder.

His father sat portrait still, then he pressed his hands together in a prayer-like manner.

"The first non-American I saw was a French girl. Cute as a button too. She had that light blond hair, sort of like Tater, and not much older than Liz." George paused to compose himself; his wounded eyes alternated between the floor and the camera. "She shot me in the foot. When I looked down, I knew my baseball career was over. Funny, that's the first thing I thought of. I wasn't worried about dying—just how could I play baseball with a chunk of my foot gone?" George shook his head in dismay. "Maybe we Donleys weren't meant to play ball," said Grampa George.

Maybe not, Joe silently agreed. If not for his father's own "bad hop," would he have made it to the big show? Joe wondered.

"I could have made it," George said without elaboration. Though he spoke softly, his next words broke the silence like Hendrix in a funeral parlor. "I had to shoot her," he muttered. "I killed her."

Joe shook. "You killed her?" Joe's bewilderment released more air into the two balloons flanking his nose.

Joe's father nodded. "Anybody with a gun, you treated them alike. It was like a field box seat on the edge of hell."

Joe suddenly feared that his parenting efforts were a distant second compared to those of his dad. George Donley was as good a man as he'd ever known. Heck, Joe remembered childhood friends complaining their dads would never play catch. Not George Donley. He poured his soul into helping Joe chase his dream, even after a French Nazi sympathizer had shattered his own. Joe felt a strange sense of relief knowing his dad could not see his current predicament.

Joe watched a lone tear streak down his father's cheek. Donley men don't cry. Hell, Donley men shun emotion like death.

"Aah, don't sweat it. Us Donley men should have learned to cry a long time ago," the old coach said. "Anyway, that's why I did it."

"Did what?" asked his son.

"That's why I wore my uniform, so people won't forget. For my money, June 6, 1944, is the most important day in modern history." George pointed his finger at the camera, his voice returning to an officer's strength. "I hear they barely mention World War II in schools these days. If we hadn't of won, you might be speaking German. Worse, you might have played soccer as a kid," Joe's father said, who held Nazis and soccer players in equally low esteem. "When I first got back from the war,

I could close my eyes and see battle. I've never touched any kind of gun again. Heck, I haven't even been hunting since the war. I almost never see my dead buddies in my dreams any more, but you never forget. And I don't want this country to forget either."

He leaned back in the chair. "Why am I telling you all this? I'll tell you why," Joe's father quickly replied. "It doesn't take Teddy Ballgame's eyes to know you're struggling a bit. I'll grant you," said George, with a slight bob of the head, "you've never fully recovered from that day. But see, I've had a day I never fully recovered from either."

A thought engulfed Joe like a turbulent wave off Normandy beach; his own longest day of over twenty years ago didn't seem so long any more.

George looked straight at Joe as hard as he had ever looked at him. "Now, I don't want it to sound like I'm fussing at you, but I think you come from a generation that's a little spoiled. Sure, things didn't work out exactly as you planned. You may not have it all, but you've got enough. You know, I used to feel the same way you do. I had an ongoing rhubarb with God for over thirty years—ever since D-day. But the day you got hurt, I told God I'd quit fighting with Him if He would just let you live. He did, and I did. Truth is, I almost felt guilty for being alive when I should have just been thankful for ever surviving the war in the first place. Life's too short to waste a minute."

Joe's father shook his head. "You can't beat the head ump, Joe. Your mom's always been right about all that religious stuff. I just don't want you to have to go through something really bad before you realize that." George simply didn't want his son to miss the good parts.

"Hey! What was that movie where the little girl twisted her head all around and puked that guacamole salad?" George asked, his tone now light as Ted William's bat.

"Movie?" Joe said, confused.

"*The Exorcist*!" George exclaimed, breaking into a grin. "I'm glad we've had this talk. It's been sort of like an exorcism, don't you think?"

"George!" Joe's mother called. "What are you doing in there?"

George's bristly eyebrows shot upward; his eyes darted to the side. His words came quicker than before. "I gotta go. Thanks for listening. Look," he added, "the war was worth it for me if you never have to go through hell like that. I've had a good life, and you can too. If I get run over by a truck tomorrow, I'll die a contented man." Joe's father paused briefly. "Especially if I know you're okay."

"George!" Mary's voice moved closer, and the screen turned to snow. George, a man who gave everything but expected nothing in return, had vanished from his son's life for the second and final time.

Not tomorrow, but today, Joe thought, sliding backward sixteen months through an electronic crack in time. Not only hit by a truck, but run over by a train. Despite the TV's static, Joe's mind was quiet to the point of numbness.

"I don't know what to say," he mumbled eventually.

He didn't know what to feel either. His watery eyes rested on the snowy screen. Joe had not cried since he was six, on the day he realized all people die, himself included.

Joe began to cry, but his tears were as peaceful as a summer shower. He cried and cried, washing away the barrier that held the darkness in him for so long. The startling sound of the doorbell stifled his tears. Donley men may have taken to crying but not in front of just anybody.

CHAPTER 40
DUKE PAYS A VISIT

AFTER three rings of the front doorbell, the neurosurgeon decided no one was home. Through a broken shuffle, Duke started to renegotiate the red brick walkway to his motorcycle.

"Duke? Is that you?" Joe's voice sounded ragged.

From the look of Joe's red-rimmed eyes, Duke wondered if he had arrived in the nick of time or at precisely the wrong time. Duke also maintained that worried look. Like a good case of jock rash, tiny seeds of doubt had irritated Duke for some time, causing him to question his experimental surgery.

"Joe, we need to have a little talk."

Duke followed Joe inside. As both men sank into opposite ends of the den sofa, a bird screeched into the room.

"Chester! Chester!" squawked the bird.

"Watch it!" Joe cried, ducking from his seat.

Duke ducked, too, but Chester only circled close to Joe's skull. After three dive-bombing runs, the mad bird fluttered out of the room.

"Joe, I'd like to explain something to you in medical terms," said Duke, his intense eyes following the bird, his voice as precise as if he were teaching surgery. "First, let me tell you about what is called the pituitary axis. The pituitary is a real small gland that sits at the base of the brain. It's connected to the brain, but it's also connected to the blood stream. It is bathed by a collection of veins. Think of a pituitary gland as the head computer to all the hormonal systems."

Duke's tone was informational, not condescending.

What did all that have to do with him? Joe wondered. Why a medical lecture in my living room?

"The pituitary gland doesn't make thyroid hormone; it makes the hormone that tells the thyroid to make thyroid hormone. It doesn't make testosterone; it makes the hormone that tells the testicle to make testosterone. It's really a kind of controlling feature." Duke stared at Joe, his face calm, his eyes sure.

"It's governed by influences that come from the brain, but it's also regulated by the overall amount of hormone that's in the bloodstream. And that's a delicate balance." Duke held up his thumb and index finger together, as if holding something delicate.

Duke was not the type of man to toss words around like Frisbees; something weighed heavily on Duke's mind, but what?

"So, let's say the thyroid hormone begins to dip below the correct level. The pituitary gland emits a hormone that goes into the bloodstream and causes the thyroid to release more hormones. It's a feedback mechanism. The pituitary gland targets the thyroid with a hormone that causes the thyroid to make more thyroid hormone and put it into the bloodstream. The bloodstream continues to bathe the pituitary gland, and the pituitary gland recognizes that there now is enough thyroid hormone in the bloodstream, so it doesn't put out any more of what is called thyroid releasing factor."

Maybe college credits were available for this course, Joe thought. Not a bad idea since it looked like he would shortly need a new line of work.

"Now, the brain can override all this procedure for brief periods. And," Duke said, perplexingly scratching his perfectly manicured salt and pepper beard, "this is something that we don't understand that well yet, but the brain can send messages to the pituitary gland that essentially tell the pituitary gland to forget what the thermostat is saying. So, it's a delicate balance that has a feedback mechanism to keep it all under control. Sometimes, for reasons we don't really understand, a small clump of pituitary cells begin to grow and multiply rapidly and then become immune to normal feedback control. As a result, the amount of thyroid hormone in the blood will rise to very high levels, but the nest of abnormal pituitary cells keeps putting out high levels of thyroid releasing hormone. So, in short order, we have the thyroid gland going like its hair is on fire in response to a cluster of pituitary cells locked in overdrive. In medicine, we call this group of cells an 'adenoma,' a benign tumor that produces one or more hormones." Duke's eyes continued to study Joe, a shrewdness in his stare.

Shit happens, Joe thought. Hope there's no pop quiz on this sucker.

"These pituitary adenomas come in a variety of types, depending on the type of cell that's involved. The best example is in the NBA. Those guys have growth hormones secreting adenoma all over the place, so they grow like weeds. Does this make any sense?"

Joe nodded. About as much sense as talking with a dead man.
"Good," said Duke. He drew a deep breath. "Cause that's what's driven this last six months—a pituitary adenoma."

A dash of interest burst onto Joe's face. Duke sounded terribly past-tense.

"Do I have anything now?"

"We'll discuss that in a minute. I knew you had the adenoma after you got back from the fantasy camp. You had all the signs. The changes in your physical make-up, the increased strength and size, the crisp vision, and . . . increased sex drive."

Joe's eyes widened. He felt like a kid caught putting slugs in the drink machine at school. Duke eyed Joe with perception as rare as it was immeasurable. "Gladys buys that damn weekly rag and brings it to work. I saw the picture." Duke's tone lightened ever so briefly. "That purple-headed love warrior can sure cause a man a lot of trouble."

Joe's eyes expanded more. That comment didn't sound like Duke.

"Actually, I got that one from my anesthesiologist," Duke explained, instantly confirming Joe's hunch.

"What caused this pituitary whatever-you-call-it?"

"I believe that when you fell out of that tree, the fall shocked the pituitary gland, producing a massive release of pituitary hormones. Didn't last long, but it was the trigger to kick off a sizable dose of hyperactivity. Somehow, that kick-started a group of pituitary cells that pretty soon started dancing to their own tune." Duke sounded like a head mechanic proud of his prize-winning car. (Pituitary, smituitary, thought Joe).

Duke, who already looked plenty serious, managed to wratch his seriousness up a notch. "I talked to Joan."

Joe's eyebrows shot upward in hopeful anticipation.

"She told me about your tripping over your daughter's skate. That fall and the blow to your head must have produced a hemorrhage that destroyed the tumor itself, but not the gland. I'm quite sure of it," Duke said. "That's why your physical condition has reversed itself. I also expect your sex drive's lessened." Duke's eyes danced conspiratorially. "It's called pituitary apoplexy, and it occurs fairly frequently with tumors of the pituitary gland."

"Does Joan know all this?"

"And more," replied the brain surgeon.

"More?" Joe said, returning Duke's words like a ping-pong volley.

"Joe," said Duke, inhaling deeply. "Not every middle-aged man that falls out of a tree and develops a balls-to-the-wall pituitary adenoma. I dare say you're the only one. But then you're the only one who ever had a pituitary gland transplant," announced Duke. "Ever," he reiterated after a brief pause.

Void of all expression, Joe tried to recall details of that fateful day. Only the image of a hardball honing in like a guided missile came to mind.

"Until recently, only my medical team knew," Duke said softly. "Ted, my anesthesiologist, got drunk and told the donor's sister this summer. The donor's parents are deceased. I've always wanted them to know the contribution their little boy made," said Duke, sighing heavily enough to disrupt Chester's airwaves.

Joe's shoulders stiffened when Duke said "little boy." Starting dimly to comprehend the magnitude of Duke's revelation, Joe stared at the surgeon as if guacamole poured from both of his ears.

"I should have told them a long time ago," Duke added regrettably, "but we didn't exactly follow legal protocol. Shit, there was no protocol then for things like this. I guess I was a little apprehensive about telling anyone. But who gives a wolf shit," said Duke, his voice and eyes returning to full strength. "We did some incredible work that day. I feel better now. Sort of like a..." Duke hesitated, searching for the right words.

"An exorcist?" blurted Joe. "Like an exorcism has occurred?"

"Yeah," said Duke through his grin. "Like an exorcist."

With both hands palms up, Joe asked, "What does all this mean? You know, in medical terms."

Hands clasped and elbows to his thighs, Duke bowed toward Joe. "It means you're a pretty lucky fellow just to be alive and not burdened with taking a hundred pills a day. It means you're lucky to have normal functions and live normally. And that's all secondary to the sacrifices of the little boy. Remember, the donor didn't have the options you've had. From a physician's perspective, it means you're unique: the only man on earth with a pituitary transplant."

A pity Bull was not within hearing distance, Joe thought. "Little Man wants to feel special. The only man with a pituitary gland transplant. How special is that?" Bull would have surely replied.

"Of course," Duke added, "that's neither to your credit or your fault. This is something you didn't have anything to do with, so the only thing that makes a difference is how you deal with it now," Duke said, his eyes catching Joe's.

Joe was silent for a long time before he spoke. "Joan knows all of this?"

"She does now."

Relief flooded through Joe like a deluge of fresh spring water. A desire to hold his wife and children so overwhelmed him, he felt a tingle in his stomach; his face felt flush.

"There's one more thing I think you ought to know," Duke warned, his eyes narrowing. He cupped his square jaw in his left hand and massaged his thick beard. "The girl in the *Enquirer* picture is the donor's younger sister." Somehow Duke made this news seem reasonable, a logic he assumed Joe could have lived without.

Maybe it was due to the piercing volume or possibly because the sound was so foreign, but Duke flinched violently. Joe was laughing so hard his sides hurt. He doubled over, slapping his thighs with both hands. What a unique sight. Joe Donley, a unique man, had learned to laugh and cry all in the same day. Like Duke said, "The only thing that makes a difference is how you deal with it."

CHAPTER 41
TOOTHPICK JOHNSON

DUKE commandeered his motorcycle with all the predictable precision and intensity of a brain surgeon. As he rode off, the cycle briefly stood on its hind wheel before landing so gently, it seemed to kiss the road. He looked like that other Duke riding off into the sunset. Only after the engine's roar faded did Joe hear the phone ringing. As if trying to leg out a slow grounder, he rushed inside, Joe longed to hear Joan's voice, even if her angered pitch rivaled the roar of Duke's cycle.

"Joe, get to the park pronto. I located Tex's bookie." Rocket's words came faster than normal, like his fastball with a tail wind. "How much money you need?" Rocket added, his voice full of intrigue.

"A cool mill."

Dressed in street clothes, Joe and Rocket dangled their feet over a row of seats in the second deck of the Rangers' new triple-deck stadium. The park held fifty thousand plus change, every seat identical in color to the natural green carpet. Massive ironwork partially obscured the sun's glare. In right field, a home run porch was as enticing as the head cheerleader in school. Right center served as the deepest part of the park, leaving an asymmetrical outfield design that also contributed to the feel of yesteryear. Only a modern, multi-tiered office complex beyond center field betrayed the park's link to the past.

The ballyard felt Roman in its emptiness, as if anticipating a duel with swords instead of wood and cowhide. Below, a handful of groundskeepers were raking the infield, which glowed a brilliant green and rich reddish brown.

"Isn't this a great office?" Rocket said, plainly relishing his surroundings.

Verifying their solitude, Joe's head rotated from left to right field. "What's the deal with Tex's bookie?"

"Don't ask me no questions, and I won't tell you no lies," Rocket drawled. "Now listen, these hitters today swing at most anything, and the only pitch most pitchers can get over consistently is the fastball. Lay off the breaking ball. Try to get ahead in the count. And wear shorter pants."

"Shorter pants?"

"Smaller strike zone. Remember, get ahead in the count. Sandbag every now and then; if a fastball comes in, pretend you're fooled." Rocket's voice began to rise in excitement. "A pitcher gets careless and grooves one," said Rocket, his right hand snapping an imaginary fastball. "Wham! You blast it."

"Interesting," Joe said. His voice sounded rusty.

"All these years, not one hitter's ever asked me for advice. Makes sense for a batter to pick a pitcher's brain. Think about it."

"Why are you bothering to tell me all this?" Joe said. "Tex loses ten million if I post an o-fer, and Jackson has a big day. I'm never going to get off the pine. You gotta admit ten million smackers will solve a lot of Tex's problems whether we make the playoffs or not."

Rocket's eyebrows bristled at the mention of New York's Henry Jackson, the son of the retired pitcher whose strikeout record Rocket had long ago shattered, the same Jackson who previously criticized Rocket's career won-lost record.

"I'm tellin' you for two reasons." As Rocket's eyes strayed to the glass infield, a rough edge surfaced in his voice. "First, I need that victory today, and you can help me get it. Remember, a loss might force a play-off, and I can't pitch again tomorrow. Second, you're gonna play."

Joe stared at Rocket as he began to get the picture.

"You've done more than just locate Tex's bookie."

"One other thing," Rocket said. "Toothpick's on the mound today."

Toothpick. The name itself would cause any sensible batter to shudder. A gold toothpick always dangled from his mouth like a six-shooter from a holster. "Skoal-tyne," a mix of Dentyne gum and chewing tobacco stained his teeth and dripped from his chin. "You can't chew it, and you can't spit it out," Toothpick would sneer through teeth stained like Grandma's formal dining table.

"Yeah, I know all about him," Joe said. "A heater almost as good as yours, and a breaking ball as nasty as himself."

"Well, if you know all about him, then you know he stands up straight for his fastball and bends more for the curve." Rocket's hardball eyes drilled into Joe. "Sometimes, it makes sense to pick a pitcher's brain about another pitcher," Rocket added, competitiveness dominating the craggy lines of his face.

CHAPTER 42

LIKE ANOTHER JOE

On the ballpark's perimeter, trees hinted at fall. Inside, a Caribbean blue sky, stretching to baseball heaven, contrasted spectacularly with the ocean of green below. The Rangers sported snow white uniforms with navy blue lettering and trim. The visiting Yankees wore traditional road grey with black. An hour before the 2:05 first pitch, the crowd was already filing in, sounding like hyper bees on the prowl.

Beyond the right centerfield wall, smoke signals spiraled into the air, courtesy of Rocket's fastballs. Toward left center, Toothpick's pre-game missiles left a jet stream of visible air. His hat sat high left, defying gravity after every pitch by refusing to fall. Though a decade younger than Rocket, Toothpick's sour disposition and unkempt beard made him look ten years older. His rumpled uniform looked like he slept in it.

Henry Jackson, now in the batting cage, trailed Joe by a mere two points in the batting race with a .367 average. Jackson's every swing sent balls out of the infield faster than bottle rockets.

Tex, flanked by his ever-present bodyguards, strutted down the aisle, greeting well-wishers along the way. His gold jewelry flashing in the sun, Tex took his front row seat by the Rangers' dugout; almost immediately, one of his bodyguards handed him a black cellular phone. Brandishing a smile as large as his ego, the owner placed the phone to his ear. The longer Tex listened, the redder his face grew. Tex's impersonation of a nice person came to a thunderous halt. Tex disgustedly airmail-expressed the phone to his aid in the aisle and then leaned over the railing into the Rangers' dugout.

"Marty! Come here!"

Joe sat in the dugout wearing a slice-of-the-moon smile, as if he indeed possessed a picture of Tex "with a sheep." He waved pleasantly to his employer, his newly found range of emotions visibly agreeing with him.

Marty's head popped through the haze of dugout smoke. "What's up?" he snapped.

Tex shot Joe a death-dealing glare. "Donley's starting at DH today."

Joe jumped so high in the air, he almost bumped his head on the dugout ceiling.

"Get lucid, Donley!" the manager practically yelled.

Too late. Joe already stood in first-base foul territory, whipping his bat at imaginary fastballs.

Frothin, running warm-up sprints in the outfield, stopped dead in his tracks and nailed Joe with as nasty a glare as one man could possibly show toward another.

For eight innings, Rocket and Toothpick conducted their own version of airmail express. Both teams had scored only one run. Joe was 0 for two with a strikeout, groundout, and walk. Jackson was three for three. After stretching a double into a triple, he drilled a single in the third inning and blasted a homer, New York's only score, in the sixth.

With the Rangers preparing to take the field in the top of the ninth, Rocket gave Jackson his due.

"The cocky shit can hit," he told Joe begrudgingly.

Rocket's hat rested in his lap as beads of sweat rolled down his forehead and into his eyes. He wiped his sleeve across his nose and face.

"I'm gonna get him out this time if it kills me," the pitcher said with surprising malice. "And we've got to score this inning." He poked Joe firmly in the chest with his forefinger. "You may as well be the one to do it."

"I will," Joe heard himself saying as Rocket headed to the mound, his stride charged with purpose.

Jackson, a lean will o' the wisp right-handed hitter with legs clear up to his armpits, batted first in the ninth. Swinging early, Jackson slashed a curve ball foul down the third baseline. Strike one. Swinging late, he popped up a fastball in the first-base stands. Strike two.

Rocket glared at Jackson with a look that said, "You're expectin' me to waste a couple. Maybe high fastballs, with enough heat to light a torch or maybe a breaking ball that falls from twelve to six o'clock and bounces short of home plate. But you're too good to chase anything out of the strike zone. Truth is, you're expectin' wrong. I got ahead in the count—not you. Your ass is wound tighter than a cat's over a wagon wheel, and it's mine." Rocket could say a lot in his look.

Rocket reared so far back into his windup, his left foot pointed straight to the sky. His right arm snapped with the pitch like a flag in West Texas. On release, he grunted loud enough to bring relief from the stigma of losing for nearly two decades, relief from Jackson's biting remarks.

Jackson gawked at the ball with strangled awe. He did not see a high hard one or a nasty curve in the dirt. Rocket delivered a change-up slow enough to need back-up lights. Henry Jackson's body refused to cooperate with his mind. He flailed violently before the ball reached the halfway point. Strike three.

Jackson walked dejectedly to his dugout, his face flush with humiliation. The efforts of the next two batters reinforced Webster's thoughts on futility. Still tied one to one, the game reached the bottom of the ninth.

The once steady drone of the crowd had become an orgiastic frenzy. Just one run, and the Rangers would clinch the division title.

From the on-deck circle, Joe scanned the crowd. No Candice, or whatever her name, in the third base stands. A man holding a large plastic beer cup, his belly drooping comfortably over his belt, occupied her seat. No sign of Joan or the girls. No Big Jim either. Only Bull was there.

Rodriguez, the Rangers' catcher, skillfully fouled off six pitches before drawing a walk to become the Rangers' first base runner in four innings.

During Joe's lonely walk to the plate, everything seemed in slow motion. From the corner of his eye, he saw Tex's hands folded in the symbolic gesture of prayer, his eyes closed. Marty anxiously prowled the dugout while Rocket sat expressionless nearby.

Joe dug his metal cleats into the dirt around home plate. He felt his throat tighten with desire. Toothpick's hostile face and squinting eyes bore in on Joe, daring him to swing at the pitch. His dad's teachings repeated themselves in his mind. Relax. Smooth swing. Close your shoulders. Keep your head still, the bat above the strike zone. Wait, then attack. Especially wait, then attack.

His mother's teaching too: I think I can, I think I can, Joe mumbled silently.

Sure enough, the left-hander offered a vicious breaking ball that dropped from Joe's shoulders to his knees.

"No, no," said the ump sharply, shaking his head. Ball one. Frowning, Toothpick swaggered off the mound like a schoolyard bully. The ump, a burly Irishman named O'Reilly, strode toward him.

"Don't start your complaining, Toothpick," O'Reilly said crisply. "The pitch was low."

Toothpick glared at Joe and pointed to his pants, which exposed blue stockings practically to his knees. "It wasn't low. He's got his damn pant legs pulled up to his crotch," growled the veteran.

Toothpick's glove snapped at the return throw from his catcher. Toothpick stalked back to the mound.

Shorter pants. Not a bad idea, Joe mused.

Back on the mound, Toothpick massaged the resin bag in his left hand like a good luck piece and dropped it beside the pitcher's rubber. Puffs of red dirt rose before vaporizing in thin air. Toothpick's next offering, a scorching fastball, arrived high and outside. Joe backed away, apparently distracting the catcher, and Toothpick's heat sailed to the screen. Rodriguez easily took second base.

"Ball," O'Reilly announced.

Pretend the pitch fooled you. Not a bad idea, Joe thought. His eyes found Rocket in the dugout. Rocket's lips moved in an urgent message that Joe couldn't decipher, but Joe remembered all of his teacher's admonitions well. Toothpick stood high on the mound, straight as a ruler, a sure sign of his next pitch.

Only a few hitters experience the phenomenon occasionally, some less than that, most never. In spite of the pitch's startling velocity, the ball appeared to stop in flight, pleading for attention. Joe obliged with the mightiest swing of his life. Lumber pummeled cowhide, sounding as loud as dynamite. A tingle ran up his arms as the ball shot toward third base, leaving a miniscule white line of resin residue in its midst.

Danny Aiker, the Yankee's lanky third baseman, stretched to the sky, momentarily taking on the appearance of posing for a Wheaties box cover. Aiker's glove not only swallowed the ball but also Tex's ten million bucks, the Rangers' division title, and Joe's batting crown. Then, like a rocket boosted to the second stage, the ball resumed flight but still inside Aiker's glove! Time froze as the giant left hand, the baseball nestled inside, soared with the predictability of a hot dog wrapper in a tornado.

Rodriguez, initially paralyzed by the sight, broke for third. Aiker's glove, weary from flight, crashed to the turf in shallow left field. After a pregnant pause, the mitt gave birth to a baseball, which trickled to a halt on the soft grass.

Rodriguez raced on toward the treasure buried in red dirt. New York's left fielder, shortstop, and third baseman simultaneously converged on the object of so much attention. Aiker scooped up the ball and rifled it home.

Aiker's sizzling peg short-hopped the Yankee catcher and ricocheted off his rigid pie-shaped mitt. Rodriguez scored standing up. The stadium detonated into a delirious sea of joy.

Time out. At this point, one might imagine that everyone lived happily ever after. Texas clinched the title. Joe won the batting crown. (No scorekeeper would rule Joe's blue darter anything but a base hit.) Tex won $10,000,000. Joan and the girls returned home. Liz wrote a best seller. Tater, overcoming her fears, ceased dressing in layers. K. C. became regular as Ex-Lax. Bull and Joe somehow saved Walrus Real Estate. Rocket became commissioner of Major League Baseball. Duke performed surgery on Frothin, instantly transforming him into a fellow brain surgeon, and Big Jim joined the wrestling tour. Poverty vanished, world affairs improved, and so on. Maybe...maybe not. Remember, life is what happens when you're busy making other plans. Play ball.

Joe strolled into second base calmly, graciously, remindful of another Joe as in DiMaggio. His mind took a snapshot of the hysterical crowd that jumped up and down in unison, as if all were riding pogo sticks. Led by Rocket, the Ranger players formed a huge pile of human flesh at home plate. Tex joined the celebration as Tom Petty's "I Won't Back Down" blared on the stadium loudspeakers.

Joe found Bull in the stands, tipped his cap, and waved. He winked with cloudy eyes, an indication he now considered loneliness a fate far worse than death without a life of distinction.

CHAPTER 43
DON'T MAKE IT FAIR

THE dressing room celebration looked seamless in comparison to other victory parties often seen on the boob tube. Heads glistened from dampness and smelled of grapes; Ranger players and management joyfully indulged in the obligatory waste of champagne. Tex had stocked the Rangers' clubhouse with the cheap stuff, the type that leaves rolling concrete inside the consumer's head after a few hours. Marty nearly downed a whole bottle in one long swallow, looking like a wino coming off the desert. Tex, showcasing his ten-million-dollar grin, stood in the midst of it all, guzzling rotgut from a $400 black cowboy hat.

Not everyone joined in. Joe stood to one side with Bull and Rocket, calmly watching the joyous melee. All three sipped on long-neck beers.

"Bull, wait here. This won't take long," Joe said.

Joe and Rocket approached Tex.

"Tex, could Joe and I see you in the privacy of your office for just a second?" Rocket yelled over the noisy din.

"Why sure, boys," Tex slurred.

Joe and Rocket followed Tex's wobbly stride to an adjacent office. The public show-off kept a shabby private space. Tex dropped heavily into a worn vinyl chair behind an old metal desk. Joe and Rocket eased into two portable chairs facing him.

"What a day," Tex hiccuped.

"It sure is," Rocket replied. His glance, sparkling with a rookie's mischief, latched onto Joe.

"What's up?" Tex asked abruptly, as if suddenly remembering he had visitors.

"I quit," Joe blurted.

"You mean after the playoffs?"

"Nope. Today."

Suddenly sober, Tex sat erect in his chair and eyed Joe suspiciously. "But why? You're coming out of your slump."

"I've got my reasons."

"What are you going to do?" Tex asked, his eyes bird small.

"Back to my real estate business," Joe said. And back to his family, he hoped.

"Aren't you forgetting something?" Tex shot back, his tone suddenly covered with frost. He forced a tolerant smile.

Rocket stood abruptly and handed the owner an envelope. Tex accepted it with the same apprehension he would accept the dinner tab. Anxiety and distrust rapidly permeated the room.

"Walrus Real Estate is no longer in your debt. You're paid in full with time to spare," Rocket said.

Tex missed Rocket's look of pure sneaky delight. His wide eyes were glued to Rocket's million-dollar check. So much for anxiety and distrust. Air laced with more tension than an L. A. courtroom filled the room.

Tex's dark brows furrowed; it was the look of a man counting lost dollars.

"You're paying off the debt? Why?" Understanding seeped into Tex's gaze. "Are you stealing those properties from me?" Tex quizzed, his voice rising like a volcano. His look could have split wood.

"No, I'm keeping you from stealing them from Joe and Bull. I'm gonna be their partner. I need a few buildings to go with my ranch."

"How can you do this?" Tex whined rhetorically. He raised his hands palm up. "If it wasn't for me, you'd still be stuck in New York. We've been together for twenty years!" he added in a higher tone than usual.

"And for twenty years, you've blamed me for not winning the title," Rocket said crisply.

"That's why I brought you home—to win us a championship," Tex said lamely. His face registered the hint of betrayal.

"By myself!" Rocket snapped, leaning across the desk close enough to smell Tex's champagne breath.

Tex retreated, the chair sliding on its rollers.

"You were too cheap to get us players!" Rocket pointed to Joe. "Hell, you got lucky here and signed Joe for the major league minimum!" He dropped back into his seat and stared balefully at his boss.

Tex cleared his throat uncomfortably. Sweat beads broke out on his forehead.

"Besides," Rocket said, his voice suddenly soft as a Texas leaguer, "you've always underpaid me. You knew I'd play for less to be near my family."

Tex's look searched the room as if seeking a way out. "You made it up in endorsements," he finally said lamer than before.

"Don't make it fair."

He stood abruptly, and Joe followed suit. Tex remained frozen in his chair.

"After the playoffs, I'm quittin' too," Rocket announced, his voice still toneless. "Playin' ball's similar to chasin' women." Rocket's glance briefly caught Joe. "It's a young man's sport. I'd like to step out on a winner. Now's the time."

Tex suddenly assumed the demeanor of a man introduced to his own assassin. Sweat ran down his face in giant rivulets as his meal ticket whirled and left the room. Joe followed and closed the door gently behind him.

Outside the office, Joe muttered, "Like an exorcism."

"Huh?"

"Ah, nothing. Man, you'd think this was the worst day of his life." Joe shook his head in bewilderment. "What about all the money he won today because of me?"

The office phone rang behind them.

"It is the worst day of his life," Rocket announced.

"How come?"

Rocket laid his ear against the door and motioned for Joe to do the same. Violent bursts of profanity shattered the silence on its other side.

"That's it," Rocket whispered.

"What?"

Next came the dull sound of flesh thumping the floor, accompanied by squeaky chair rollers in need of oil. All went quiet. Rocket slowly opened the door and looked smugly inside. He pushed the door open further so Joe could see. Inside, Tex lay passed out on the floor, his skin white as home plate after an ump's sweeping.

"That's the call that tells him his bookie's been busted." Rocket placed his famous right arm around Joe and walked him toward the locker room. "Now tell me a little more 'bout this reel state bizness."

CHAPTER 44

FALLING OFF A TURNIP TRUCK

Marty, exhausted from the game, from the season, from his life, sat at one side of the dressing room taking in the festivities. Soaking wet, he seemed even smaller. His bloodshot eyes traveled around the room like a red searchlight. Where was Tex? Finally, something good happens, and the dickhead misses the celebration. Marty visibly cringed. What deviate couple could have possibly conceived the lumbering half-wit that was steamrolling toward him?

Duren's uniform, still dry, clung tightly to his frame. His eyes bulged dangerously, and his face glistened with rage-inspired sweat.

"I I I I," he stammered, his stutter squeezing his throat. In desperation to speak, he raised his hands above his head. "I qu qu quit!"

Marty took a swig from his bottle of champagne, then gulped audibly.

"Don't forget to take the dog," he called to Frothin's backside through a mirthless chuckle.

Bull was in no hurry for his buddy's return. How often, he wondered, does a sports fan get a chance to sit in on a major-league victory party?

He watched Duren and Marty's confrontation with mild pity. Poor Frothin. His mind was loaded with more crap than the Trinity River and fallen too far down for any possible rescue. But Bull's internal VCR had stored a tape like a squirrel stores nuts for the winter. Frothin's stutter! Bull's heart shot up his throat, beating sixteen to the dozen. The night of Liz's kidnapping, the masked man had yelled that hell-crazed stutter: "I'll...I'll...be baacck!" And the tone was identical to today, a deep pulsating assault on Bull's ears.

Duren Green, a bonafide major league ballplayer, had kidnapped Liz Donley? The possibility struck Bull with the force of one certain train.

Bull could not solve the jigsaw puzzle in his mind. Think, man, think! No time. Bull dashed out the dressing room door.

Duren's size-sixteen feet fiercely pounded the parking lot pavement as if it were the skull of his father. His eyes flashed like a light show at a rock concert.

Frothin's mind was not tuned to the crowd of gawking fans shuffling along the asphalt nor to the slow trickle of cars leaving for home. An old horror movie played that turned up at the most inopportune times. Roll 'em. Location: the middle of nowhere, Blue Ridge Mountains of North Carolina. Time: fifteen years earlier. Set: a wooden shack, small, dilapidated, by an isolated dusty road. A few worn-out pickups occupied a gravel parking area by the front entrance, a place where Duren's father bought cheap moonshine. Duren, fourteen years old and nearly his adult size, sat dejectedly chained to the bumper of a pickup, its color hidden beneath a cover of dust and rust. The heavy wool fabric of his baggy, gray uniform would draw sweat on a cool day. Today was not a cool day, and sweat raced down his sunburned face. Misfits and drunks, all appearing of the same mutation, milled in and out of the establishment. The air reeked as much from hard times as from booze.

, Duren's father stumbled from the shack, wearing his familiar soiled overalls. Uneven growths of hair sprouted from his oval head, courtesy of his wife's unsteady hand. Black steel stubble covered a face more red from booze than the sun. With bloated cheeks and his face distorted, the elder Green's hell-bent eyes devoured his teenaged son.

"Boy!" His growl revealed a missing front tooth; his remaining teeth matched the puke yellow trim on Duren's uniform. He bent down to his son and Duren flinched at the harsh smell of moonshine.

"One pissant sangle ain't gonna brang a lot of pro scouts!" his father roared.

The senior Green drew back the palm of his hand to strike. Looking a little older but none wiser, the Dalmatian raced toward the enemy at warp speed. Direct hit, right above the ankle, his teeth penetrated the drunkard's leg.

Duren's father, anesthetized from 100-plus proof, displayed no ill effects of the attack. The whimpering Dalmatian released the ankle and dropped to his master's side. Duren's father stormed inside the shack but quickly returned with a shotgun.

"Spot! Look out!" screamed Duren.

Spot's head exploded with the first shot. His brain, pink and fluffy, splattered on Duren's face. His face instantly went blank, expressionless, and his mind permanently moved over to the dark side.

An hour later, oblivious to Duren still chained to the pickup, his dad stumbled into the back of another truck loaded with turnips. After the truck had traveled less than a mile, Duren's father, higher than a major league pop-up, accidentally tumbled from the bed of the truck onto the dirt road where a trailing pickup squashed his head flatter than home plate. Duren's father held the unique distinction of falling off one turnip truck and then being killed by another.

"Mister Green." A high voice jarred Frothin to the present. A small boy was shoving his red Ranger cap and felt pen toward Duren Green. "Would you autograph my—?"

With eyes half open, Frothin, wearing the same damaged expression as fifteen years before, stopped and lifted his head in the general direction of the boy. He managed to do this without further raising his eyelids.

"Fuck off," Frothin said in an eerie disembodied voice. Saliva drooled from both sides of his mouth. The kid took off in a mad dash for parts unknown.

Once again, a child had slowed Frothin, allowing Bull to catch up with him. Bull immediately recognized Frothin's grim lips and hostile squint.

"So, it was you that night," said Bull. Winded from the run, his words and breath escaped with a rush. "Seems like you and I have been here before," Bull added defiantly.

Frothin's body was too big and his mind too small to frighten easily. The demonic look on his face would have inspired men of less bravery than Bull to run for cover. Both men, one large and the other larger, stared at one another with mutual scorn.

"You weren't terrorizing Lakewood. Just the Donleys," Bull accused, shattering the heavy silence.

Frothin's rage was automatic. While flashing the same disposition of his father, Frothin drew back his massive right fist. Bull instinctively raised both hands, but Frothin's devastating right cross easily pierced Bull's protective shield. Bull slowly dropped to one knee, like an injured horse attempting to kneel.

If Frothin looked surprised, it was only because Bull's face displayed no signs of blood. After Frothin's second blow, this changed as Bull's face assumed the puffy texture of an overripe grapefruit. His eyes became blank screens. He weaved a downed fighter's weave, melting into the pavement. Frothin continued toward his destination.

CHAPTER 45
CAN DADDY COME HOME?

Joan, along with Big Jim and her daughters, huddled around the television in the Donley living room. Though they saw no sign of Joe, all wistfully watched the post-game locker room commentary of the Rangers' division title. Tears slow as molasses trickled down Joan's cheeks, taking make-up along the way.

"Thanks for inviting me to come over and watch the game," Big Jim said to Joan. "And please don't be sad," he begged.

"What's the matter, Mom? Are you kind of blue?" K. C. asked. "You don't love Daddy anymore because he's a baseballer?"

"Please, Mom, can Daddy come home?" Tater quizzed, her tone lighter than air, her shocking blue eyes percolating with hope.

Joan paced the living room with pantherish grace, her eyes nailed to a Persian rug. Memories that she didn't have use for flooded her mind. Family vacations, BIOYA softball games, outings to Keller's or church or school. "This is neither to Joe's credit nor his fault. The only thing that makes a difference is how you deal with it." These words, which Duke also said to Joan, sounded internally, as though piped in through a hi-tech set of headphones.

"It's not fair!" she blurted. "Your daddy messed up everything!" Life had thrown her far too many curves, Joan decided. "Crap," she added under her breath.

Big Jim's oval eyes swept the room, either looking for crap or wondering what his dad could have possibly messed up now. K. C. and Tater rushed to their mother's side.

"I'm sorry, girls. I should never talk about your dad that way."

Liz stood nearby, steady and solid. "Go to the park, Mom." Noting the fear on her mother's face, she paused. "They got the guy, remember? He's dead now. We'll be okay."

Joan nibbled her lower lip. With complex eyes, she looked at Liz, at Tater, at K. C. Then her look narrowed, then narrowed some more. Questions stirred in her mind. Even if she swallowed her pride, should she visit Joe? Patrick could not have kidnapped Liz. But who? Surely her children would be safe at home for an hour or two. After all, the area attacks had stopped. Joan's mind, running from her thoughts, felt fuzzy like TV reception without an antenna.

"Crap," she said again, louder. "Liz, watch after things." Joan grabbed her purse off a coffee table and headed to the front door. "I won't be gone long. Stay in the house and keep the doors locked."

"Don't worry, Ms. Donley. I'll look after things," Big Jim said.

Joan shut the front door behind her. Her glance shot upward. Pale clouds hovered below a low gray-blue sky. Big Jim's words had almost sounded ominous, like a large black cloud's warning of thunder.

Inside the Donley home, after watching a few minutes of *101 Dalmatians*, boredom set in. Tater spread her arms and stretched to her tip-toes on her skates. "I think he'll come hooooommmme," she sang. "I think he'll come hooooommmme!"

"Shut up, dork," Liz said, though her tone implied only mild irritation. Her eyes quickly took in everything and everybody in the room. "Let's go out and play," she commanded.

"You're not the boss! Momma told us to stay inside," K. C. huffed.

"Shut up, dork," Tater snapped, reproducing the exact inflections of her older sister's voice.

Liz strode purposefully to the front door. Wordlessly, Tater and K. C.

fell in line. Fearing dork implications, Big Jim did the same.

When the Donley's phone rang, only Chester, who was flying reconnaissance missions, occupied the home. After four rings, the girl's voices, sounding like playful chipmunks, responded in unison: "You've reached the Donleys. We're never home these days. At the beep, leave your message."

After the beep, Joe's voice exploded through the receiver. "Joan, it's me. If you're there, please don't leave. I'm coming home."

CHAPTER 46
JOE AND JOAN TAKE A RIDE

WITH his hair wet from the shower and swept straight back, Joe re-entered the locker room, which still resembled the inside of a bee hive. He spotted Marty wearing an off-center smirk and tottering drunkenly amid the mayhem.

"Hey, Skip," Joe called, "have you seen my buddy?"

The puffiness in the Rangers' skipper's face made his eyes seem too small. Marty pointed to the exit and managed to mumble, "Went that-a-way. On a fast track too. For reasons I cannot fuckin' interpolate, I think he was following Green."

Joe, mainly curious, walked briskly through the huge parking area. He expected—even wanted—people to stare, but few noticed him. The exiting fans seemed more preoccupied with a huddle about fifty yards in front of him. Was that an ambulance? Trying to fine tune his vision, Joe squinted repeatedly. An equal mix of concern and acknowledgment shone through the squint in his eyes. Paramedics were lifting a man onto a stretcher. Big guy. Blond.

Joe's legs turned to Jello, and he stumbled as if mired in too much soft dirt at home plate. Recovering, he raced toward Bull, flailing his arms and spitting out cuss words.

Joe arrived just as the paramedics prepared to load Bull into the ambulance. "Bull," Joe gasped, "are you okay?"

A flicker of recognition glowed in Bull's eyes. A tomato-red bandage concealed much of his face, and tufts of hair sprouted from his head at untamed angles.

"What the hell happened?" Joe asked frantically, a huge catch in his throat.

"It was him that night at your house," Bull moaned.

"Who?"

Joe's wide eyes clung to Bull as paramedics loaded the stretcher in the ambulance. With the rear doors still open, Joe stood by Bull's head.

"Duren Green. He took Liz," replied Bull, his voice weaker than Joe could ever remember.

"How do you know?" Joe quizzed, pricking up his ears.

"Little Man." A hard edge surfaced in Bull's tone. "Do I have to explain now? That Paul Bunyan-lookin' son of a bitch just left here, and he's not in a real good mood. Get your ass home, pronto."

A paramedic tried to shut the doors, but Joe held him back.

"Frothin did this?" A needless question. Bull's look said it all. Joe released the paramedic's arm. "You're my best friend, Bull," said Joe, his voice breaking.

"I know, Little Man," said Bull softly. Bull looked to the paramedic. His manner and voice managed to recharge a bit. "I've never ridden in an ambulance before. You think the driver could turn on the siren?"

"I don't think you have to worry about that," said the paramedic. The door slammed shut.

"Don't die," Joe whispered. "You can't die."

Siren blaring, the ambulance disappeared from the parking lot.

Joe commandeered his black Beemer through the lot as if all other drivers had personally insulted his manhood. He recognized Joan's blonde hair and her white van simultaneously. The two cars, on a course to meet head on, skidded to a stop within a few feet of the other. Joe left his car like it was on fire. He ripped open his wife's front-passenger door and slid in the front seat.

"Where are the kids? Why aren't they with you?" Joe asked urgently. It sounded like an order and significantly louder than Joe had intended.

These were the first words spoken by Joe to his wife since the release of the *American Enquirer*. "I've missed you" or "you look good" or even "I'm sorry" would have probably served as a better opening.

Joan stared at Joe with a face so guarded it would block home plate.

"You've got a lot of nerve getting in this car, much less asking about the kids, Mr. Super Star!" Her voice and body trembled with humiliation.

Joan started to repeatedly pound Joe's shoulder with her large Nordic fists. A left, a right, left right, left right.

Joe, by now intimate with the symptoms, recognized this attack as Joan's own exorcism. Joe initially offered little resistance, but the punch to his nose constituted more abuse than he could accept. His hands grasped both of hers; she bit deeply into his thumb. He clasped his palm over Joan's mouth; she jabbed his gut.

As if someone turned off the power, Joan suddenly lost her aggressiveness and started to wind down. Joe released his hand from Joan's mouth. Expelling breath, she also started to cry, a hard cry, like a hard rain.

Joe gently pushed blonde strands away from her face. He saw an expression on her face unlike any he had ever seen before. Fear? Humiliation? Anger? Rejection? Disappointment? Maybe all. Joe grabbed his wife and held her so close they appeared to share one anatomy.

"Duren Green's the guy that took Liz," Joe spoke into his wife's ear with remarkable calm. "He's gone bonkers. He's already hurt Bull."

"The ballplayer?" Joan said incredulously, pushing away for a better look.

Joe nodded. "You know that ambulance that just screamed out of here? That was Bull. We need to get home."

Joe leaned back into his seat, each studying the other. Joan looked stricken, pale as white ash. After a moment's silence, Joan tilted her head toward Joe in sort of a measuring way. Abruptly, she stomped the accelerator so hard Joe's head snapped forward. With the rear tires screeching like angry pigs and propelling tiny rocks into the air, the minivan raced for home.

"Is Bull okay?" Joan asked shortly after the van reached Interstate 30.

"I don't know," said Joe solemnly.

"What happened?" Joan wondered, her eyes full of mist.

"I'm not sure, but evidently Green was the hammer and Bull the nail."

"Dear God! If he could do that to Bull, think of what he could do to . . ." Joan paused, leaving the rest of her thought unspoken.

Joe knew what Joan was thinking. His mind shrank from the notion.

"Where do you think Green's headed?"

"He's on his way somewhere," Joe said grimly. "I don't want to take any chances. Let's get home."

"Joe, what are we going to do if he's there?" Joan paused, irony suddenly consuming her face and voice. "That's probably the last act we'd try together." She took her eyes off the road and looked at Joe; a worry crease appeared between her brows. "Funny. When all this started, I knew that before it was over I'd wish things were like before."

"Sounds good to me," said Joe, regret running through his voice the size of construction cable. Feeling Joan's glare, he kept his eyes ahead, watching the car swallow white road stripes.

"I guess I'm supposed to be a liberated woman and just accept what's happened." Joan's voice not only escalated but quivered as if restraining tears or anger or both. "Well, I'm an old-fashioned girl from Hutchins, Texas, and I don't know if I can." Joan waved her hands vigorously before reclaiming the steering wheel. "Every time we made love, I'd be thinking about that girl. In that picture, her boobs are big enough to make me vomit."

Joe could feel the temperature in the car rising. He wisely chose to remain quiet. Weather the heat wave calmly, like facing an opposing team on a roll.

"You too probably," Joan sighed.

Presumably, Joan was referring to the boobs and not the vomit, Joe very silently mused.

"Whatever possessed you, Joe?" Joan's voice cracked; her fingers brushed her cheekbones, wiping away raindrop-size tears. "You've never even looked twice at another woman."

"You talked to Duke?" Joe asked hopefully.

"Yeah, I know. It's not to your credit or fault but how you deal with it or something like that," Joan said, waving her hands but with less animation than before.

"It was all a setup. Duren hired her to disrupt my game, I guess."

"Well!" cried Joan in mock disbelief. "Anyone should know better than to think some T & A would disrupt my husband when playing ball," Joan said so sharply Joe felt a tremble. "Pretty effective performance, though. She's even got a hit play," Joan said, a trace of envy in her tone.

"Joan, I apologize for what I've done. I'm not asking for forgiveness. I just want you to know I'm sorry."

Joe felt less anxiety his first big league at bat. He heard only the sound of Interstate traffic rushing by.

After what seemed too long a silence, Joan blurted out, "God, please let those kids be all right."

"God, please let those kids be all right," Joe repeated, looking respectfully to the sky.

CHAPTER 47
FROTHIN RETURNS

A T dusk, the air still smelled of summer fragrances. Climbing English ivy covered much of the front and side of the Donley home. Enhanced by a sprinkler system, a blend of Bermuda and St. Augustine grass in need of a cut made a solid green blanket of the front yard.

A child's voice, innocent and pure, drew a hulking shadow closer. The little tenor appeared in a holiday mood. To the tune of "Twelve Days of Christmas," the high voice happily serenaded:

> "On the twelfth day of Christmas my true love gave to me: twelve taters crinkling, eleven potato wedges, ten baked potatoes, nine potato skins, eight stacks of hash browns, seven potatoes of mashing, six fries of Frenching, and five o-n-i-o-n r-i-n-g-s. Four tasty French fries, three potatoes scalloped, two tater tots and a baked potato with melted cheese."

The hulk lurked undetected behind an oak tree. Duren Green, near three hundred pounds of delusion with the disposition of a mad bull, had returned to further investigate this family that seemed to have it all.

As he had lumbered along the median of Interstate 30 in his uniform, an admiring fan stopped to give a real-life major-leaguer a ride. Frothin flashed a look so threatening, he had little trouble persuading the driver to relinquish his car.

It was perfect this way, thought Duren. If anything went wrong, no one could trace his car to the Donley home. The insanity playing inside Duren Green's mind had progressed to the bottom of the ninth inning.

On the way over, he'd wondered if someone had left the door unlocked like the last time. No need to concern himself with that now as he watched the children and a chubby man playing in the Donley front yard, all grinning as if they'd found a pirate's treasure.

The kid wearing skates had hair blonde enough to throw off light; her blue eyes reminded him of the mountain streams back home. Singing all the while, she was tossing a baseball to fatso, who usually missed it completely. Faking disgust, blondie would spit ferociously to the grass.

The littlest one, the redhead, sat off to one side, totally mesmerized with an assortment of little dolls. Every now and then, she turned and spoke to someone he could not see.

Ah, the one from that night, the one with that smooth dark skin and those grown-up lips, so full and wet. She stood near the little redhead, watching, and appeared to be mulling over what order to give next.

Frothin stood at attention, as if in his stretched and torn mind he heard "God Bless America" or maybe "Psychotic Reaction." He was soaking in Liz's youthful beauty. It had got the best of him that night, and he took her. Besides, from his part of the country, she was marrying age, and he needed a wife. With a toss of her head, the girl rearranged her honey brown hair and laughed a bright, inviting laugh.

Seized by inspiration, Frothin stepped from behind the big tree. Other than his eyes glowing like a lit torch, he showed no sign of emotion.

Frothin's eyes met with those of his kidnapping victim. He saw recognition in her glance, and she started to run. Frothin, with the mountain man in him, snatched Liz so efficiently, the others initially failed to notice. Liz squirmed, but to no avail.

"Let me go!" she screamed, with as much anger as fear in her plea.

Frothin cupped his massive hand over her mouth.

"L-e-t h-e-r g-o," Big Jim stuttered, arriving to the rescue.

"You a retard?" Frothin asked, his voice rattling from the general vicinity of his belly button.

Misery loves company. Frothin exposed an alarming grin, and Big Jim started to step backwards slowly as if realizing he faced a live bomb.

A brittle sound of teeth clacking came from Tater's direction. Though her skates were riveted to the ground, her knees shook in early Elvis fashion.

The little redhead missed it all. "I hate my own brain," chirped Hollywood Barbie through her master. Hollywood Barbie had hair and an upper body like the female lifeguard's on *Baywatch*.

"Don't be sad," comforted Ken Barbie.

"Everybody in my family hates me," responded Hollywood Barbie.

Frothin related instantly to the dialogue, especially the "everybody in my family hates me." With one hand still over Liz's mouth, he toted her toward K. C. as easily as toting his Louisville Slugger.

"My life has no meaning," moaned Hollywood Barbie.

K. C. looked up at Frothin through bright eyes. "You're a baseballer like my dad!" she blurted.

She started to giggle but then saw the hostile gleam in the visitor's eyes. Taking note of her oldest sister's confinement, K. C.'s laughter died a sudden death. K. C. now understood everything was going wrong at warp speed. "A crazy Mormon if I've ever seen one," she said privately.

Big Jim shuffled toward Frothin. This time, he spoke with the reluctance of a new kid on the block. "P-p-put Liz d-d-down."

Only Big Jim went down. With one granite fist, Frothin dropped Big Jim to the grass. A collective gasp filled the air.

"Everybody run!" K. C. yelled. "Avery, run!"

She bounded to her feet, but Frothin's heavy hand clamped her shoulder, bringing on a sudden case of paralysis. His other hand still held Liz.

"Who's Avery?" Frothin asked, with eyes narrowed too long from life's disappointments.

K. C. glanced to her older sister. With an assassin's stare, Liz nodded. "Avery's my brother," K. C. answered, her voice trembling.

"Where is he?"

"He ran to the backyard," said K. C.

"I didn't see him," mumbled Frothin, cocking his head to one side as if looking for invisible people or hearing secret voices.

"I'm the only one that can see him," said K. C.

Liz rifled the wide-eyed Tater a quick wink, who remained still and mute.

Frothin studied K. C. "Can you see my dog?" he finally asked.

K. C.'s eyes searched all around the front yard like dual searchlights before spotlighting on Liz. It was a "what now" look. Everyone remained still. Liz lowered her chin in response to her sister's unasked question.

Unsure of the signal, K. C. repeated the gesture which Frothin took as an affirmative nod.

"What's he look like?" he asked, a gleam of suspicion glowing through the murk in his eyes.

Suspense hung in midair. With a harrumph, K. C. cleared her throat. The last movie she'd seen had all those little spotted puppies. "Polkadotted?"

Frothin's grin exposed teeth long enough to resemble Hershey's teeth.

"I'm sure Avery climbed in the tree," K. C. volunteered, relief flowing through her voice like a busted fire hydrant.

"The tree?"

"Yep. The magic tree," said K. C., her head bobbing cork-like.

"Magic tree?" Frothin asked.

"After my dad fell out of that tree, he became a great baseballer," K. C. said proudly. "Like J. C. Penney."

"K. C.! Shut up!" admonished Liz. "What's she going to do now, ask him to spend the night?" Liz grumbled under her breath.

# CHAPTER 48
THE SECOND SHOT WAS FOR YOU

Joan's van made a screeching pit stop in the Donley driveway. The sight of Big Jim sprawled across the front yard gave Joe chilling spasms. Joe reached Big Jim first, but only by a nanosecond.

Big Jim's smashed nose had taken residence beside his right ear and blood oozed from one corner of his mouth.

"Big Jim, where are the girls?" Joan cried, her face contorted and flush.

Big Jim's eyes remained closed. His lips parted, but only air came out. He pointed to the back yard, and Joe took off.

As Joan followed, Big Jim's voice came up from the ground, slow and faint/ "Get 'em, Joe."

In the back yard, a slight breeze brought the odor of an abandoned dog pound into Joe's face. Joe's concerns with the scent of dog crap quickly left him. He and Joan found their two oldest daughters, gagged and bound to the trunk of the old pecan tree' Tater was pale enough to pass for a descendant of the Holy Ghost. Liz wore a somber adult-like frown. Both looked older than he remembered. Instinctively, father and mother sprang toward them but quickly slammed on the pedestrian brakes. Like a giant two-legged predator prepared to strike, Duren Green was perched high in the tree, holding K. C.!

Joe's saliva, suddenly too dry to swallow, tasted of fear. With his new range of emotions, he felt equally capable of exploding into violence or tears. Unsure of what to do next, he stared at Frothin and mumbled something to Joan. Joan, her terror total and complete, ran into the house.

Why hadn't Hershey protected the girls? Joe wondered. The chocolate lab wagged his tail contentedly, as if he just single-handedly eliminated the entire meow-meow species. Joe could not know that Frothin's love and respect toward canines had easily disarmed the chocolate lab.

Frothin was mumbling some slow, foreign wail through thin lips that were blue in tint. Drool formed a Fu Manchu mustache along his jaw line. Although his eyes were ablaze, Frothin showed little surprise at the sight of Joe. His own eyes, Joe supposed, were overcome with horror and disbelief. Frothin looked to be the sort of moron who could enjoy jumping from a tree practically the height of a ballpark's second deck.

A thread of relief, though tiny as Duke's surgical suture, ran through Joe. Joe's baby, at least, looked hopeful.

"Hi, Dad," K. C. said meekly. "Mr. Green wants to jump from the magic tree," added K. C., the weight of her words crushing Joe's brief optimism.

Joe's stomach was in free fall. Could he ever feel more Christ-like? To know that without hesitation he would sacrifice his own life to save the life of his children.

Frothin clutched K. C. to his chest. If he landed on her, he would smash her to jelly. Joe drew a deep breath, storing this fear in the back of his mind.

"Aw, I wouldn't do that," Joe said, dismissing the idea with a warm sweeping gesture of his arm. His voice somehow passed for nonchalance.

"I-i-i-it's a ma-magic tree," stammered Frothin defiantly. "You, you, you're a-a-afraid i-i-it'll h-help me, too. I-i-i won't b-b-be p-p-p-o-o-or again! I w-want wh-what you… you h-have."

In spite of Frothin's adrenaline-inspired stutter and the mounting evidence that he was crazy as a loon, he orated quite convincingly. Joe made a mental note, if the opportunity ever presented itself, to ask

Frothin exactly what he possessed that Frothin craved so badly.

"Nobody wants you to be poor. Besides, I got a strong feeling that tree only had one good fall in it. The second one could kill you," Joe said, trying to cram his voice with sincerity.

"N-no, it w-w-won't. W-w-w-w-we're a-a-all g-g-going t-t-to jump," Frothin announced, his baritone voice now more scary than an alien's voice.

"All?"

"M-m-me and h-her and Sp-spot and, and . . .," Frothin said, his stutter trailing off into nothingness.

"Avery," reminded K. C., forever the helpful one.

"I don't think K. C. wants to jump," Joe said, holding his hand up in the symbolic gesture for stop.

Joan stood on an aluminum ladder and searched the cupboard over the refrigerator. She found the small revolver, which lay still, as if in hibernation. Joan's cheeks burned at the thought swirling in her head. She wanted to blow off Frothin's head, massive in size and misdirection. Upon further consideration, a shot in the vicinity of her husband's other head, not so massive in size but recently misdirected, didn't seem like such a bad idea either.

Joan's hand swallowed the little gun that would complement well the butcher knife in her back pocket. She heard the sudden heart-rendering sound of K. C.'s whoop hanging in midair.

Joe's yell followed. "K. Ceeeeeee!!"

A short silence followed, dark and more disturbing than a child's runaway note.

Joan bypassed the ladder's four steps, causing the kitchen floor to shake on impact. She sprinted out the back door, but by the time she reached the tree, K. C. was sitting up.

"My God! K. C., are you all right?" Joan asked, hovering closely over K. C.

K. C. said nothing, showed nothing.

Joe, already kneeling by K. C.'s side, caught the flash of the butcher knife in Joan's pocket. He yanked it out and cut the rope that held Liz and Tater. It was the most rapid and emotional hug he had ever given his two oldest daughters.

Meanwhile, Frothin was in a mess—a pile of Hershey's to be exact. He lay on his side babbling incoherently, his body twitching sporadically. Abruptly, as though the scent of Hershey's dung was poisonous, Frothin went deathly still.

Miraculously, K. C. seemed uninjured. Before Joe or Joan could stop her, she abruptly stood and quickly started for the back door.

"Take it easy," said Joe, catching up to her.

Joan sprinted inside to call for an ambulance and the police while Liz and Tater clung tightly to Joe's side.

On the way to the back door, Joe turned back to look at Frothin. "Damn, I think he's dead," Joe mumbled.

Inside, K. C. suddenly took a turn for the worse, flopping onto the living room sofa. She wailed hysterically as the family formed a tight huddle around her.

"It's okay, K. C. The ambulance will be here any minute," Joan said, stroking the child's forehead.

"Don't cry," Tater crooned.

"She's faking it," Liz whispered sardonically to Tater.

A rank odor, clinging all around K. C., suddenly worsened. "Did Hershey come inside?" Joe snarled, his nose sniffing and straining toward the smell. He looked around but saw no sign of Hershey. What...

Joe sprang toward the back door but promptly collided with Frothin in the kitchen. With the muscles in Frothin's face pulsating so violently, Joe overlooked Joan's knife that Frothin now held by his side.

Joe's and Frothin's eyes locked on each other. If Joe Donley and Duren Green had one thing in common, it was this: as automatically, as absentmindedly as carrying a wallet, both men carried around the influence of their fathers at all times.

An old lesson hit Joe at that moment, and it blurted out uncontrollably. "Wait, then attack, wait, then attack." Joe quoted with authority.

The conspiracy in Frothin's mind continued. He waited before attacking, providing the mistake Joe needed. In a frenzied flourish, Joe charged into Frothin's chest, driving the giant's back into the refrigerator. Amid one loud barking grunt, Frothin lost the knife and crashed seat-first to the kitchen floor. Cereal boxes, loaves of bread, and fruit rained down from the refrigerator onto the entangled men.

Joe rode Frothin's chest and wrapped both hands violently around his neck and throat. Holding Frothin down proved impossible. Frothin heaved Joe across the kitchen floor like a human shot put. Where in the hell is Joan with that gun? Joe wondered during flight. While scrambling to his feet, Joe saw Frothin retrieve the knife from the floor.

Joe fronted Frothin the way a matador faces a bull. Save one difference, the bull held the cutlery. Bet on the big guy with the knife, Joe decided. A high frenzied sound came from some other part of the house. Few cockatiels existed in Frothin's past, and he froze like a bird dog on point.

"Chester! Chester!"

The screech came closer. With the stunning ferocity of a fighter pilot gone too long without battle, the mad bomber entered the kitchen. A great mystery will always remain with regard to Chester's intent. One thing was certain... Joe knew to duck; Frothin did not.

If Chester intended to harm Joe, the accuracy of his attack rivaled that of scud missiles. Upon impact with Frothin's forehead, Chester, in his multicolored splendor, exploded with the brilliance of a July Fourth firecracker. He damn near sounded like one too.

Dropping the knife, Frothin's hands went to both sides of his head, as if to remove a helmet. He stumbled a few steps in the manner of a stunned boxer, but eventually righted himself. Brandishing a shark's grin, he bent over and picked up the knife.

Click. It was the sound of a gun cocking. Joan stood in the doorway with the pistol in her hand. She faced Frothin, who stood in front of the refrigerator. Through eyes that had become nuclear warheads, Joan aimed the pistol toward Frothin's own bulging eyes. The heads of Liz and Tater timidly poked forth from each side of their mother. Claustrophobia suddenly ruled the small room.

"Come on, dickhead! Just try it, and your fat head will be splattered all over the icebox!" Joan urged, her voice two decibels short of a scream, her face red enough to incite a bull's charge. "Come on! I'm begging you!" Yep, she said it. "Make my day!"

Frothin, in his smartest move since running away from home, dropped the knife. Too late. Joan fired the gun—not once, but twice.

A deafening silence accompanied the gun smoke permeating the air. In a sort of delayed reaction, Frothin fell across the kitchen floor like a light pole.

"Damn! You killed him!" Joe said incredulously.

From behind their mother, Tater and Liz observed the aftermath with disbelieving eyes.

"No. I shot the icebox," Joan said calmly.

"Twice?" wondered Joe.

"Nope. The second shot was for you."

Joan's icy tone, more than her words, caused Joe's insides to squirm. Joe approached the giant reluctantly. No sign of a bullet wound, no blood either. Frothin's body lay still, but his eyes remained open. Joe inspected the refrigerator, immediately noticing, taped to the door, the Bible verse that read: "Do everything possible on your part to live in peace with everybody. Never take revenge, my friend, but let God's anger do it."

One bullet hole had dotted the "i" on the word "friend." Joe detected no sign of the other bullet and quickly decided against making further inquiries.

CHAPTER 49
A CHAPTER FROM LIZ'S DIARY RECORDED A FEW DAYS LATER

Boy, was Mom mad. We still haven't found that second bullet. I don't think she really intended to shoot Dad, but if she had, I bet I know where that bullet would have gone.

In a matter of minutes, two police cars arrived, then two ambulances. Dusk had turned to darkness. With so many red lights flashing, our front yard and driveway looked like the entrance to an emergency room on Saturday night. Or as Mom said, "A night club after a pretty bad ruckus."

One ambulance took Duren Green, but not before police and paramedics strapped him into a stretcher. One of the paramedics told us Duren had probably entered a catatonic state. His eyes looked as big as ping-pong balls and didn't blink. His body was stiffer than a marble statue.

Big Jim entered the other ambulance on his own, though his face was lopsided. Mom climbed in after Big Jim as paramedics loaded K. C. into the same ambulance on a stretcher. I tried to lighten the mood a little. "Hey K. C., how's Avery?"

"He died in the fall," she snapped, glaring at me like I just kicked her in a private place.

Just before the ambulance door closed, Mom fired me one of her own, slant-eyed killer looks. With still no word on Bull, I guess things were still a little tight for her to appreciate any humor. I grieved as much for Avery as I'm sure Dad did for Chester, who still lay splattered on our kitchen floor.

By now, a couple of dozen curious neighbors had wandered into our front yard. Dad, Tater, and I were walking to our car to go check on Bull at the hospital when I heard that familiar nerdy voice.

"Mr. Donley."

We turned to see our neighborhood dork and baseball memorabilia collector, Noah Schmidt, heading our way. With those glasses and slicked back hair, he reminded me of a teenage accountant.

"Was that Duren Green in that ambulance?" Noah asked.

"Sure was," my dad said.

It's a wonder Noah didn't ask if we could flag down the ambulance and get Duren's autograph.

"He did something bad, didn't he?"

"Yep, Noah. He sure did."

"Why?"

I was really impressed with what Dad said next.

"I think he wanted something so bad his mind snapped."

Noah thought about this awhile before he asked, "What did he want?"

Dad also paused, but not as long, before he answered, "The same thing we all want—to feel important."

Noah stared off into the stars and, I thought, here it comes, another Noah special like "Duh, Mr. Donley, do you think Rocket will pitch until he's seventy?" Or something equally retarded. But Noah fooled me with a change-up, you might say. He actually asked something halfway intelligent.

"Mr. Donley, have you ever wanted to feel important so bad that your mind snapped?"

"Yeah, Noah, I'm afraid so," my dad said. He wrapped one arm around Noah and smiled. I don't remember seeing my dad ever smile like that. Not a huge smile, but warm as a pitcher's warm-up jacket on a sunny spring day. "But I'm okay now," he said, "and hopefully, Duren will be too."

A few minutes later in our car, my father said he'd just figured it out. Duren Green wanted more than his designated hitter's spot back. He wanted to belong, to have a family like ours.

CHAPTER 50
SAFE AT HOME

SIX months later, Rocket towered over the mound, powerful and proficient. Wearing a menacing scowl, he leaned into home plate. A packed crowd anxiously anticipated the first pitch. Rocket started into his famous windup.

Rocket's pitch failed to generate the customary hissing noise of an angry snake. As it floated to home plate, a voice from the stands yelled, "Way to fire, Rocket!"

Laughter erupted. The batter, short and broad, missed the pitch by three feet. Through a jack-o'-lantern grin, Rocket watched the ball land softly as a feather into the catcher's mitt. Smiles were everywhere, and through these sunny expressions, most everyone gawked at the pitcher as though he were on display at the Hall of Fame.

"Did you see that?" Bull asked Big Jim excitedly.

Bull, wearing a bright yellow hard hat, pointed reverently to the mound. He and Big Jim stood in foul territory close to first base.

BIOYA's black lettering, not Rangers' blue, spanned the front of Rocket's jersey. His muscular thighs threatened to burst through his Wranglers. Dark brown lizard boots and a cream-colored cowboy hat completed his uniform. Rocket toiled in the anonymous world of slow pitch softball—-sort of.

Under a distant blue sky, a cool breeze carried the scent of fresh air mixed with diamond dust. Liz Donley hunkered down alone on the BIOYA bench, dictating into her tiny black recorder. A black cap with a white B on its crown set off her bronze face; a short ponytail dangled through an opening in the rear of her cap. She wore one of her dad's BIOYA T-shirts knotted at the waist, exposing a pair of tattered jean cut-offs. Liz's serious brown eyes and high cheekbones made her look older than fifteen as she continued to spin the Donley story.

"Unbelievable! Here we are at the same park where it all started just a little over a year ago, the day Dad fell from the tree after a softball game." She wrinkled her nose at the sun and shook her head. "It seems like a lifetime ago."

"My grandmother's helping me with my book." Liz's loving glance shifted to Joe's mother. "She's getting out more these days." Mary sat in the small bleacher section behind home plate. She wore her short white hair pulled away from her face and bound in back in a clip. A faint smile played at the corners of her mouth in a delicate face that had given way to slight jowls.

"She's probably thinking of Grampa George right now," Liz said.

"Rocket's retired," she continued, her glimpse traveling to the pitcher's mound. "He occasionally comes to town to check on the properties." A look of mild amusement cut across Liz's face. "Rocket's had a slight impact upon attendance." His adoring public stood shoulder to shoulder along both foul lines, and more spectators crammed the bleacher section.

"Rocket's family usually travels with him," Liz added. "It's not hard to pick them out of the crowd."

A strikingly attractive woman, fortyish, with honey-colored hair, and two teenaged children sat in the bleachers. All dressed identical to Rocket, from western wear to the BIOYA T-shirt.

"Rumor is that Tex will be forced to sell the Rangers because of his gambling activities. Another rumor is that a group put together by Rocket will be the new owners. Dad thinks Rocket will figure out a way for him and Bull to be a part of that group." Liz's face broke into an approving smile.

On the sidelines, Big Jim was guffawing about something. "Bull and Big Jim are okay now, but Duren Green broke Big Jim's nose and punctured his right eardrum. Duren actually crushed part of Bull's skull. Bull wears a hard hat around everywhere now and looks like a construction worker. It's a good thing Duke fixed Bull right up because I don't think us Donleys could have taken it. Or Duke's nurse for that matter." Liz grinned like a kid caught sneaking her first kiss. "Bull and Gladys are getting married," Liz announced, her tone changing from heavy to light faster than a TV weather map. "I can't wait to see what their kids look like."

A high pitch drifted Liz's way. Tater sat behind home plate. Her yellow hair glistened brighter than the sun, and her bangs nearly concealed her eyes. She was singing to an imaginary packed house at Carnegie Hall. From the exaggerated wave of Tater's hands—a trait obviously inherited from her mother—a rock-n-roll symphony appeared the musical choice of the day. Tater wore a grey cotton sweatshirt, lettered GAP on the front, along with Cardinal-red satin shorts and white tennies.

"Tater's still a pain, and her constant singing gives me migraines. At least she's quit wearing all those clothes on top of each other. I think Dad got rid of the skates."

K. C. sat next to Tater. With her red hair flashing like a blinking stoplight, K. C. was carrying on multiple conversations simultaneously.

"K. C.'s fine," Liz told the black box. "That fall unplugged her. By the time she landed, her pants had more padding than a Wonder-bra. She's as regular as the mail now. She claims Avery jumped on his own trying to save her, but died in the fall. I'm sure the shrinks would have a field day with that one."

Naturally, Liz's father manned centerfield. Joe's eyes would intermittently gaze at his children as if seeing them after a long road trip. The batter lifted a fly ball to center field; Joe, his loving expression still intact, glided across the outfield and stabbed air for the catch.

"Dad's changed," Liz whispered in a voice that hovered between maturity and youthful innocence. "He's not so cool anymore. Even though Tater and K. C. make things difficult at times, I know Dad's happiest when he's with us and Mom."

Despite Liz's uncommon wisdom for her age, she could not truly understand the why of it all. Indeed, her father himself had only recently begun to understand that the best a man can do is tickle the light, and that if he does, darkness just might take care of itself.

Joe no longer concerned himself with the quest for a life of distinction. This obsession had consumed enough of Joe and had contributed to his hurting the people he loved most. If Candice, or at least Carla's interpretation of Candice, thought of life as x-rated, a tamer PG-13 would suit Joe just fine. Joe felt content for life once again to be "passing him by."

Joan sat in the bleachers beside Tater and K. C., one row below Rocket's wife and children. Her gracefully clasped hands rested in her lap, and the knees of elegantly crossed legs leaned toward home plate. She had emerged from an exorcism of her own with a stoic calmness and quiet dignity and only occasionally did a distant sorrow linger around her face.

"Mom let Dad move back home," Liz said, raising the volume a notch, as if proudly showing off old family pictures. "We kept making her watch *The Parent Trap*. I guess it worked."

Liz looked to the sky in deep thought and made several clucking sounds with her tongue. "Even though people still occasionally ask Dad for his autograph, I think Mom's a hero too. She's letting us live as a family again. I wish whoever said parents shouldn't stay together for their children would go make a shark happy," Liz said, her face suddenly fixed in a frown.

With eyes older than her years, Liz stared at the tiny recorder as if it presented a problem but not insurmountably so. "Maybe Mom hasn't forgotten, but she's forgiven. She decided the bullet dotting the 'i' in the Bible verse on the refrigerator door was an omen. She's forgiven Dad. She's even forgiven Duren Green." Liz shook her head in disbelief and exhaled audibly through her nostrils. "I guess you can only take forgiveness so far. When Carla Big Boobs came to town with her play at the State

Fair Music Hall, she proved she was crazy," Liz said, unable to suppress a wry grin. "The woman's clearly nuts," explained Liz with another shake of her head. "She told the paper some story about my father having one of her deceased brother's body parts. Think about it."

"Liz!" boomed an upbeat voice from center field. Liz snapped her head toward her father. Joe's stern face was void of expression, his hands planted firmly on his hips.

"Hey!" he yelled. "I need a substitute out here!"

Liz stared at her father, her brows furrowed in brief confusion. It was a cautious response on her part to prevent false optimism from setting in. Slowly, Joe's brown eyes began to twinkle, and he cracked a baiting grin. The harder Liz tried to confine her smile, the more the smile fought for freedom. It was a smile that would light ball diamonds and render teenage boys helpless.

Liz deftly swapped her recorder with a baseball glove, an official Walter "Rocket" Nolin model. Looking more like a future homecoming queen than a center fielder, Liz sprinted toward her father. As their paths crossed, Joe gently patted Liz on the shoulder and said, through a wide grin, "Go get 'em Tiger." He then loped over to take a seat beside Joan and Tater in the stands. K. C. climbed onto his lap. And Liz Donley finally succeeded in breaking the gender barrier for the BIOYA's slow-pitch softball team.

More than the gender barrier would tumble this day. It was not surprising that Rocket on the mound had drawn out one Noah Schmidt, baseball fanatic and secret long-time admirer of Liz Donley. Yet to Noah's own surprise, it was Liz whom he couldn't take his eyes off in the field. After the game, as Joe was shaking hands, slapping shoulders, and hugging his children, he discovered Noah practically standing under his feet.

An oversized red Rangers' sweatshirt and baggy jeans swallowed Noah whole. Behind black-rimmed Buddy Holly spectacles, his apprehensive eyes looked like swollen marbles.

"What's up?" Joe responded warmly.

Noah cleared his throat and stood as tall as he could. "Mr. Donley, I'd like your permission to ask Liz for a date," blurted the youngster.

Liz, unaware of Noah's intentions, stood nearby lecturing Tater on the art of playing center field.

In a weighted silence, Joe cast an assessing eye down at Noah.

"I don't know about that," Joe finally said, his brows arched, his voice rigid as Noah's posture.

"What?" Noah's voice dropped a dozen notches.

"First, I'm going to have to ask you something." Joe folded and unfolded his arms in vintage fatherly seriousness.

Noah swallowed, his eyes fixed on Joe's.

"Noah," Joe said, a grin too nuclear to be contained from spreading across his face. This bubbly expression darted around his insides speedier than a hyper-fastball before racing across Joe's entire body and exploding through the soles of his rubber-nibbed shoes.

Draping a warm arm around Noah's shoulders, Joe finally asked with boyish delight, "Tell me, have you ever had a pituitary gland transplant?"

Joe Donley was finally safe at home.

Illegitimi non carborundum